THE COMEBACK TOUR

JOELLE SPERANZA

A TRASH THE DRESS NOVEL

DEDICATION

For anyone who has ever loved a boy band.
For the Trash the Dress community.
For my kids, who will chase their own dreams.

1

CAILIN DECLARES "I DON'T WANT HIM BACK"

CAILIN

OUT OF ALL THE positions I've tried, this is by far the most awkward one to be caught doing in public. With both legs tucked behind my head, I'm definitely experiencing new sensations and can't help but let out a moan. But once I realize it's not as easy to get out of this position as it is to get into it, my moans turn to screams. And now, my sixty-five-year-old neighbor, Mrs. Sanders, is standing in front of me pointing her finger.

"Cailin, you really shouldn't be doing yoga in this dingy basement. You're probably inhaling mold and who knows what else. There's a nice studio down the street. Why are you doing this here?"

Good question. I came down to the storage area of our New York City apartment building because today is moving day. To help ease my stress—and stall—I thought it would be a good idea to unroll the old yoga mat I unpacked and do a few relaxing poses. Now, Mrs. Sanders is staring at me stuck in Dwi Pada Sirsasana, a pose that is considered to be a deep, spiritual pose for achieving calmness. However, I just look like a turtle stuck on its back with its head sticking out of the shell.

I debate which pain I would rather endure. Should I continue straining my leg muscles or announce that I just became a twenty-nine-year-old, jobless divorcée?

"I find dark, damp basements the ideal place for my spiritual practice. Do you mind helping me get my leg out from behind my head?"

Mrs. Sanders shakes her head. Once both of my legs are firmly on the cold ground in front of me, I thank her.

"Now, what's the real reason you're down here?"

"Collin and I got divorced and I just bought an apartment back in my hometown in New Jersey. The movers are going to be here in a few hours, and I need to sort through these boxes filled with all the sentimental items I've collected in my life, and decide which memories I am going to keep and which ones I can set free."

"I see. I didn't realize you and Collin were having problems. I never heard you fight over the three years you've been here."

"That's because we hardly spoke to each other."

I walk over to a pile of boxes and stare at the one with "wedding gown" written in thick black marker across the top. There's no more time to choose between donating it or booking a trash the dress style divorce photo shoot, during which I would splatter it in paint. Each flick of color would unleash the pent up regret I have for staying in a stagnant marriage too long. By the end of the photoshoot, I would have forgiven myself and begun the healing part of my journey. But it's 8 a.m. and there's no photographer here, so I slide that box to the donate pile, next to Mrs. Sanders.

"I'm sorry to hear that, Cailin," she says. She stresses the syllables of my name as usual to pronounce Kay-Lynn.

"Don't be sorry. I had enough of living in a loveless marriage. In fact, I would have felt less lonely if I actually lived alone. The divorce was mutual."

That's all I'm going to reveal to Mrs. Sanders. If I say any more, by the time I go through the Lincoln Tunnel back to Jersey, the whole complex will be buzzing with the gossip. No one needs to know that Collin wanted out of everything—including a commitment, mortgage, and my future dreams of a house filled with children and dogs. Or that my plan up until last week was to keep the condo. But then I was abruptly fired from my job as Vice President of Publicity for a pharmaceutical company, so I decided to downsize and move closer to my family and best friend, Gemma. Don't worry though, I'd say I'm doing good for someone who just wasted what should have been the best decade of her life married to the wrong man, lost her job, and is uprooting her life to move back to her home-town. I'll even awkwardly smile to myself to prove it.

"Good for you, then. You're too young to be miserable."

"Thanks for helping me out, Mrs. Sanders. You take care."

Fortunately, Mrs. Sanders takes that as her cue to leave. She wishes me luck and walks back upstairs to her first-floor apart-ment. That leaves just me and about twenty more boxes. Not all of them will fit into my new, smaller apartment. The calendar notification on my phone reminds me every hour that time is ticking and the moving company will arrive shortly to transport my belongings.

I scan the room and locate where I placed my coffee mug, which unfortunately says "Wifey" across the front. I take a sip of lukewarm black coffee, but I don't know if caffeine is enough to fuel me for this task.

Don't get me wrong. I'm totally ready to move on with my life, despite the phrase on my mug. Note to self: order new mugs that say something empowering like, "Stronger Than Coffee," or "Better Not Broken," so I can post selfies and reas-sure all my old high school classmates and friends of Collin, who follow me on social media and I have yet to block, that I am totally fine. If they made a mug that crammed the phrase, "Don't Pity Me Because I'm Young And Divorced And You're

Happily Married And Having Babies. I'm Great," onto it, I would sip to that. A girl with an empowering mug would know exactly how to tackle starting her life over from scratch.

Maybe I'm a coward, but I just don't want to confront the girl I used to be: the creative go-getter who didn't settle for anything less than her dreams. I let that girl down. And I know I must forgive myself before I can fly. That's what this cleaning haul will do. I'll free myself of any remnants holding me back from being the best version of myself moving forward.

I find a box of wedding photos. Collin and I looked great in pictures, but life together exposed the negative and we were out of focus. We could not sustain a marriage. I'm keeping these for the reminder.

I open the box which contains every diary I've written in since I was in second grade. When I was younger, I kept diaries with heart-shaped locks that could only be opened with keys. But as I got older, I started to sum up my days on tattered notebooks. Their edges frayed as I quickly recapped days. I was too busy living life to its fullest to stop and neatly print.

I reach in the box and pull out a purple diary, which I kept during my senior year of high school. Flipping through the pages, I stop and read an entry:

Dear Diary,

Today, Ethan met me at my locker and handed me a note. He told me not to read it until I got into class. Then, we held hands as he walked me to science. We've been dating for a few weeks now, but people still stare at us. Are they wondering how the school newspaper editor scored the football player? Why he's not with a cheerleader? Or, maybe they are all rooting us on because they know we grew up together at the lake. And I've been crushing on him since third grade. Either way, he's mine now. In the note, he asked if he is my favorite boyfriend. "Check yes or no," he wrote. Well, he's my first! So yes, I would confirm that he is my favorite boyfriend. It's ironic how he is so cute, yet a tad bit insecure. He always teases me about my 5 Leo Hearts obsession and the photos of Jax on my walls. Gonna wait to tell him Gemma and I are going to road trip to Philly to see their show. And then, hit NYC. And of course, Jersey. A girl can never attend too many 5 Leo Hearts shows. Maybe one day, we'll actually meet them. Or get a photo with them. Or even more dreamy, get front row seats and pulled up on stage for one of their serenades...

I smile, reflecting back on that iconic time of my life. I need to call Gemma, who answers on the first ring, as usual.

"Guess what I just found?"

"The lipstick I just spent $20 on and lost in Stella's diaper bag?"

"My old diaries about our love for 5 Leo Hearts. Remember how we went to every concert hoping to meet them and seriously thought we stood a chance among their millions of fans? I was going to marry Jax and you were going to marry Ridge."

"It was a solid plan," Gemma says. "Your bedroom was wallpapered with posters of Jax—though I don't know how you could prefer the rebel over Ridge. Gah! Ridge was such a heartthrob. And if we married cousins, then we would have been officially related."

Ahh, to be so young and naive. As if 5 Leo Hearts—named after the members' shared astrological sign, with each of their birthdays falling between July 23rd and August 22nd—would fall for normal girls, while they topped every music chart and performed on the biggest stages across the world.

"Hey now, my results from that teen magazine quiz even confirmed that Jax is my dream guy," I say.

"Can you believe you married the exact opposite of your

dream guy?" Gemma, on the other hand, married Mark, who is a bread-winning husband. He even comes home every night and caters to her needs, whether she stayed home or took their daughter, Stella, to work at the boutique she owns, and had the nanny watch her in the backroom nursery.

"Ok, Gemma. Way to dig it in. I know Collin wasn't exactly good for me, but we did have some good times."

"Cailin, are we talking about the same guy? The one who refused to buy you flowers on Valentine's Day or on your anniversary because they die?"

"In hindsight, I should have seen the red flags."

"I told you to never trust a man who waxes his eyebrows," Gemma says.

Ok, so maybe I was a bit blinded by Collin's dark eyes, perfectly tanned skin, and ambition. I watched every day as he got dressed in expensive clothes and a designer watch, just to sit on the couch and check his phone to see if any investors responded to his emails. Collin captivated me—and everyone else who falls for well-groomed men over six feet tall. Back then, I felt like I won the boyfriend lottery, but in reality, I only scratched the surface to learn that nothing matched up.

"Lesson learned."

"So, how's it going packing for the move? Is he even coming to help you?"

Gemma can't see me roll my eyes. "Of course not. He sent professional movers for all his things to ensure they were handled with care."

"Darn, I was hoping he would leave those white sneakers he cleaned every night so we could burn them in a bonfire." Gemma lets out a loud sigh, as if someone just told her that her favorite designer sold out of a virtual sample sale before she had a chance to log online. "We'll have to celebrate another way."

"Once I'm back, we'll have plenty of time to hang out. I'm gonna hang up now and force myself to finish sorting through this mess."

"Good luck, love you."

"Love you, too."

The box of diaries is going against my "keeper" wall. Reading that journal entry reminded me that I possessed limitless imagination. It was a nice detour, but my real destination, I remind myself, is my new apartment. I take a gulp of coffee, pull up the puffy sleeves of my sweatshirt, and get down to business. I have a few hours to compress my life and get through this task. I have to close the door on this era of Cailin. The version of me that lost track of her thirst for life and settled for the familiar. The one who compromised to avoid change and still found herself in upheaval.

I was served lessons that can't be taught while growing up. No one tells you that people will be brought into your life and then removed once the universe decides you deserve more. That you'll wonder why you had to go through it at all. Or why you worked so many years in a job just because it paid well, when all the while, it left you unfulfilled and you end up getting fired.

Tomorrow, I will be a new version of myself. Cailin 2.0. Get me a cute pair of combat boots because I'm about to kick some butt.

Sure, I'm going back to my hometown. But I have to stop viewing this as a failure or some big mistake. I will not let anyone look at me like I have the scarlet letter, "D" on my forehead. I will own my divorce. And I will claim what's mine.

Trash the Dress Online Chat

Cailin: Hi. I'm Cailin. Thanks for the add. I just signed my divorce papers and it's so weird. I'm ready to move on—my divorce was mutual—but a part of me still feels empty. Like something is missing in my life. Maybe it's because I also just lost my job. Hoping to connect to others who can relate. Anyone else comparing your life to reels right now?

Mae: Welcome to the other side. I'm still working through my divorce, but this group has been a lifesaver!

Tori: Another marriage bites the dust! Just kidding.

Noreen: @Tori! I will apologize for you. Please ignore her @Cailin. She's getting over her first post-divorce breakup and starting to doubt love again.

Cora: So nice to meet you @Cailin!

Alexandra: @Cora where have you been!? We were worried because you haven't posted in a few days.

Cora: @Alexandra Didn't mean to worry anyone. I didn't have power to charge my phone for a few days but I'm OK now.

Alexandra: @Cora Does that mean you finally left him?

2

JAX SLATER VOWS TO CHANGE DIRTY
DAWG WAYS

JAX

Stroke after stroke and nothing relieves me. My trusty right arm is especially aching. Usually swimming calms my nerves, but lately I've been so stressed. After years out of the spotlight, I'm about to go back into the public eye, release my first solo album, and go out on my first solo tour. As soon as I make those announcements with my new PR team, I'll once again be relevant. I'll have to beef up security on my property to make sure no paparazzi hide in trees with their giant lenses. I'm also opening myself up to scrutiny.

I'm so stressed that I've even resorted to attending online meditation sessions at the suggestion of my therapist. He tells me learning techniques to manage my worries will help me get more comfortable going out in public post-breakup with my almost fiancé and fellow pop star, Maxine.

The problem is, I don't want to be more social and I don't want to go out in public alone. When you're a pop star as famous as I am, everyone is always watching you. That's why I quit yoga classes after one session. I thought going to a 5 a.m.

class would be safe, because who wakes up that early in Los Angeles? A lot of people, apparently. I walked out.

The last thing I need is someone sneaking a cell phone picture of me in class and then selling it to the tabloids. I can picture the headlines poking fun at my escapades. **Jax Slater Perfecting Positions For The Bedroom**. Or, **Downward Facing Dog: Womanizer Jax Slater At It Again.**

I disagree with those who accuse me of being addicted to women. I've just had the opportunity to meet and have one-night stands with many willing females. That's what happens when you join a boy band at age fifteen. By the time you're in your thirties, like me, you've spent half of your life in the public eye and have millions of women vying for your attention.

With 5 Leo Hearts, I've traveled the world, sold over 100 million albums, and won countless awards. I'm so grateful for our fans. My career with 5 Leo Hearts would not exist without the dedication of our followers. They propelled us to the most popular musical group in the world at one point.

They also are responsible for stereotyping us into roles where we've felt trapped. Mario is the sensitive one. Jack, the oldest, is the responsible one who holds us together. Oliver is the fun, goofy one. My cousin, Ridge, is the youngest one, a.k.a the heartthrob. And I am the resident bad boy.

I got labeled the bad boy when I started to get tattoos. Coupled with the fact that I prefer to wear black, everyone just assumes I'm a rebel. For many years, I fed into it. I was raised by my single mother and my grandma near Orlando, Florida and didn't have a male role model. Therefore, I did what I thought men do: date a lot of women. My mom always taught me to treat women with respect. And I respected their decisions to have one-night stands.

That's where the paparazzi had their field days. Always photographing me leaving a club with a new woman by my side. That all stopped when I started exclusively dating Maxine. She tamed the beast.

I never thought someone could make me settle down, but I wanted to commit to a life with Maxine. I even set down roots and bought a big house in Los Angeles because she wanted to pursue a movie career. But things slowly fell apart when I brought up getting engaged.

"Baby, I love you, but look at my thighs," Maxine said the night I mentioned us taking the next step. "They are perfect. Do you really think now is the time to talk about getting married and having kids? I just paid for the sculpting of this body and I'm not about to let pregnancy ruin it."

I did love those thighs. And all her other surgically-enhanced curves. But I also wanted something real. "We don't have to have kids right away. I just want to show the world you're mine. Get you a big, sparkly ring."

"Why don't you just buy me some diamond earrings, babe? I'll love those. I can wear my hair up on the next red carpet and tell everyone you gave them to me."

It became obvious that Maxine and I were headed down two different paths. She lusted for fame and I merely put up with it as a condition to my career. I sewed my oats and was ready to settle down and get married. But Maxine, who is a few years younger, was just getting started acting. She didn't want to put her career on hold and have kids. We eventually decided to call it quits.

"I think it's time I move on," I told her one night when she was soaking in a bubble bath. Part of me hoped that in her relaxed state, she would change her mind.

"Move again, Jax? We just unpacked! I'm not about to stuff all my precious jewelry in my purse again so the moving people don't touch it with their grimy hands. Besides, I like the tub. The jets really massage my back. Standing all day on set in heels can really take its toll on a girl."

I stepped into the bathroom and turned on the lights. Maxine lifted her head above a pile of bubbles as I blew out the candles on the edge of the tub.

"Our relationship is over, Maxine. I think we both know that. I want to get married and you don't. There's nowhere else for us to go."

"I love you, babe. And I know you love me. Can't we just wait a few years? We're so good together."

"We *were* good together. And I will always care about you. But there's more to life then VIP parties and celebrity gifting suites. And I don't want to hold you back." I knew if I phrased it like that, Maxine would understand.

After a few moments of silence, Maxine sunk under the bubbles. I worried she was making an over-the-top scene. However, she was actually digging for the tub stopper. As sounds of the tub draining filled the air, she stepped out of the tub. I reached for her robe and handed it to her, as she said, "I agree. You're right. This relationship is holding me back. How am I ever going to travel on set for roles while I'm worried about you here alone, missing me? This is for the best."

"You should move out, Maxine. You can stay in the guest room tonight." Then, I left the room without waiting for her response. I knew it didn't cause her nearly as much pain to hear those words as I felt saying them aloud.

The next day, Maxine left and was officially moved out a week later. Now, I've been alone in this huge house, with an elevator I don't need. I spend all my time in either my music studio or the gym, trying to ignore the emptiness.

Since then, I've gone on a few dates. But no one has held my interest enough for me to want to form a long-term relationship. The last girl I dated was a friend of Ridge's wife, Kelly. She was a nice girl and I liked hanging out with her, but I think it was more because I also got to hang out with Ridge and Kelly. Once a guy gets tied down, it's hard to get quality bro time. But, I totally understand that Ridge is in his newlywed phase. Anyway, I ended things with that girl. No sense in dragging things along when I knew I'd be leaving for tour. Luckily, she took it well. I wouldn't be surprised if she expected to be just another one of bad boy Jax Slater's conquests, anyway.

I pull myself out of the pool and pat myself dry with a towel. It's a gorgeous morning so I decide to lounge. I used to host a lot of parties outside here with Maxine. We would fill the pool with oversized floats like swans and llamas. The more ridiculous, the better. Maxine liked to make a spectacle. I don't miss those days, but I do wish I had someone by my side.

"What's on your mind?" Lily, my housekeeper, asks. She hands me a glass of ice water. Lily knows me better than anyone. She's like my second mother.

"Everything, Lily. My solo album is nothing like 5 Leo Hearts music. I've been writing hundreds of songs that reflect who I am now, but I don't know if that's going to resonate with my fans. Can I live up to the pop star I once was? Or will I let everyone, including myself, down?"

"Are you proud of your songs, Jax?"

"I am. I've never written my own songs before. We've always had award-winning songwriters for 5 Leo Hearts. Between the songwriters and professional musicians backing us, the guys and I carried the vocal harmonies and choreography. We're entertainers, for sure. But am I an artist? Sometimes I can't help but feel like an imposter because I didn't write the songs or play an instrument."

"But you're doing that now."

"I have to prove to myself that I can do it on my own, Lily. The problem is, my A&R team at the label—the department that determines which song is a hit and will be a single—hasn't chosen a song they want to release first. I'm worried that means there isn't a hit."

"You're fearing that you're a failure before you even start, Jax. Don't do that."

"The one thing I am counting on to help get me through this is my publicity team. It's the same team I've worked with for years with 5 Leo Hearts. They'll know how to handle any negative press that comes my way and position me in the best light."

"You're hoping they can clean up your reputation as the bad boy and convince people to take you seriously, aren't you?"

"If they can do that, then maybe—just maybe—I'll feel less anxious about going out in public."

Going back out on the road will be a big deal for me, and my therapist is encouraging me to push myself out of this cocoon. My mom actually started me in therapy when I was young. She wanted me to have an outlet to discuss fame and keep me grounded. At least that's what she told me.

I think she also had another motive: to process feelings around being abandoned as a toddler by my father, who left one day with no explanation. I stuck with the therapy because it just became a part of my routine, and it does actually help to have someone you can tell anything to without judgment. Especially when the world studies your life through a magnifying glass.

"I know it's going to be hard at first, but once you get back out there, Jax, you might even meet a nice woman. The right woman."

That would be nice, but I just don't know where to start. Pop stars really can't go on dating apps. Heck, even if I tried, everyone would think I'm a fake. Do celebrities get verification checkmarks on swipe-right apps? I'm not interested in anyone near my inner circle. Been there and tried that. Anyone else my industry friends would hook me up with would probably be a celebrity. If there's one thing I know I don't want in a future partner, it's someone who is in the public eye. For this new phase of my life, I just want to meet a normal girl.

How does someone who was once named one of the most attractive men alive get the girl next door? I've yet to figure that out.

Trash the Dress Online Chat

Cora: I don't want to keep hijacking Cailin's thread. So, I'll post my update here. I did it!!! I left!! I slept in my car for a few nights, but I drove and now I'm a few states away. He should be served with divorce papers any day now.

Alexandra: I am so proud of you! I know how long you've been trying to leave. Sending you big virtual hugs. WE ARE HERE FOR YOU. YOU GOT THIS.

Rachel: YES, GIRL!! Remember to change the password on all your mutual bank accounts. Do you have enough money to get by? Let us know how we can help. Please don't sleep in your car. We can chip in and get you a hotel for a little while.

Harper: I was so worried about you. Glad you are safe. Now you can heal!

3

CAILIN MCCALL SAYS BYE, BYE…AND BUYS NEW HOME

CAILIN

THERE'S nothing left in my condo, yet I can't seem to find my keys. The movers just loaded up my furniture and are on their way to Jersey. I stand in the middle of the living room, trying to focus on where I misplaced my keychain, but get lost in my thoughts.

When Collin and I first moved in, we were so excited to order new furniture. It was like we made it. We were married, had our own place, and were financially stable enough to purchase new couches. No more hand-me-downs. The first night we were officially moved in, we cuddled on the couch to watch a movie. We microwaved a bag of kettle corn a little too long, and despite the burned smell, sifted through the charcoal pieces in the bag to find the perfectly popped kernels. Whenever Collin found one, he took it and ate it. Part of me wished just once, he would take that perfect piece, trace his fingers over my lips, and feed it to me. A little sexy gesture here and there would have meant the world to me, but Collin didn't put in extra effort.

Collin was too practical for surprise romantic gestures. He

was physically next to me, but often I wondered if his mind was off brainstorming a new project, or thinking about emails. That first night on our couch, I made him pose for a selfie with me and I uploaded it to my social pages with the caption, "First movie night in our newlywed home!" I added a ton of hearts and #homeiswheretheheartis. Maybe I was a little extra showy in order to make myself believe it was the truth.

Now, I've been sitting alone on that couch, but I'm somehow happier. I was ready to embark on this new chapter of my life the day Collin told me he didn't want to be married to me anymore.

"I think you're holding me back from being successful," Collin said.

"By holding you back, do you mean covering the mortgage and all our bills while you invest our money in developing apps that continue to fail?" I asked.

"We can't all become Vice Presidents of companies overnight, Cailin. Sometimes it takes people a few years to find success."

Always an optimist, my tragic trait might be ignoring warning signs. I did with Collin, and now, I've just done it with my job. I should have seen it coming.

"Who is this guy moving into the spare office?" I asked my boss. I felt the eyes of my colleagues on my back when I walked into his office and closed the door.

"Take a seat, Cailin," my boss said.

"I'll stand."

"Cailin, we're letting you go."

"Excuse me? You're *firing* me?"

"I know this may come as a shock. You've been with this company for years and have developed so many award-winning campaigns."

"I've brought in millions of dollars, Troy. No one is more qualified than I am to do this job."

"I'm sorry, Cailin. But part of the terms of agreement for

the merger were that they keep their PR team." Troy tapped his fingers on his desk. Perhaps he was just as uncomfortable as me with the conversation.

"I see what's happening here. They want a man leading the company initiatives. I'm being pushed out because I'm a woman. Plain and simple."

"It's not that he's a man. He's just more passionate about pharmaceuticals. You have to admit, you don't really have that spark anymore. I know it may not seem like it, but I'm doing you a favor by letting you go, instead of keeping you on to work with their team. You'll get a generous severance package and the opportunity to figure out what you're really passionate about for work."

"I hate that you're making that decision for me. I've dedicated my life to this job, you know that."

"Please don't cry, Cailin. Now is a good time for you to evaluate things."

"Over all these years, we've gotten really close, Troy. And it hurts to lose my job at the same time my marriage is ending. But I do think you're right. I may have had an office with a window overlooking New York City and a fancy title, but I don't feel like I belong here. I'm not sure where—or who with, for that matter—I belong, but I'm going to find out."

"I know you will. And I will be happy to be a reference for you. Take your time to pack your things and say your goodbyes."

With that, I walked out of Troy's office and vowed to find work that gives me creative freedom and purpose. And I'll get that. As soon as I move out of this condo of false hope, settle into my new apartment, and update my resume.

I walk through each vacant room of my condo to make sure I didn't leave anything behind and eventually find my keys next to the kitchen sink. I look out the living room window overlooking New York City. Millions of people, each with a story as to why they are walking down the sidewalk outside the building. I'm pretty sure I'm the only one that's about to walk down this particular city street for the last time.

I need anthems, I decide, as I choose a playlist for my car ride home. Songs that make me happy and fill me with power. I can and will find a new love. Obviously, I choose my boy band mix. This playlist features my favorite songs from 5 Leo Hearts, as well as my favorite groups from England and Ireland. All five-member harmonies that make me swoon and believe that rom-com love really exists.

As I drive down the highway, I put my windows down, and turn up the radio as a solo verse from Jax comes on. He has the sexiest voice, hands down. It's rugged and rough, not smooth and youthful like the other members. That's probably why he never got photographed in the center of the group for pictures. He wasn't America's sweetheart and that's why I crushed so hard. Jax rocked tattoos and scruffy facial hair. He wore mostly black clothing to further establish his identity in the group. I wondered what he smelled like. He was edgy and mysterious and everything I wanted in a boyfriend when I was in my early twenties.

An hour later, I arrive back to my hometown. I pull into the lot of my new apartment and see Gemma standing outside with balloons. As I walk over to her, I cover my face in my hands and then look up to quickly scan the area for passersby.

"Surprise!" Gemma is wearing a maxi dress and straw hat, which signifies summer mode in Jersey, but would never be seen on the streets of NYC.

"It sure is," I say. "What are you doing here and why do you have balloons? This is so embarrassing."

"I just wanted to officially welcome you home," Gemma says. "How was your ride?"

"It was great. I listened to 5 Leo Hearts. Do you remember

when you were caller number 100 on the radio and won tickets for us to watch the show from the VIP area in front of the stage?"

"Those were the days. I wonder when Stella is older if she will beg me to take her to pop concerts. That would be amazing."

"We should start getting her into the music now. She'll grow up loving it. Where is she, by the way?"

"Home, napping with the nanny. I snuck out to go to the shop to check on things, but it's a slow day so I decided to wait here in my car like a creep and read a book until I figured you might arrive."

We open the door to my apartment and are greeted with the smell of fresh paint. Crisp white walls stare back at me: a fresh canvas for whatever mood I want to create. This will be my sanctuary. The apartment has a mostly open floor plan. You enter into the living room, which is open to the kitchen. There's a small dining area and I already imagine placing an accent rug under the table to define the space. We wander into the spacious bedroom, which boasts a walk-in closet that I can't wait to fill. The bathroom is clean and recently renovated with white subway tile. I'm going to add splashes of color to make everything pop. Maybe lots of greenery and bamboo.

"This is really cute," Gemma says. We walk back into the living area and wait for the movers. I can tell her mind is also going in circles with décor ideas.

"It's perfect for what I need. Plenty of natural sunlight for selfies, closet space, and I can easily access outside to walk the dog."

"Wait, what dog?" Gemma asks.

"Well, the dog I am going to get," I say. Putting this intention out into the universe will help me claim it. "One of my post-divorce goals is to adopt a dog and shower it with all the love in the world."

"Dogs provide more love and loyalty than men. I'm sure

there's a study somewhere that proves it."

"If not, maybe I can conduct one. Cailin 2.0 will become a researcher."

"What was it that Collin said on your first date when you asked him if he was a dog person?"

"He said, 'They shed and slobber, take up space in the bed, and leave you heartbroken when they pass away.' That should have been my first red flag."

"You totally should have excused yourself to use the bathroom and then snuck out the back window."

"I did consider it. But the thought of landing on a thorny bush seemed less appealing than continuing with the rest of the conversation."

"How did you respond?"

"I told him, 'You just haven't met the right dog yet. The dog that makes every day better, even if all you have left are memories.'"

Gemma's facial expression changes to one of concern. "Okay, how are you really feeling though? You can tell me. This is a big change. Do we need a night out?"

I appreciate Gemma for checking in on me beneath what she sees on the surface. "Honestly, I cried all the tears away a while ago. I mourned the marriage, forgave myself, and allowed grace, and now I'm ready to move on."

Gemma gives me a hug. "I'm proud of you, really. That sounded inspirational. Like something more women need to hear. It's okay to cry, be gentle with yourself, and don't replay mistakes or lost time in your mind. Just move forward."

Gemma dabs her eye and I notice her lip quiver. "Are you crying?"

"Hormones."

With that, we both burst out laughing, and I realize how much I needed to let go for a moment. Soon after, Gemma leaves to go check on Stella. As soon as the door closes behind her, a sudden feeling of loneliness washes over me. But that only lasts a second, because my mom is texting me, telling me she's on her way to help me unpack.

———

With my mom's help, I have mostly everything organized where it belongs. I'm glad I have her support, but wish she would back off a bit when trying to help me find a new relationship.

"You know, Ethan is single," my mom says. "He's doing really well as a financial analyst. Wait 'til you see the size of his house. It's way too big for one man. He must be waiting to find the right woman to get married and have kids."

We ordered pizza from my favorite restaurant. When I was little, we got pizza every Friday night. My older brothers and dad ordered pepperoni, and my mom and I dug into the white pie. My brothers have both moved out of state for work, but I video chat with their kids every week. My dad is retired and off on a fishing expedition with his friends at the moment.

I sigh and pull my second slice. "Mom, Ethan was my boyfriend in high school. We were kids. Please stop trying to set me up."

My mom swallows a bite of pizza as she contemplates her response. "I'm just saying that he could be good for you. I'd like to have grandchildren who live nearby."

I nearly choke on my food. And this foreshadowed the rest of our conversation. Later, when my mom leaves, I collapse on my bed and start mindlessly scrolling social media to decompress. Yes, it's against every therapist's advice. But, I'm tempted to look up Ethan's page. We're connected, but really never interact. I can't help but admit that I am curious about the size of his house...and maybe other things. Ethan was a good kisser back in the day. Not that I had anything to compare it to back then. But maybe a little post-divorce action is just what I need.

As I'm trailing off into a heated fantasy, my social feed updates and my heart skips a beat. There's Jax. He just posted a photo of himself working out, shirtless, sweaty, and covered in more tattoos. Gosh, he still gets my heart racing. I follow him, but not religiously, since I grew up and have established my own life as a daytime drama series.

"Back at it. Big news coming soon," Jax captions the photo. I double tap to like it and log out of the app. I decide I should shut down my phone. If I stay on any longer, I'm going to start looking up jobs, and I just want to relax and forget about the state of these matters for the rest of the night.

Before I can power off, I get a text from my college room-mate, Imani. We bonded over our ambition to succeed in media relations. We both became publicists, but Imani leaned more towards music publicity. I left the entertainment side of PR and ventured into the world of corporate PR because I straight-up wanted to make money, and working with indie rock bands didn't cover my cost of life expenses. But at times, I always envied Imani, because she was doing work that made her exhila-rated and she got paid well by her company. It's what I yearned to feel and achieve. I click on Imani's text.

> Imani: Call me ASAP. I have a great opportunity for you.

I debate calling Imani. I'm interested in what she has to say, but I'm also exhausted. However, I give in and pull up her number.

"Cailin, you can thank me now. I have the solution to your problems. You need a job and one of the senior publicists at my company just resigned. We need to fill her spot ASAP and I already told my boss about you. I just need you to update your resume and send it to me tomorrow."

I'm stunned. Could finding a new job really be this easy? I was expecting to be applying for roles and crying over countless rejections for at least a few weeks. I even made a list of my favorite ice cream flavors that are made in tub size.

"Whoa, slow down," I say. "I just moved out of the City and I haven't worked in music PR in years. I am totally out of the game."

"PR is PR. You know how to manage accounts, lead calls with clients, and you're creative as hell. The media loves you and you form strong connections with everyone you work with, so all that will translate here. You just need to brush up on the state of the music industry and learn the key contacts and outlets. I can help with that. And this role is totally remote, like most of our company. You won't have to commute to the office."

Imani is slowly selling me on this idea. I feel my heart start to race with excitement, like when I spot the roasted nut vendor on the street and there's no line. "Okay, it's worth a shot. I have to pay the mortgage on my apartment, after all. I'll update my resume tomorrow and send it to you."

"You won't regret this, Cailin. There's a new tour starting that's going to be a big deal. I don't have the details yet, but I know we will need all hands on deck."

"Maybe this is just what I need. Thank you for always supporting me and for pushing me out of my comfort zone. Working in healthcare is what I know, but not what I love, and if I'm going to be the best version of myself moving forward, that means not settling for anything less than I deserve. That goes for love and work."

"Now is your time," Imani says.

We hang up and I feel lighter. I'm nervous about the job interview and potentially being thrown into a new position at a new company while working on a major account. But I know I can handle it. Things are accelerating quicker than I expected, but I'll follow the direction I'm being led in by the universe. It wouldn't steer me wrong, would it?

Before I turn off my phone for good this time, I click back open my social media app and click on Ethan's profile.

Trash the Dress Online Chat

Alexandra: My ex wants to introduce his new girlfriend to the twins. Seriously? They are too young. Why does he have to confuse them? I don't want them to think she's their mother when they are with him on the weekends. HELP!

Leila: Is this the chick he met at the club? It won't last long.

Chelsea: My ex did this once and then the girl he was dating realized he had too much baggage so she dumped him. Maybe it will work out in your favor? But it's sooo hard at first to go through this. I know. I miss my kids so much when they are with their dad. I worry about all the little stuff too. Video chat helps but it's not the same.

Tori: You had to expect this was going to happen.

Harper: @Tori Remember the rules of this group. Alexandra has posted multiple times about cheating on her husband but that's not what this thread is about. Please be kind.

4

JAX SLATER IS FORCED TO FACE THE MUSIC

JAX

MY MANAGER, Harry, is knocking at my door. He's here for a meeting about the upcoming tour. I open the door and give him a man hug. Harry's been the manager of 5 Leo Hearts from the start. He gave us a chance and chose us out of hundreds of groups who auditioned to be represented by his agency. Harry's talent firm represents a lot of high-profile musicians and he somehow finds a way to give everyone his full attention. Maybe his secret is never getting married. But Harry doesn't seem to care about being alone. He's in a love affair with his work.

"My man," Harry says. He walks in and helps himself to a cold bottle of water from my refrigerator. It's filled with enough food to feed an army, thanks to Lily. I usually end up donating half of it to a local homeless shelter at the end of every week. Maybe one day, I'll have a family to share my riches with, but for now, it's hard to find the joy in the excess of everything. All I see is what's missing.

"What's the deal?" I ask. "Any word back from the label?"

"The pressure is on from A&R. They love the album, really. But they don't feel like one song in particular is strong enough to go out and wow everyone as the first single. This is a big move and we have to do it right."

"So, basically they hate the album." I start to second guess myself again. Why did I think I have what it takes? I'm just a singer, not a songwriter.

"No, I didn't say that. They just feel like this batch of songs are the filler songs. You know how every 5 Leo Hearts album had three or four singles and the rest just backed up the hits? The fans still love and request the other songs, but they live and breathe the singles."

"I think a few have potential to be singles." I rattle off the names of the tracks to Harry.

"I agree. The label likes those songs as well. However, we need that one anthemic song to kick things off. The one that makes the whole stadium sing in unison. You still have time to write and record one. The album doesn't come out until after tour wraps up."

"Then I'd have to write and find a place to record while we're on the road." This added stress is the last thing I want before I emerge from my years-long hiatus and get back on the road.

"If anyone can do this, I know you can." Harry always encourages me and somehow convinces me to start believing in myself when I am blinded by doubt.

"I'll keep writing. We still have a few days before tour starts and miracles can happen."

"Maybe it would help if you got some new inspiration. Get out. You're always hiding in this house."

"That's the benefit of a big house." But in all seriousness, I understand Harry.

When I go out, everyone sees Jax Slater, the pop star. Everyone will want to talk to me about the group and how much they love us. No one ever really wants to get to know me. I just want to have a boring conversation like everyone else and talk about the weather. Have someone tell me about their life.

They know about mine. Maybe my struggles really aren't a big deal in the grand scheme of the world.

"I just think that getting out might do you some good. Get your feet wet before you're thrown back into things."

Harry does have a point. I'm going to have to get used to going out in public again. I used to thrive off that attention from passersby. I loved meeting my fans when the band was in our prime. Maybe I just need to go back to who I was and then I'll be inspired to write a hit song. Yet, my conscience is still whispering that I'm an imposter. Can I be a success on my own without the band? I have to give it my best shot, despite my reservations.

"I'll give Oliver a call and see if he wants to meet up later." There's strength in numbers. If Oliver is with me, we'll get more attention. But he'll also shield me from being the focus.

"Atta boy," Harry says. He pats my shoulder. "I'll leave you to it."

I say goodbye to Harry and make plans to meet Oliver for drinks tonight. Here goes nothing.

I meet Oliver at some swanky LA bar that he insists we go to because it will make us look hip. I tell him there's no way we are competing with the new crop of Hollywood elite, but go along to humor him.

Since the band has taken a hiatus, Oliver has begun dabbling in real estate. He buys and oversees a renovation team as he flips properties. He doesn't seem to miss touring that much, but I know he misses the attention.

I walk through the room, wishing it was acceptable to wear sunglasses indoors. The room is brighter than the street outside. Each wall is decorated in a different theme to pose and take photos. They've even gone as far as to set up tripods for your cell phones and ring lights, to make taking selfies and tagging the establishment a breeze.

It's like I've entered a jungle and I can't make my way out of the quicksand. But finally, I see Oliver. He's dressed to impress and sitting at the bar, flirting with the bartender.

As I stand next to him, she does a double take. It's been a while since anyone has seen 5 Leo Hearts out in public together. The only glimpse people have gotten of the "where are they now?" version of our stories is when the media covered Ridge's wedding. We were all groomsmen. I was Best Man, which by the way, is a massive task if the groom is marrying Kelly. I found that out the hard way. I might as well have been a bridesmaid for the amount of times her sister, the Maid of Honor, texted me.

"Is this seat taken?" I sit down next to my bandmate.

"Jax, dude," Oliver says. We do a one-arm hug and hand-shake move. "Never thought the day would come when you asked me to hang out. But here we are."

"Yeah, yeah. Harry wants me to get out a little before touring starts."

"I can't believe you're doing it," Oliver says, taking a sip of his drink. He's matured but still has what I think women would consider a sexy nerd vibe, thanks to his black wide-rim glasses. "The first of us to break out and go solo. I honestly thought it would be Ridge."

"Me too. It probably would have been if he wasn't shacked up with Kelly." I order a drink. It's a nice change from making my own at home.

"That's true." Oliver shoots the bartender a smile and her cheeks turn a rouge color. "Once she got her hooks in him, he was whipped. Now that she got him down the aisle, forget it. He's gone the way of Mario and Jack. Wedded bliss and all that."

"At least we actually like all their wives. What about you?" I dart my eyes to the bartender, who is now serving some young stars who look like they're only recently licensed to drink. Pretty sure one of them is an actor on a popular teen drama. They have no clue that Oliver and I are famous. If they do, they aren't letting on that they recognize us. We are has-beens. And I love that. Except, I need to be relevant.

"She's hot, right?" Oliver says about the bartender. "I might get her number. But I don't want to get tied down right now. I'm in the middle of negotiations to get this house in Beverly Hills. It's not even a flip. I want to get it and then make a few updates and put it back on the market."

"Look at you, trading work for women. I like this new you."

"Hey now, look who's talking, The King of Players. I haven't seen you with anyone on your arm lately."

There goes my reputation getting thrown at me again. Even from my closest friends. I know he's slightly joking, but it still irritates me. "Nah, I'm just focused on writing songs and getting this album out. No distractions for me, either."

"That's awesome. I can't wait to hear some of them."

"The label says I still need a single," I say.

"I'd offer to give input, but I know you want to do this totally alone."

"Thanks, I appreciate it. You're right though, I have to do this alone. To prove that I can, ya know?" I take a sip of my drink and swallow the truth.

"I get it. You still want a career in music, so you should. Who knows if the band will ever reunite? You need to figure out how post boy band life will be for you."

"Yours is looking pretty good, Oliver. You're well on your way." I raise my glass to him.

As Oliver and I talk, I start to feel more confident being out in public. This isn't so bad after all. I just had to rip off the bandage. A few casual acquaintances spot us and come over to chat. Before I know it, a few hours pass and I'm ready to go home. I might be getting adjusted to going back out, but I haven't done it enough to want to spend all night socializing with crowds. I want to get up and start my day early tomorrow. I'm feeling a new motivation.

Before we head out, Oliver gets the bartender's number. I knew it. Good for him.

"Isn't that weird? I'm leaving with a girl's number and you're going home alone. Things are definitely not like the old days."

"Definitely not." Except, I'm oddly not jealous or feeling a need to compete with him. I'm different now, and for that, I am grateful.

Tomorrow I'm one day closer to going on tour. And that means I'm either one step closer to public scrutiny or one step closer to everything I want. Hopefully the upcoming meeting with my PR team will help ease some of my worry. I wonder who will be working on my account this time. Marisol, Carlos, and Imani have all been great. But I'm not sure who will be the one assigned to come on the road to manage tour press. Whoever it is, I'll be working closely with this person every day.

Trash the Dress Online Chat

Rachel: Happy divorce anniversary to me! Two years ago, I never thought I'd be where I am today.

Cora: Happy divorceaversary! I can't even think about what my life might be like two years from now but I know it'll have to be better than these past two years.

Alexandra: I hope you are doing something special tonight!

Cailin: Wow, I didn't know this was a thing!

5

CAILIN MCCALL RUNS INTO A FAMILIAR
FACE

CAILIN

Ethan doesn't post a lot on social media. But when he does, it's about the lake. He's on the Board of Directors and apparently working on a fundraiser to renovate the clubhouse. I scroll deeper to search for a recent picture. There's one from a few months ago. He's still handsome, in a lumberjack way, beard and all. His light brown hair is cut short, his hazel eyes still shimmer, and his body is toned, but not overly muscular. He surely works out, but I bet he participates in more nature-based activities and sports, like bike riding, swimming, and hiking. I wonder why he's still single. He's successful and obviously attractive. I'll have to ask Gemma. She always comes through with the details.

With that, my curiosity is filled and I shut my phone off and attempt to go to sleep.

It's weird sleeping alone my first night in my new place. Everything is so quiet and dark here. Back in the City, there's always noise and lights from the hustle and bustle. But here in suburbia, I can hear the clock tick. Well, I would if I had a wall clock.

My bed, sheets, and comforter are the same. The leggings and T-shirt I'm sleeping in have been worn a million times. They're familiar, but I feel different. I feel new. Full of possibility. A little scared, but mostly positive. I close my eyes, hug my pillow, and quickly drift off and fall asleep as exhaustion overcomes my body.

Light shines through my window at 6 a.m. and I awake to the sunrise. The sky is pink and purple, but a hint of yellow is breaking through and illuminates a gorgeous glow. I snap a photo and then make a mental note to get black-out curtains. Since I'm up, I decide to make the most of the day and take a walk around the lake.

After I shower, I start to get dressed but debate what to wear. Should I look put together, in case I run into anyone? It's my first real day out in town since my return. With small lake communities, news travels fast. On one hand, I want to at least have a good outfit for them to talk about when they gossip. On the other hand, it's early morning and I'm going for a casual walk so I can get away with workout clothes. I decide to blend my two ideas. I slip into a pair of black leggings that have a bit of shine, so they look more lux. Then, I choose a white tank-top that screams casual, but looks chic. I brush my hair and leave it down, and throw on a black baseball-style hat and sunglasses. The motivational bracelet stack on my arm reminds me to manifest my goals and trust fate. I look at my naked left ring finger, slightly missing the diamonds that once shone there, but also excited for the opportunities that can fill my life thanks to that blank space.

When I get to the local coffee shop, I'm greeted by the smell of freshly ground beans. I don't recognize anyone as I make my way past the couches to the register, but the barista is friendly. She doesn't even ask my name for the order, because in this town, everyone knows each other. I leave with a black Americana in my hand, and faith that the barista will have my order ready for me as soon as I walk in tomorrow, and drive four minutes to the lake.

A familiar musty smell welcomes me. The lake is the same as the pictures ingrained in my mind. There's a narrow beach, a playground for the kids, and picnic tables. The clubhouse does look run down. I have so many memories there and think about all the little kids who are enjoying it these days. I hope Ethan's renovation project is a success.

I walk over a little worn and torn bridge near a small waterfall, and stop to admire a mother and baby geese as they swim.

Someone yells out, "Careful, that bridge is a little unstable in the middle."

I turn around and see a glistening guy in a tank top, shorts, and sunglasses, wearing a bandana across his head. He's holding a blue water bottle in his hands and stops jogging to lift up his sunglasses. As he wipes beads of sweat off his forehead, I register his identity. It takes me one second to look at those hazel eyes and realize this is Ethan.

"Oh, thank you," I say. I'm suddenly off balance. I'm unsure if he recognizes me, so I take off my sunglasses. I awkwardly pause and let space fill the air.

"I heard you were moving back, Cailin. Good to see you." Ethan pets his beard and takes in every inch of my body. I don't mind one bit.

"You too, Ethan." I let my eyes drift down to admire his toned calves and arms, but catch myself and bring them back to his eyes. All I can do is take in the glimmer as the sun hits his pupils just right. The corners of his eyes have a few lines. He's aged well.

"So, what do you think?" Ethan asks. "Still breathtaking?"

Yes. I almost say it aloud. That comment catches me off guard. For a moment, I think he's referring to himself. Then, I realize he means the lake.

"Oh, yes," I say. "Everything looks the same, just with more history. The clubhouse has certainly seen better days, though."

Ethan lights up at the mention of the clubhouse and tells me, "It's definitely worn down and falling apart. There's so much work that needs to be done on it, that I'm trying to raise money to rebuild it from scratch. So many of us have happy memories here and I'd hate to see them end. There's a new generation of families that deserve the same opportunities we've had here."

He takes a sip of his water and I watch as he swallows. His Adam's apple is prominent now. Suddenly, I find Adam's apples sexy.

"That's a great idea. If there's anything I can do to help promote it and get the local media involved, let me know. I'd love to give back for such an important cause."

"I'd love that," Ethan says. He places his hand on my shoulder and lets it drift down my arm, making it tingle. This is the first man who has touched me since Collin. I didn't know my body could still have physical reactions to men. "I'm just out for my morning run and have to get showered and ready for a client meeting, but how about we meet up later? Or whenever you're free?"

"Sounds great," I say. "I'd like that. Here, let me have your phone. I'll give you my number." I'd rather leave the ball in his court.

Ethan hands me his phone and I type in my number. He takes it, flashes me his pearly whites, and puts it back into his pocket. His shorts tug down, revealing the V-shape of his abs. "It was really great to see you. I'm glad you're back."

"Me too," I say. I think I actually mean it. Things are looking up.

Ethan dashes off and I watch him run. I wonder if we could rekindle the flames of our youth. But I also wonder how much he has actually changed and if he's the same old possessive Ethan. For now, I'm just going to enjoy it and let things unfold.

Back at home, I open up my laptop and get to updating my resume. I need to highlight all I've accomplished and also show what I can bring to the table at an entertainment firm.

As I ponder what I can spotlight as an entertainment PR success, I wonder if any of my past boy band chasing escapades count. Surely, designing a sign on poster board that got featured on music television the day Gemma and I stood outside the TV studio for 5 Leo Hearts' appearance counts as creativity and recognition. Competition among fans was tough those days. Everyone wanted to stand out. Some made signs, others, gift baskets. Gemma and I did it all. We conquered the toughest crowds, pushing our way to the front of the stage, snuck cameras in venues, and even survived gum getting thrown in our hair by other fans.

The one thing we always took pride in was that we were not the girls who set out to sleep with the band. That was never our intention and we made sure we didn't associate with the groupies. Gemma and I were simply dedicated fans who wanted to meet our favorite singers, the guys whose music made us happy even on sad days. We cherished their songs, which connected us to our generation, and made us hope for a love like the songs they crooned. You know, totally attainable things in a teenage girl's dream.

After a little while of focusing on my actual career experience and talents, my resume is updated and sent off to Imani. I figure it's a good idea to update my profile on my professional networking page, too. Because I don't want to put all my eggs in one basket, I search job openings and see if there are any positions I might want to apply for, but there's nothing. I really hope Imani's team is impressed once they read my resume. I'll take this job, even if it means a step down in ranks. Passion and purpose are more important than a title.

Titles are so annoying. Right now, mine are "jobless" and "divorced." I hope I don't have to go to a doctor's office anytime soon because circling those boxes on check-in forms will not be fun. Why are there no petitions to remove marital status off forms where your relationship is no one's business? All they really need is your emergency contact name and number. If they're going to put that question, they should at least leave a line for comments. This way, I can write, "Send hot, emotionally, and financially stable men my way."

As I walk into my living room to start unpacking a few pictures I want to hang on the walls, my phone dings. It's a text message from Ethan. He's wasting no time in contacting me.

> Ethan: Hey there! I was just thinking about running into you this morning. I don't want to be too forward, but I'd love to spend more time catching up. Would you like to have dinner with me tonight? I'll cook.

Whoa. My first reaction is to think he *is* bold for asking me over to his place on our first... is it a date? But then again, we already had our tongues in each other's mouths 1,000 times before, so this really isn't a big deal. It's just two people who dated when they were teenagers and are now old enough to own their homes, so they can invite guests over for proper meals that they cook.

I don't want to appear too eager, so I wait ten minutes before I respond. It's just enough time to make him question if he was indeed too forward, but to also create the illusion that I'm not totally glued to my phone hoping for human interaction.

To pass the time, I check the social media group I recently joined for young divorced women, called Trash the Dress. I read an article about it online and it sounded like a really empowering group that is right up my alley, so I requested to join. I've been enjoying following the posts. Some are basic divorce conversations, like how to navigate child custody agreements, but there's also a special camaraderie among these women as they cheer each other on through moves, new jobs, and dating.

So far, I've made quite a few new close friends. I wonder if I should make a post about Ethan, but decide that I should wait until I actually have more to share.

Enough time has passed for me to respond to his message.

> Me: Sounds great. Hope your skills in the kitchen are as good as they were on the football field.

I send my response to tease and hope Ethan catches that I'm open to concluding dinner with dessert.

> Ethan: Much better with my hands in the kitchen than on a football, if you can believe it.

I'm slightly blushing at the thought of making out with Ethan in his kitchen. It's fun to flirt again, to feel like someone desires me. I want to keep calm, but I can't. I'm going on my first post-divorce date.

Trash the Dress Online Chat

Tori: Can you believe lumberjack dude tried to booty call me last night? As if.

Leanne: I'd give anything to be a guy's booty call right now.

Alexandra: I'm swearing off sex until I meet my next husband.

Cora: @Alexandra stop punishing yourself for cheating!

6

CAILIN MCCALL DITCHES EX-HUSBAND FOR —GASP!—OLD BOYFRIEND

CAILIN

AFTER THROWING half of my clothes across the bedroom, I give up. I can't find my favorite shirt. It's a cornflower blue color and just oversized enough so that it drapes off my shoulders. It would have been perfect for dinner tonight, but since it has disappeared, I pick up my keys and head over to Gemma's boutique, Boho Bliss + Co., with hopes of scoring the perfect top. What else can a young, recently divorced woman wear to give the illusion that she isn't trying really hard to convince herself she's still got it?

It's been a while since I've been inside the store. I'm greeted by the smell of sweet candles. They aren't lit, but they smell so good, they just emit deliciousness. It's a mix of coconut, rose, vanilla, and cinnamon. Gemma's store has a bright white and airy atmosphere accentuated by lush green plants. It feels like southern California in New Jersey. The store displays jewelry, home décor gifts, and carefully curated artisan clothes. Everything in stock appears to be specifically chosen, and knowing Gemma, she spent hours selecting each item.

"Hey," I say to Gemma. I walk past a table filled with NJ-shaped wooden cutting boards and debate getting one.

"Cailin!" Gemma peers out from behind the register. "What are you doing here? I didn't know you were coming? How is it being back in town today?"

So many questions. Typical Gemma. "It's good. I ran into Ethan this morning when I took a walk at the lake."

Gemma puts down the clipboard she was holding and gives me her full attention. "Oh really?"

"We just spoke quickly, but I gave him my number and he texted me to go to dinner at his place tonight." I walk over to the candles and take a whiff of the coconut one.

"Stop it." Gemma looks around to make sure no other customers are near. "Do you think he's hot? I mean, he's hot. And single. You should go."

I roll my eyes and laugh as I put down the coconut candle and wander over to a display of necklaces. "He is hot. And yes, I'm going. But I don't know if it's a date. I told him I would help brainstorm promotion ideas to raise money to rebuild the clubhouse." I pick up a rose gold charmed necklace and admire it against my chest in the mirror.

"Sure, the clubhouse. You two go ahead and explore those ideas, and maybe each other, while you're at it. Ethan has been single for so long. I don't know what his deal is, but maybe you'll find out. So, what are you going to wear?" Gemma walks over and puts a summer fedora on my head.

"That's why I'm here," I say. I quickly remove the hat. I love it. Sold.

"No," Gemma says. "That's why I'm here." She grabs my arm, shows me to a dressing room and begins throwing shirts over the door.

I step out and show her each option. I like something about all of them, but decide one is the winner. It's a red crop top that looks super sexy, but also super laid back. We pick out a long gold necklace, beaded with colorful stones that will drape nicely down my chest.

"Please send me a selfie before you leave so I can see how smokin' you are." Gemma rings up my order. I refuse to accept her friends and family discount, though my bank account statement will probably scare me in a few weeks.

"You got it." I hug her goodbye and head home.

Home. My new home. In my old town. Where I'm going to meet my ex-boyfriend for dinner. Somehow, my new start is beginning with my past. I wonder if that's a good thing. But progress is progress. I'm moving forward. New apartment, maybe a new job, sooner rather than later, and a new dating life that is maybe starting now. As I walk down the sidewalk to my car, I look up at the sky, take a deep breath, and exhale. For a second, I feel limitless.

Okay, I also feel really nervous. My stomach feels like one hundred butterflies were just let loose. Do I even know how to go on a date? If this is a date. I'm worried the crop top might be overdoing it now. I debate just wearing a T-shirt so Ethan thinks I'm totally uncomplicated and casual. But of course, that is the furthest thing from the truth.

A while later, I decide I still need to calm my sudden nerves before I get to Ethan's. In my car, I turn on my playlist and pick my favorite 5 Leo Hearts pump up jam. This will do the trick. The ride to Ethan's house is literally the same length of time as the song. I turn off my engine, step out of my car, and close the door with a mission. Tonight, I'm going to let go and let fate take the wheel.

Ethan's house is stately. It's a corner house with dark blue siding and gray stone in the front. There's a complementing gray stone wall surrounding the house. The lawn is a lush and hydrated dark green. There are yellow tulips planted in a small garden in front and perfectly landscaped bushes. It's well-kept, just as I would expect.

I don't get a chance to ring the doorbell, because Ethan has the front storm door open and can see me coming through the glass screen door. He immediately opens it and embraces me in a hug. Ethan lifts me off my feet and then places his arm around my waist as he welcomes me inside. I see him glance up and down and know I chose the right outfit. He's wearing cargo shorts and a T-shirt.

"This is gorgeous," I say. Ethan leads me inside.

"Thanks. I put a lot of work into this place when I renovated it. I want this to be my forever home. Hopefully raise a family here one day to give kids the memories I had growing up. It's such a special community."

We walk through the living room. It's sterile and filled only with essentials, like a TV and couches. Total bachelor pad. There's not one sign of a woman's touch.

"There's definitely no other place like it. As much as people love New York City, and as much fun as I had there, I'd never want to raise kids there. There's something about walking down the beach that makes me feel more alive than walking down a city street."

Ethan brings me into the kitchen, which is basically the size of my apartment. The center island is navy blue and all the hardware on the cabinets is gold. He has a spectacular eye for design. On the island, he has laid out a salad bowl and tossing utensils.

"I thought we'd make a salad," Ethan says. "I recently saw a post online about mango, walnut, and cheese drizzled with balsamic vinaigrette dressing. I'll grill some chicken to throw in, if that's cool with you. You're not a vegetarian, are you?"

I'm impressed he asks if I'm vegetarian. Usually people just assume that everyone eats meat. "I actually try to stick to a mostly pescatarian diet, but I do eat chicken from time to time. Sounds great. What can I do?"

Ethan hands me the lettuce and salad spinner. "You can start washing the lettuce and I'll prep the chicken."

"It'll be nice to have a home-cooked meal. Since the move, I've been mostly living on take-out."

"Speaking of the move, if you don't mind me asking, what happened with you and your husband?" I can tell Ethan is trying to get the details out of me as smoothly as possible. And I'm ready for this conversation. I've rehearsed my response in preparation for an ambush of inquiries upon my arrival back home.

"Honestly, it was a long time coming. We were unhappy together and mutually decided to divorce. I'm looking at the end of my marriage as a new beginning." I spin the salad, hoping this topic won't continue in circles.

"I'm sorry you had to go through that. Speaking from past experience, I know breaking up with you can be hard on a guy. But it sounds like you have a really forward-thinking outlook on things."

Ethan stops slicing the mango, wipes his hands on a towel, and hands me a glass of sparkling water. He must remember that in high school, I never drank. I've remained straight-edge my entire life. Abstaining from alcohol, drugs, and smoking was not hard for me because I was never interested in altering my mind or behavior. I accept the glass of water as Ethan picks up his own. He clinks his glass to mine.

"Here's to new beginnings," Ethan says.

"To new beginnings," I say. There's a sizzle between us that I think we can both feel. Ethan's hand lingers near mine for a second and I'm transported back down the halls of high school, as he held my hands on the way to class. But now, when I look at his eyes, I see tiny creases in the corners. There's a history behind those crevices. And I want to know the story of how Ethan, the varsity football player that every girl crushed on, became Ethan the successful financial analyst, still single at age 30.

We grab plates, napkins, and our drinks, and head to Ethan's yard. The sprawling space is lush with a vegetable garden and flowers. The patio is set with twinkling lights that illuminate a cozy outdoor couch in front of a fire pit. A hammock is nestled between two trees in a far-off corner. This is the backyard of dreams.

"Make yourself comfortable," Ethan says. He ignites the grill in one try.

"Wow. This is the perfect place for summer parties. Do you entertain often?" I sink down on the couch and sip my water.

"I host parties, but mostly I just hang out with everyone at the lake. I was dating this girl who lived down the Jersey shore for a while, so I was spending weekends there. But I recently ended things with her. I could tell she was going to want a bigger commitment. I wasn't ready to have her move in and didn't want to do the commute anymore."

"That was noble of you, in a way, not to lead her on." That must be why everyone thought he was single. He was leaving town to hookup.

Ethan shuts the lid on the grill as the chicken cooks and turns to look at me. "She wasn't the woman I would want to spend the rest of my life with."

I don't reply. I'm wondering if Ethan has been in love with me for all these years.

"Anyway, I'm sure we can find something more fun to discuss."

"Like the lake fundraiser," I say, circling back to what brought me here tonight.

Ethan and I eat dinner on his bistro dining set. The sun is setting and we're sipping rose and lemon flavored iced-tea that he apparently brewed himself. Our conversation reflects back on old memories from school and the lake. Then, we catch each other up on our current interests. We talk about promotion ideas to help raise money for the clubhouse at the lake to be rebuilt. As we debate over the best new streaming TV shows, Ethan tells me, "I have a surprise. I'll be right back."

Trash the Dress Online Chat

Sydney: My sister got engaged last night. All the feelings.

Leanne: Hugs.

Harper: True love does exist!

Cora: If I ever get married again, I want to be the one to propose. I'm not going to let a man dictate my life anymore.

7

CAILIN MCCALL'S FIRST POST-DIVORCE DATE GOES UP IN FLAMES

CAILIN

ETHAN IS inside for a few minutes and comes out carrying skewers, a bag of marshmallows, chocolate bars, and graham crackers.

"We're making s'mores!"

"Hope you have room for dessert." Ethan takes a seat next to me.

"I will never deny myself s'mores. Oh my gosh. I haven't had these since we used to all sit around the lake at the annual campouts. Do you remember how that one time my skewer caught on fire and I freaked out? Gemma started screaming and everyone ran away, but then you poured water on it and everything was fine."

We laugh, like no time has passed between us. I feel like I can easily settle back into this life. Most people try to leave the small town they came from to explore life and gain more opportunity. I tried that. I enjoyed my adventures. But there's something so simple about spending your nights outside in a backyard, making s'mores, and laughing. I want to fill my life with mini moments like this one that create a mosaic in my heart.

Ethan finishes sliding on the marshmallows and hands me a stick. "I totally forgot about that. But if you think I need to get my fire extinguisher, let me run back to the house now."

"I think I have things under control this time," I say.

The flames aren't just coming from the fire pit tonight. Ethan scoots closer to me on the couch so that our knees are touching. I pull my charred dessert out of the fire and take my first bite. The warm, gooey flavors melt together to make my taste buds dance, and I want to devour the entire s'more at once. But I restrain.

"This is so good. If I were you, I'd eat these every night outside here."

"Nah, there's no fun in s'mores when you're not sharing them with anyone." He points to my lips, "Here, you've got some marshmallow on your mouth."

Ethan takes his thumb and softly brushes it against my upper lip to remove the melted treat. Only it doesn't budge. So, we laugh and he tries again, to no avail.

"Let me try this." Ethan leans in. He's going to kiss me. I'm going to have my first post-divorce kiss, with my ex-boyfriend. My heart nervously thumps.

Our lips softly touch. Ethan pulls back, and we look at each other and both smile.

"I hope that was okay," he asks. "It just felt right in the moment."

"That was nice. This is all really, really, nice. I'm glad I came."

"I'm glad you came," he says.

We throw our skewers down and Ethan pulls me in for a deep kiss. I throw my arms around his neck and hold him tight. His hands are wrapped around my waist. As our bodies press together, I'm reminded that Ethan feels safe and familiar. His slightly chapped lips run along my mouth, settling back to where they've explored so many times before. Before things can get too heavy, we are interrupted as bright lights shine in our faces. There's a car pulling in Ethan's driveway.

"Oh no," Ethan says. He looks over his fence. "Gary's here."

"Gary?" I wipe my lips and pat my hair down in place.

"He's on the Board at the lake. I forgot he told me he was stopping by one night this week to drop off some papers I have to sign to move forward with the charity event. He has awful timing." Ethan sits up and straightens his wrinkled shirt.

I'm disappointed, but understand. While making out with Ethan was fun, I didn't feel the pow-pow-pow of sparks I was hoping for. Maybe it was just my nerves. Or, we needed more time. Either way, Ethan kissed me with more passion than Collin showed the last year of our marriage. I have confirmation that I deserve to be treated like I'm desired.

"No worries. I should get going anyway. It's getting late and you have work tomorrow."

By this point, Gary has stepped out of his truck and sees me next to Ethan. He's an older man with gray hair and is oblivious to the fact that he crashed our date. Ethan introduces us and we exchange pleasantries. I collect my belongings, thank Ethan for a lovely evening, and tell him we'll talk soon.

Ethan is trying to be polite with Gary, but I can tell he feels seriously cock-blocked right now and I kinda do too. Maybe my first post-divorce escapade isn't supposed to be with Ethan and the universe is sending me signs. I turn on my car and the DJ on the radio introduces a throwback song from 5 Leo Hearts about all our tomorrows. I raise the volume and drive home wondering what the new day will bring.

I was almost late for a video conference call with Imani's boss and I have no one to blame but myself. Sure, I'm unemployed, but I shouldn't be acting jobless. I should still wake up early and check my email and text messages, like I've done every day for years. But last night I turned off my alarm clock.

Luckily, I awoke with enough time to spare to get ready for this last-minute video call request. Imani's boss emailed me over a non-disclosure agreement to sign before we speak. This must be a really famous client.

What does one wear for a video chat to discuss working for a major celebrity? I go with a black shirt, statement necklace, and cotton shorts that I slept in, since this video will only show my face. Since I didn't have time to blow out my hair, I simply curl the front two pieces. I'm sure there's a beauty influencer somewhere who has posted a video about that hack, so I try not to let myself feel too bad for not washing it. Along with natural looking makeup and some light pink gloss, I look confident, but not overdone.

The anticipation for the other participants to join the video chat slowly makes me crazy. Finally, a woman who appears to be in her mid-fifties appears on camera. She pushes her bold red eyeglasses to her nose and greets me with enthusiasm.

"Cailin! So nice to meet you. I'm Marisol. My colleague, Carlos, will be joining us as well in just a moment."

"Hi Marisol, nice to meet you. Thanks for taking the time to speak with me."

"Imani has told me a lot of great things about your work. While we wait for Carlos, I'll tell you a little about myself. I started my career as a publicist and led the Latina music division of the company where I began. I eventually transitioned to a pop music account team, which was our biggest division. The thrill and pressure of those accounts exhilarated me, but I always wanted more for myself. That's how this company was formed. Today, I oversee all the clients and employees and am available to strategize or handle crises, but for the most part, our account leads handle the day-to-day and direct contact with clients."

I nod and smile, as Carlos appears on the chat. He's wearing a bright yellow hoodie. I immediately love him. "That's very impressive. Thanks for sharing."

"Here's Carlos now," Marisol says.

"Sorry, I'm late. Putting out a fire with a client who missed an interview this morning."

"Hi Carlos, nice to meet you," I say.

Marisol leads the conversation, "Cailin, I believe Imani told you that one of our senior publicists recently left and we are in urgent need for a team member to come on and manage a new account that's beginning soon. Did you sign the NDA that we sent over this morning? We don't usually have candidates sign them for interviews, but our firm is under agreement not to share the information of an upcoming tour that's going to be announced."

"I received and submitted it. No worries, I totally understand."

Marisol smiles and continues, "Great. Carlos has worked with this client in a previous capacity for many years and was originally slated to manage the details of this tour, but dates got pushed back and now Carlos and his partner will be honeymooning in Hawaii."

"Sorry, not sorry," Carlos says.

I can tell they have a laid-back banter between them and this is a comfortable and inclusive work environment. We talk a little longer about my experience and the details of the job. I thank them for considering me and they tell me they will be in touch later today. That sounds promising, but I don't want to totally get my hopes up.

I need a distraction. I decide to do something on my post-divorce bucket list that I've been thinking about for a while. I literally have nothing to do and no one to stop me.

Trash the Dress Online Chat

Cailin: I had my first post-divorce make-out session. Eeek! This is happening. I'm back out there.

Fiona: Isn't it the best feeling?!

Harper: I felt so alive my first time.

Tori: Did you get it in?!

8

CAILIN MCCALL CELEBRATES DIVORCE IN HER 20S WITH NEW TATTOO

CAILIN

THE BUZZING IS loud and I can hear the vibrations as a needle hoovers above my arm. I always get nervous when the needle is just about to start digging into my flesh. I have seconds to decide if I want to back out, but I never do.

"What brings you in today?" Rob, the tattoo artist asks. He's slender, has a pierced nose and is wearing a metal band shirt. His tattoos are all black outlines. I wonder if that's intentional or if he will eventually fill them with color. One is of a box of french fries, so I wonder how badass he really is. Or maybe, he just really likes fries.

"Documenting my goals and keeping them top of mind as I start a new chapter," I say. My eyes are focused on the needle.

Most of my tattoos are for show, meaning that they're cute and I like to look at them, but they don't have much meaning. I have a star behind my ear because I thought it was cool. The flowers on my shoulder were strategically placed to show off when I wear tank tops in the summer. Those turned out to be a bad move because no one told me how painful it would be to sit through that session. But nothing at all prepared me for the pain of my foot tattoo. It's a tiny arrow with the word "believe" between the end and tip of the arrow. But the pain was big. Tattoo studios should have pain level charts to warn you, but I suppose if they did, not many would stay in business.

This tattoo I'm getting is symbolic to me. The heart-shaped lock with a vintage keyhole in it represents the lock I had on my diaries when I was younger. This is going to symbolize that I'm not going to open my heart again and settle for another man unless it's completely right. It's going to remind me to follow my passions and all the dreams I wrote about when I was younger. I'm going to make myself proud.

But first, I need to make myself stop squirming.

"Sorry," I say. Rob already wiped down the inside of my wrist and placed the outline of the tattoo on my skin. He's ready to start and waiting for me to give the okay.

"I'm ready for this." I close my eyes and clench my jaw.

The needle sinks into my skin and in an effort to distract myself, I make conversation with Rob. "So how long have you been tattooing?"

He doesn't look up as he replies. "You're actually my first. Can you tell I'm nervous? I don't think that line I just made looks too shaky, do you?"

I take a minute to process that information and try not to show that I am completely freaked out. I didn't sign up to be someone's first real client.

"Oh, wow. Did you practice a lot on oranges? Or whatever tattoo artists practice on?"

I look at how much progress Rob made and debate asking him to stop right now.

Rob bursts out laughing. "You handled that better than most people I tell that line."

"You're joking with me?" Thank heavens.

"Gets 'em every time. I've been doing this for about ten years, so don't worry, you're in good hands." He wipes off my wrist to show me his work and relief washes over me.

About twenty minutes of minimal pain later—thankfully—my tattoo is being covered with a special gel and wrapped. I'll have to keep it like this for about an hour. I can't wait to remove the bandaging, wash my tattoo, and snap a picture.

I missed a few notifications while my phone was on silent in the tattoo parlor. The first thing I see is a text from Ethan. I click on it and read:

> Ethan: Just thinking about you and hoping your day is going well. Bummed Gary interrupted us last night. I'd love to pick up where we left off, though.

He left that open ended, which means the ball is in my court. Before I respond, I see an email come in from Marisol. The subject line reads: "Offer letter."

My heart races as I open the email.

Dear Cailin,

It was a pleasure speaking with you today. I feel that your experience and passion for the work you do would make you an incredible asset to our team. Attached is an official offer, which details salary and benefits, as well as additional information.

Should you accept, you'll be leading the new project for a longtime client account that starts tomorrow. The client is Jax Slater, from 5 Leo Hearts. He is going to announce his new solo album and tour later this week. The tour kicks off next week and since Carlos is not available, we will need you to fill in as on-site media relations, coordinating press for each tour date. It's a one month run across the country. You'll have your own

> tour bus. We can go over further details after you—
> hopefully—agree to come on board. We look forward to
> your response.

I'm dead. I don't think I'm breathing, so I must be dead. I also think that if I'm not dead, I am going to pass out, because my head is spinning and my heart is probably near having an attack. I debate going to the emergency room and then assure myself that I am not having a weird out of body experience, and this is real life.

I literally stopped reading the email after I saw the name Jax Slater. I first stopped breathing because all my teenage dreams came flooding to my mind. Cailin at age nineteen would be freaking out knowing that she was not only going to meet her favorite musician, but work on his team. That thought is exactly what made me begin to hyperventilate and nearly pass out.

Working with a celebrity of Jax Slater's caliber is an immense amount of responsibility and pressure. Arranging media for the tour is going to be a beast of a job. There are going to be so many requests for guest passes to review the show, backstage meet-and-greets, and interviews. I'll be in charge of granting people access to Jax and making sure his story makes it across all the major morning shows and news sites. If his tour fails to meet expectations from his managers, label, and pop culture, a brunt of that guilt will fall on his publicity team. My neck is on the line at a new company, where I haven't proven myself. At the same time, I'm being thrown out for the biggest opportunity of my life. An opportunity beyond my wildest dreams.

I'm going to be working with Jax Slater. No, wait... I'm going on tour with Jax Slater. I don't even care what the rest of the offer letter states. I could be agreeing to work every major holiday for the next five years and that's fine, because I'm going to accept and I am going on tour with the guy whose shirtless poster lined my bedroom walls for years. And I'm going to play it totally cool and establish myself in the music publicity industry, just as I did in the healthcare PR sector. This can be the start of a career that energizes and inspires me. And the perks are already better than anything the HR department will offer.

I get to my car and sit there in shock for a few minutes. I'm in no condition to drive right now. But there is something I can do to see if I am hallucinating. I pick up my phone and scream into it.

Trash the Dress Online Chat

Cailin: Anyone else have a divorce tattoo? I just got mine!
Leila: I have a phoenix rising from ashes.
Cora: I should get a tattoo of the date I set myself free.

9

JAX SLATER, THE LONELY LEO HEART, HIDES BEHIND THE CURTAIN

JAX

THE GARBAGE BIN in my studio is overflowing with crumbled paper. I don't like anything I'm writing. Maybe I'm not cut out to be a songwriter and I took on too much with this dream. I should just set aside my pride and call in a professional songwriting team. They'd have something for me to record by end of the day. Then, I can make the label happy and go on tour without this weighing me down.

The easy way out is tempting, but I'm not going to take it. I remind myself that I'm an artist and the path to creating art isn't always easy. Sometimes the most beautiful things grow out of devastation. I just need to keep watering the dirt. I'm already at rock bottom. I've started to plant the seeds. Eventually something will sprout, right? Or whatever the self-help gurus spew.

Just as I'm about to go for a jog to burn this negative energy, Harry calls me. "Got some news," he says.

"Hit me."

"Marisol is hiring a new publicist for your account. Someone with a strong background and great reputation.

Sounds like a force to be reckoned with based on what I've been told."

"Awesome, just what we need. Is this dude going to come out on the road?" I don't know why, but I assume this new publicist is a dude. When I hear 'force to be reckoned with,' I automatically think of a guy.

"As far as I know, yes. We'll get the PR contact all set up on a private bus."

"I'll kinda miss Carlos," I say. "He always trash talked the tabloids for posting about me and he kept things running smoothly."

"Carlos is off to marry his partner, but he'll be overseeing things virtually."

"Good for him." But I can't help but hope that doesn't bring me any added stress as I adjust to a new publicist.

"Since we're talking about buses..."

Here we go. Harry is going to try to convince me to fly on my private jet between each show. He's not exactly a fan of roughing it and has come to enjoy and expect the luxury that comes with representing the biggest musical stars.

I cut him off. "Not happening. We went over this. If I'm going to figure out who I am outside of 5 Leo Hearts, then I need to get outside the life I am accustomed to and change things up a little."

"I know, I get it. Just worth a shot," Harry says. "Anyway, we'll get a video chat scheduled so we can meet the new publicist."

"Okay, sounds good. Let me know when it's confirmed." It's not like we have to work with my schedule. I'm always available. If I'm not working out, I'm getting frustrated with songwriting, and I can surely use a good distraction.

Harry and I hang up and I decide to start packing for tour. I need to figure out what I'm wearing. I could ask the stylist who worked with 5 Leo Hearts, but then I wouldn't be authentic to myself. The whole point of this tour is to break my stereotype and redefine my reputation. I need to do that by picking out my own clothes because I'm a grown man. I can handle that. Can't I?

In an effort to break out of my shell, I muster up the motivation to go shopping. A new tour calls for new clothes. I'm not looking forward to this. But I'm gonna go to my usual shop and pick up more of what I like. I don't know how often we'll be hitting laundromats on the road, but since I didn't hire an assistant, I can guarantee that my clothes won't get washed often. I better stock up and make sure I have enough to wear.

I drive into town, valet park my car, and head into the shop. Everyone here knows me by name. This is nothing new. I can do this.

"Mr. Slater, welcome," Julie says. She's one of the shop owners. Julie is always flirting with me. She's one of the few women I've encountered during my whirlwind of fame who I haven't taken to bed. It's not that I'm not attracted to Julie. She's your typical LA girl, half-plastic, and dressed to the nines. Any guy would find her attractive. But she's not someone I can just have some fun with because when things end—which they inevitably will because I don't want to commit to another woman who tries so hard and is so materialistic—then I can't shop here anymore. And this is really the only store I like. I can't risk that for a few rounds of sex.

"Hey, Julie," I say. I lean in to give her a hug. I know that will drive her crazy. It's kinda fun.

"What brings you in today?" Julie stands up straighter. She knows it's been ages since I've been there.

I lower my voice and ask, "Can you keep a secret?"

"Anything for you." Julie lights up like I just gave her the key to the world.

"I'm going to be doing a few shows and I need to look good."

"You look good in anything, but I'll help you find some options that would work for performing." Julie blushes.

"Let's do it."

Julie pulls a bunch of pants and shirts for me to try on. I can tell she's waiting just outside the door as I undress. However, I'm not about to come out and model. After what seems like hours, I've made my selections.

"All set? Anything you need a second opinion on?" I knew Julie would try to catch me in my underwear to see if I'm a boxers or briefs guy. I admire her determination, but she'll never know I prefer boxer briefs.

"I think I'm good. You can just ring me up."

"Wonderful," Julie says. She grabs the piles of clothes and looks like she's about to topple over.

"Let me help you." I grab the bulk of the items.

"Such a gentleman."

That's the first time in a while someone has called me a gentleman. It feels good.

"I'd love to come see one of your shows, if they're around here."

Nice try, Julie, but I'm not telling anyone what I'm really up to until I meet my new publicist and we strategize on how we're going to formally announce the tour and album. Instead, I just smile and tell her, "I'll be sharing the news soon."

An assistant at the shop helps carry my bags out to the valet area. That's one of the perks of my status. I can get people to jump at the chance to help me with anything. I tip him well and thank him for the help as my car arrives.

I feel accomplished. I'm proud of myself for getting out in public again. Sure, I went somewhere familiar, but I went out alone. And no one harassed me. I can get used to this.

For a split second, I consider getting wild and taking a drive to the beach. It's been so long since I've been there. I long to smell the salt air and feel the sand sift against my bare feet. Bask in the warmth of the sun on my body. But as tempting as that sounds, I'll just get depressed watching everyone there have fun with someone. I'll be alone. The old pop star photographed walking by himself on the beach. Headlines would make people pity me. And that's not how I want to get back out in the spotlight.

Instead, I turn towards the direction of my house. Back to where no one can pigeonhole me as **Jax Slater: Lonely Leo Heart**. I'm going to have to bring this up to my new PR team on our call. Hopefully this new guy will know just what to do.

Trash the Dress Online Chat

Alexandra: Where are the hot divorced dads?

Chelsea: If you find some, let me know. I'll cross the pond.

Leanne: @Chelsea Come to America! You can stay with me!

10

CAILIN MCCALL FINDS OUT SHE'S GOT THE RIGHT STUFF

CAILIN

GEMMA ANSWERS the phone after what seems like eternity, but is really only thirty seconds. I yell into the phone.

"Oh my gosh, Cailin. Are you okay?" I hear her drop something in the background.

"I don't know. I feel dizzy and my heart is racing. I don't know if I am hallucinating."

"Where are you? I'll call 911." Gemma is in full-on mom mode.

"No, no. I'm fine. I just got some news."

"Don't ever do that to me again. What's going on?"

"So, I got the job offer from Imani's company."

"Okay..."

"And I found out the client they want me to work with..." Just then, I realize I signed an NDA and I can't discuss the company's client because the tour hasn't officially been announced yet. How am I going to keep this information a secret from my best friend?

"And?" Gemma asks, desperate for more information.

"Well, um, I signed an NDA, so I can't tell you the client.

But I can tell you this is a big deal and I'm really excited. I freaked out. I'll tell you as soon as I can, I promise."

"You're killing me, Cailin. NDAs don't apply to best friends, let's be real."

Her begging can't break me and I let her know.

"Well, this mystery client sounds like something you're happy about, so I assume you'll be taking the job?"

"Definitely. And I'm going on tour."

"Tour? Like on a bus?"

"Yes, technically my own bus. It's a month-long tour across the country. It's a great opportunity for me, really."

"I'm sure it is. I'm just wondering how you are going to do living on a bus. Like, you probably can't wash your hair every day, or shower. Oh no. Should I get you some baby wipes in bulk from Cost Savers Shopping Club? Can you rough it?"

Gemma makes some good points. "Okay, so I didn't totally consider all of the logistics and I don't have all the answers yet. I still need to formally accept the offer and I am sure I will get all the details. But I am pretty sure hotels will be on the itinerary."

"Okay, that's good," Gemma says. "When do you leave?"

"I'm not sure, actually. But I start working virtually tomorrow." As I say that aloud, it hits me that I have a lot to do today. Like create the perfect background for virtual conference calls. And decide what to wear in case I have to go on a chat with Jax Slater.

"Wow, they must really be desperate for help." Gemma must feel me shooting her a look, because then she adds, "I mean, eager to get you onboarded."

"We have to announce the tour. As soon as we do, I'll tell you. Seriously. I can't hold this in for long. I'm about to burst."

Then I realize I can reveal other information to Gemma. "Also, I just got a tattoo and last night I made out with Ethan."

Gemma is speechless for a few seconds. "Um, okay there. Way to drop a bombshell."

"Also, it turns out Ethan was dating a girl from out of town. So that must be why everyone thought he was single."

"Interesting. Ethan definitely seems like he has some secrets. But now that you're going on tour, I'll have to figure them out another way."

"Maybe he's just private with women, Gemma."

"I don't know. The last serious girlfriend I knew he had was you and that was years ago." Stella cries in the background. "I need to hear everything, but Stella just woke up from her nap. Text me every detail and I'll text back when I can!"

Gemma and I hang up. I feel grounded now. Confident I can drive home and not crash my car. I fasten my seatbelt, turn on the ignition, and put my foot to the pedal. A new road has opened for me and I can't wait to reach my destination.

I totally forgot about Ethan in the midst of everything going on, until he texts me again. I left his last text hanging in cyberspace and that's unlike me. I'd hate it if someone ghosted me, but I'm not into this level of neediness, especially when we're not a couple.

> Ethan: Hey. You up for a run at the lake today? I'd love some company.

I feel guilty. I would totally meet Ethan to go for a run. I don't want to brush him off immediately because he is a good guy and maybe there can be something between us again. But on the other hand, I didn't feel fireworks in his arms. And at this stage in my life, I'm not going to settle for anything less than the grand finale. My tattoo reminds me of that each time I look at my wrist. So maybe it's best not to lead him to think otherwise.

Me: Hey! Crazy day yesterday. Got a tattoo and a job offer. I'm actually starting my new gig remotely this morning. Have a great run!

That should suffice. I'm letting him know there was a reason for my ghosting, that I have social manners, and that I clearly have pressing matters that need my attention, so dating is not at the forefront of my mind.

Ethan: That's amazing! Congrats. You'll have to fill me in over dinner soon.

Welp. At least my communication skills are direct and confident at the office, if not in my personal life. I leave it at that with Ethan. I get dressed in a dark gray shirt that looks professional, but also music industry cool with its faux leather sleeves. My hair is straight and cascading over my shoulders, stopping precisely where my bold blue necklace lays across my collarbone. Today's makeup look is a little extra, because I need to look good on camera. My blush and lipstick are heavier than I usually wear, but translate beautifully on video chat. I'm ready.

I click the link to my virtual meeting with Marisol. I'm set against a plain wall in my apartment, wishing I had the chance to hang scenic art.

"Cailin. Good morning and welcome." Her background is a built-in bookshelf adorned with plants, books, photos, and other décor. "We're so thrilled to have you on our team and excited for you to lead the Jax Slater account. I'm not sure how familiar you are, but this tour is a big deal for him since it's his first solo album and tour apart from the band."

"I'm so excited to be here and am very familiar with 5 Leo Hearts. I look forward to learning more about the campaign details." I hope my smile hides the fact that I can recite every song on each album in chronological order.

"Great! We're going to jump right in. Jax and his manager,

Harry, will be joining us on this call. Carlos should be popping on soon, too. You and Carlos can connect afterwards and he can fill you in on his previous work with 5 Leo Hearts. Jax wants to announce his tour tomorrow. So this morning, you'll be working with his manager to draft the official announcement for social media, along with the press release."

My stomach begins to flip flop. "Everything sounds great."

"I'll let everyone into the meeting now," Marisol says.

Slowly, everyone pops into chat. I see Jax Slater's name appear, but his camera is turned off. I'm instantly disappointed, but maybe that's better so I won't awkwardly stare into his eyes. Harry and Carlos each say hello. I'm familiar with Harry because he's in the media often and known for discovering new talent. He's been a fixture in the music industry for years. It's going to be an honor working on his team.

Suddenly, the black box formally titled "Jax Slater" disappears and Jax appears on camera. "Sorry about that," Jax says. "My personal trainer made me do an extra set of push-ups and I called in from my cell. All set up on my laptop now. Morning, everyone."

Jax Slater is on video chat with me. He's glistening in sweat and my mind wants to drift towards visions of him doing push-ups, but I must stay focused on the present. Like how his broad shoulders look in that black tank top. And how his brown hair is ruffled from the morning and clearly not washed, yet still looks sultry. He's growing a beard. Well, either that or he really needs to shave the stubble. Either way, I like it. His eyes are a deep blue and peer intensely across the screen. I wonder whose face on the chat he is focusing on, but then Marisol speaks and breaks my train of thought.

"No worries at all," Marisol says. "I was just briefing my team. You already know Carlos, and I'd also like to introduce you to Cailin McCall. She comes to our firm with an award-winning background in public relations and is going to be leading your campaign. I know you will just love working with her."

"Hi, nice to meet you," I say. I can feel my face turn beet red. Probably didn't need to apply that extra blush. "I'm really excited to work with you both. And I can't wait to hear the new music."

Jax's eyes widen like he is surprised to learn he has a new publicist. He curls his lips upwards, but doesn't get a chance to say anything because Harry eagerly jumps into the conversation. "Pleasure to meet you, Cailin. Marisol just sent over a link to your website this morning, and at first glance, your work is impressive. You're just the creative and organized mind Jax needs."

"Thank you. I'm ready to jump in wherever I'm needed." I hope the redness on my face is reducing to a shade of strawberry.

"Sounds great." Jax stumbles on his words. Even though we are miles away and looking at each other over video, I can feel like he's trying to stare into my soul. His eyes have remained fixed on one spot of the screen and they didn't move when he responded to me. Has he been staring at me?

More importantly, Jax Slater spoke to me. "Sounds great" never sounded so...surreal. But I'm not going to get distracted. My initial jitters are fading and I'm in full-on work mode. Right now, Jax Slater is just another client. Just another man. A jaw-droppingly hot man with morning scruff on his face, seriously sexy rumpled hair, and bulging muscles that I want wrapped around me. But I can never act on the instinct to touch him. One, because he's a pop star. Two, because he's my client. Three, because I'm a professional with years of credibility that I can't throw down the drain for a man. Even Jax Slater.

Marisol directs the conversation. "Since we want to announce the tour tomorrow, our focus is on helping Jax create a social media post to announce the dates, and Cailin will also be drafting a press release for you both to review. I'll send a formal email to everyone here so you all have each other's contact information. We'll be working closely together before tour kicks off to get things started, but once the tour is in full swing, Cailin will be on the road with you and act as your main point of contact."

"Have you toured before, Cailin?" Harry asks.

"This will be my first official tour managing press, but if years of experience attending concerts count, I'm a pro. But don't worry, I am ready to hit the road and will be stocked up on baby wipes."

Oh my gosh, why did I say that? Now, my face, which I am pretty sure returned to its natural color, is rising back to red. I'm thankful that I made everyone laugh.

"Oh, Cailin, don't worry. You'll have hotel stops every night to shower," Marisol says. "We'll go over all those details, don't worry. You'll hardly be roughing it." She waves her hand in the air and I girl crush on her poise, perfectly painted nails, and effortless power.

"Trust me, I've been trying to convince Jax to just use his private jet for this tour, but for some reason, he wants to get back to his roots—whatever that means—and suffer like an indie musician. I'll never understand it." Harry shakes his head.

Jax's eyes move across the screen as he says, "And I keep telling Harry that I appreciate him trusting my gut on this one. I've spent more years in airports than I can count. I'm a professional traveler. It's a luxury I'm blessed with for sure, but with all those opportunities, I've also missed a chance to really see the world the way everyone else sees it. Touring on a bus will allow me to interact with my fans more, give back to everyone who made my career what it is, and I'll have a chance to explore each city. I want to eat the local food, breathe the fresh air, and get inspiration for new songs. You can't get that when everyone is waiting on you hand and foot while flying on a private jet."

He seems to have pulled himself together from the fluster he felt earlier. I was not prepared to hear such a down-to-earth statement come from one of the world's biggest pop stars. And now, I fear my teenage crush has become my post-divorce crush.

"That makes a lot of sense," I say. I watch Jax's eyes dart back from their usual corner of the screen. What I am hoping is my corner. "In order to keep your art evolving, you need to experience new things in your life. You need to feel the highs and lows of not just your own world, but also draw on the feelings of others. Meet people, learn their stories. Feel their pain and happiness, put yourself in their shoes." I fear I maybe went off on a tangent, but I can't help it. With all the changes in my life, I've been very philosophical.

"Exactly." Jax motions his eyes up and down the screen as if he is checking out to see how far down my body he can view on camera. "You get it. You hear that, Harry? Cailin gets it. Touring on a bus is a good move." I can feel his eyes stay on me as the conversation continues.

"It all sounds inspirational until you're driving hours through nothing but highway and crave a pepperoni slice, but the next pizza parlor is fifty miles away," Harry says.

Jax rolls his eyes and everyone starts sharing stories of old days on the road. Then, the conversation steers back to the logistics of the tour and the campaign. I quietly observe, in awe, that I will be a part of this chapter.

"Now that we have our marching orders, my team is ready to kick things off," Marisol says. "Cailin will you also please touch base with Jax later today as you work on the press release? You two should set up a call to discuss quotes to include and use for media outreach. The press is going to eat this up." Marisol rubs her hands together in anticipation.

"No problem, Marisol." Sure, I'll call Jax on his cell and have a one-on-one conversation about his inspiration behind the album and thoughts about embarking on a solo tour. No pressure. My palms are already sweaty. I wipe them on my shirt as I say, "I'd also love to hear the new album if possible, so I can properly describe it in the release."

"Done." Harry slaps his hand on the desk. "I'll send you the confidential streaming link now. Look forward to your thoughts on this. It's a bit different from the dreamy pop songs 5 Leo Hearts fans know and love. Though, Jax will still perform some of them on tour as part of a nostalgia melody. Gotta give the girls what they love, you know?" He pauses and then asks, "Hey, were you a 5 Leo Hearts fan back in the day?"

And there it is. The question I've been dreading being asked for fear I will have to admit that I know every lyric to every song.

"Who wasn't?" Let me just pat myself on the back with that smooth response.

"Well, fans of Cute Boys Band," Harry says. "Boy band fans were pretty competitive."

"Tell me about it!" I can't help it. Word vomit is spewing out of my mouth. Why am I saying that? I can't think clearly in the presence of Jax Slater. "That was always so frustrating because 5 Leo Hearts came out first and Cute Boys Band was clearly trying to cash in on their success with sub-par songs and less attractive members. Their style also lacked, too."

"I told you she knows her stuff," Marisol says.

"Sounds like she does," Harry says. "Just the addition our team needs."

"I'm looking forward to it. Thanks for sending over the new music. I see the link in my inbox. I'll give it a listen and reach out to Jax later today to discuss press release quotes. Oh, and the social media post."

"Perfect," Harry says. "Once the tour is announced, the NDA ends and everyone on our team can promote the tour from their social pages too, and tag Jax, if you don't mind."

"Our team is on it," Marisol says.

As our call concludes, I focus on my next steps for the day, which include a private phone call with Jax Slater, whose phone number is now in my inbox. And then I have to tag him in a social media post, which means he is going to look at my social profile and everything I've posted. I'll need to clean up my page.

"Interested to hear your thoughts on the music, Cailin," Jax says. "I'll wait to hear from you about the press release."

And with that we all nod and log off. Jax Slater said my name. And he's waiting to hear from me about what I think of his new music. There's only one thing to do now: get to work and impress him.

Trash the Dress Online Chat

Cora: Leanne got me thinking. Since I'm in my car, maybe I should road trip to meet some of you!

Alexandra: Please tell me you are not still sleeping in your car.

Leanne: Yes! Let's map out where we all are and you can come stay with each of us while you figure things out.

Cora: This actually might be a good idea. I'll think about it.

11

BREAKING NEWS: JAX SLATER IS CRUSHING ON NEW PUBLICIST

JAX

My new publicist is not what I expected. For one thing, it's not a dude. Harry apparently found out shortly before our video chat with the team and didn't even warn me. I mean, not like it matters, or that I needed advance notice. But it would have been nice to see the website he was referring to when he spoke to Cailin on the call.

Cailin caught me off guard and I couldn't stop myself from staring at her across my monitor. I hope she couldn't tell. For all she knows, I could have been looking at Harry. Okay, I hope she doesn't think I was staring at Harry. But it's better that she doesn't think I'm gazing at her because she's working for me. She's untouchable. The worst kind of torture because she's gorgeous.

Cailin's a brunette, which is super refreshing to see. Her hair is long and straight, giving her a fierce look. She's the opposite of a California girl. Definitely New York vibes, but through the professional shield she put up, I can see she's also a little shy. I saw her flushed cheeks and immediately pictured myself whispering dirty words into her ears to deliberately make her temperature rise. This intense, immediate attraction is, of course, bad. I can't sleep with my publicist. Especially if I want to shed my bad boy reputation.

I tried to concentrate on what everyone was saying on the call, but mostly I was focused on Cailin's mouth. Every time she spoke, I watched her glossy lips move. Sweet, juicy lips that spewed actual knowledge and strategy. That drove me wild.

I know I shouldn't be thinking this, but I wonder if she was by any chance attracted to me. And how old she is. She looks old enough to have been an OG, one of the original 5 Leo Hearts fans, and she seems to have knowledge of the era when boy bands exploded. She might be around my age.

I try to rein in my thoughts. It's a good thing if Cailin knows the history of boy bands, especially 5 Leo Hearts. Then, she can help position me to the media in the way I'm hoping to come across. On the other hand, if she is familiar with my reputation, I'm sure she will be totally turned off to me personally. She might even think I'm a scumbag.

That shouldn't matter though, because, I remind myself yet again, I'm her client. It's her job to make me look good. It doesn't matter how I feel about her. She's off limits. The worst thing I could possibly do for myself would be to put the moves on Cailin.

Yet, that's all I can think about now. What if she is the girl-next-door that I've been waiting for? She works in the industry, but she's out of the spotlight. That gives her an understanding and appreciation for my line of work. She wouldn't get jealous or anything that someone outside of the industry might feel. She could just support me.

There I go, getting ahead of myself again. I gotta keep it in my pants with this one. Positive publicity and refining my reputation are even more important than the clothes I wear, so I need to put Cailin on the list of women I can't date.

Then, a foreign concept comes to mind. Just because I can't date Cailin doesn't mean I can't get to know her better. We can be friends. We're going to be working closely together on tour, after all. At that moment, it hits me. Cailin is coming on tour with me. This is going to bring a whole new set of challenges.

The crew slated to come on tour with me are mostly people who have toured with 5 Leo Hearts. All are guys except for Hayley, the merch girl. But she's dating one of the musicians, Jayce, and has helped out at some of our one-off charity shows. Therefore, she counts as one of the guys. Cailin will be the first single girl on tour. That is, if she's not dating anyone. I can't just assume she is single because I want her to be available. Actually, it's better for me if she is in a relationship. Then she really would be unavailable. The world may think I'm a womanizer, but I would never set out to steal someone's girlfriend.

I need to get my mind off Cailin. But first, I need to learn everything I can about her. I ping Harry and ask him to send me her website. He sends it right over to me, totally unaware of my real motives. I text him back.

Jax: Thanks. Is this all they sent us over about her?

Harry: That's all I got. Sorry I didn't think to send it to you before the call. Got it last minute.

Jax: No worries. Just wanted to see what you all were talking about and get her background.

Harry: I think she'll be great. And she seems to know a lot about the band.

Jax: Agree. Thanks again.

I quickly end the chat with Harry because I'm eager to check out Cailin's website. As soon as the site loads, I see her headshot on the homepage. Her hair is different, with loose waves. They look soft and bouncy, like my fingers can get lost in them. I can picture those curls flowing in front of her eyes as she laughs, and me gently moving them behind her ear before I steal a kiss. She's wearing a navy-blue shirt. Somehow, it brings out her light brown eyes. I'm envious of the photographer who took this photo because they were close enough to her to see the light reflect off them.

This is not good. Looking at this photo of Cailin brings a spark of life back to me, but I can't ignite it. That's way too risky. I move my attention away from her photo to read her bio. Her career history is impressive. She's led large corporations and been recognized for her work. She's a powerhouse, and I totally underestimated her by automatically assuming she was a man when I heard her credentials. Gotta work on that automatic bias.

By the time I'm done reading the information on Cailin's website, I feel like I have a good grasp on some parts of her life. She's clearly career-driven and goal-oriented. But I still want to know more about her. No, that's not true. I need to know.

Trash the Dress Online Chat

Cailin: Posting to make sure I'm not dreaming. The most amazing thing just happened.

Tori: Did you get it in?

Harper: Well, don't leave us in suspense!

12

CAILIN MAKES THE PHONE CALL THAT MIGHT JUST CHANGE HER DESTINY

CAILIN

IN ORDER TO write the press release, I need to completely immerse myself in Jax Slater—as if I haven't spent years and countless daydreams listening to his voice and imagining his lips travel up and down my body, sending shivers through my spine with each gentle brush against my skin. But I was a teenager, and now I'm an adult who is getting paid for my years of boy band knowledge, particularly my 5 Leo Hearts expertise. If someone could hold a Master's degree in pop music with a specialty in boy bands, it would be me. And now I need to use that knowledge as power. Determine what makes 5 Leo Hearts the best, why Jax is a standout star, what he's trying to convey with his new solo music, why people should give a damn and buy this album, and go see him on tour.

I click open the email of tracks from Harry and begin to play the songs. They are not what I expected. At all. I was expecting Jax to break solo with a harder pop rock sound, something to further establish himself as the bad boy. Maybe throw in some EDM to cater to the pop music fans who have grown up and now go clubbing. But this music is raw, mostly acoustic based, and his voice is the focus. I wonder if he's the one playing the guitar and make a note to confirm with Harry. If Jax is playing his own instruments and writing his own songs now, he is gaining leaps of credibility in the music world that will set him apart from other pop stars who work with backing bands and professional songwriting teams.

After listening to the songs, I feel like I was given a glimpse of Jax naked. Stripped down, covered in nothing but tattoos, revealing all that's there for me to absorb and learn the meaning behind. It's obvious he's hurting. Those songs are clearly inspired by his headline-making breakup with a particular female pop star named Maxine that he dated for years. She is the definition of a sex kitten, with bright red hair, a tiny waist, and voluptuous boobs, and has the voice of an angel. They once released a duet together and the video was filled with steam. Their natural chemistry was intoxicating to watch from afar and the tabloids loved them. But according to reports, they broke up when she began to see success as an actress.

Some songs, though, shed light on other areas of his journey. Jax clearly has experienced love and loss, but I can also hear that there is so much more about him that he wants the world to know. And I use that insight to draft a few questions I want to ask him. Which means I need to text Jax Slater.

My palms are shaking as I open a blank text draft.

> Me: Hi Jax. This is Cailin from the PR firm. I'm working on your press materials and was wondering if now is a good time to maybe ask you a few questions before I draft the release. Sorry for bothering you if now isn't a good time!

I cringe at my text. "Sorry for bothering you?" Why am I apologizing? This is my job. So much for channeling any of my past leadership roles and coming across as confident. Before I can obsess over my text any further, a message comes across my screen.

Jax: Now is great.

Me: Perfect! I'll call you now.

Before I pull up his number, I need to ground myself. I dig into my brain and try to recall calming techniques that so many self-help therapists and coaches I follow on social media share. Then, I remember one where you should focus on your senses. Things you can see, hear, smell, or touch. Okay, that one is no help because now I am painting a picture in my mind of how my senses are going to go into overdrive the day I meet Jax and look into his eyes as I shake his hand. Get it together, girl. I focus on the feeling of the floor. It's smooth against my feet. Actually, my feet are really smooth too. I take pride in my at-home pedis. I wonder what it would be like to have Jax rub my feet.

Stop, Cailin. Call Jax.

Jax answers the phone immediately. "Hi, Cailin."

I pull myself into work mode. "Hi, Jax. Thanks for taking a few minutes to talk to me. Like I said, I wanted to get a few quotes from you and a little background behind the album for your press release."

"Happy to answer any questions you have," Jax says. "This announcement is a really big deal for me so I want to make sure we nail it."

Clearing my throat and any visions of Jax based on that comment, I begin my questions. "These songs are a clear departure from the pop music that your fans know and love. Was that intentional? Did you set out to reinvent your musical style or did it just happen naturally during the process?"

"That's a great question. Since 5 Leo Hearts naturally faded away from music and I was out of the spotlight for a little, I took some time to really stop and evaluate my life. I asked myself if I was truly happy and fulfilled. I was able to admit to myself that being on top of the world might look amazing from the outside, but something was missing in my life. Don't get me wrong, I've lived it up with the best of them. But I felt myself changing and that's reflected in the music I created."

"What did you realize was missing?"

Jax takes a deep breath and pauses for a second before replying, "Ultimately, passion. I started in this group when I was basically a kid. I grew up in the spotlight with stars in my eyes. I dreamed of performing and I mastered it with singing, choreographed dancing, and all that. Singing cheesy love songs when I was younger came naturally. I'm not even gonna lie about the benefits of having millions of girls throwing themselves at my feet. But as my life changed and I got into a serious relationship, I realized love is not like a boy band song."

Jax is cracking open and I feel like I'm getting a glimpse into who he really is as a person—the man he's kept private from the media. "So, you needed to start making music that reflects your life and feelings." I ache for him to further confide in me. "It translates for sure. The vulnerability and the pain...I can feel them."

"That was my goal," Jax says.

"It's like this is Jax Slater, unzipped. Even more intimate than the love songs."

"I really like that perspective, Cailin. I know it's not what people might expect from the 'bad boy,' but I really hope to break that stereotype with the press surrounding this album. I got labeled the rebel based on my looks, just because I started to get tattoos and Ridge had the baby face. So, we were naturally positioned as opposites. I went with it and obviously lived up to it at some points in my life..." he trails off.

Jax seems uncomfortable so I take that as my cue to change the subject. "I didn't get any liner notes with the songs Harry sent over, so I was wondering if you wrote the songs yourself or played any instruments."

"I did, actually. It was a freeing process for me to have total control over what I want to say. I found the writing process very therapeutic after the breakup. I found myself with a lot of time alone to reflect and pick up a guitar. I learned to play a little on my own, but then was fortunate enough to get lessons from some buddies who have toured with us before."

"Are you worried about the feedback from fans?"

"I'd like to think that most 5 Leo Hearts fans have grown up with the band. Most of them are now probably married with kids, just like most of my bandmates. Mario and Jack have kids and Ridge just got married, so I'm sure he's not far behind. While our fans may play our songs for nostalgia, I can only hope that they have gone through things in their life that can help them identify with my new lyrics. Not that I want them to have experienced soul-tearing breakups. I just imagine they've had their own struggles and their journeys have led them back to my music as a source of comfort."

This is my natural segue into discussing his breakup. I'm a little nervous, but I go for it. It's my job, not a question on a date. "If you don't mind me asking, since you had a very public breakup, I think we should address it because questions will come up as you do press."

"I've thought a lot about how to respond if reporters dig into my personal life. I know it comes with the territory. Honestly, she broke my heart. I never want to paint her in a bad light. I wanted to take the next step in our relationship and get married and have a family. All that stuff that people naturally do when they've been together for years. But her acting career was taking off and she didn't want to be tied down. She wanted to be free to travel on location for roles and win awards. And that's her right. I wouldn't take her dreams away from her."

"But her dreams weren't your dreams. I totally get that. I've been there." I realize I might have overstepped into sharing my personal life. For a minute, I forgot this was a work call.

"Exactly. Look, it's no secret. I've dated around enough to know what I want. I thought I had it, but I was wrong. I think the songs reflect the fact that I've been learning, maybe even rediscovering myself. I've emerged new and different, and I might lose some fans along the way, but I hope they know I'm only human and this is my journey."

"I love that for a quote. Really, that's the ultimate rebel move, breaking out of your reputation." Jax Slater knows what he wants and he will stop at nothing to get it. I jot down a note.

"Damn, girl. I never thought of it like that before. I've always felt like I had to live up to this image people had of me to maintain my role in the group's success. Always push the boundaries on stage, be the most eccentric. And for most of my career, I was true to myself. But as I've gotten older, I definitely don't want to be stuck in a box or be defined by other people's expectations."

I suddenly feel closer to Jax. I'm seeing him beyond the posters that were taped on my wall, slowly peeling back layers to his soul. But I have to remind myself he is off-limits. Not only is he my client, but he's a major celebrity. Even if I was not his publicist, there is no way he would be interested in a normal girl like me. Anyway, nothing can happen between us, so I can just put a hard stop to this fantasy. I don't have the liberty of teenage dreams anymore. I need to face the facts of life.

"Well, I think I have a lot of information to work with. Is there anything else you want to make sure I get into the release or even the social media post?"

Jax goes over a few more details about producers and people he worked with behind the scenes, and also gives Harry props for all of his support. I know exactly how I want to write this press release.

An hour later, I'm putting the final touches on the most emotional press release I've ever written. That's one thing about working in music PR, compared to healthcare, that I already love. My writing doesn't have to be forced and straight-forward, filled with facts. As I describe the new album Jax wrote, it's my job to evoke emotion and create a connection between the fan and musician. And I'm confident I did just that. I draft an email and hit send. Now, we just have to see what Jax and Harry think. No big deal.

Trash the Dress Online Chat

Ana: I need a second job to make ends meet. No MLMs. Any ideas?

Julie: I have a few sites I can send you.

Cora: Right there with you. Hoping to find something virtual.

Cailin: I JUST got a new job. Beyond my wildest dreams. Maybe consider changing industries?

13

JAX SLATER CAUGHT BETWEEN HIS HEAD AND HIS HEART

JAX

I HAVE Cailin's number now. This is dangerous. I should edit her name in my phone and change it from Cailin McCall Publicist to Cailin Text Only For Work Matters. Although our conversation was more like an interview for Cailin to get information to write my press materials, I feel like she cracked me open. She's so easy to talk to and I felt that our conversation just flowed.

With all the women I've dated, I've always kept them at arm's length. I knew each of them was temporarily in my life for a night, or a week if they were lucky. There was no point in sharing feelings or getting to know them, because I knew I wasn't going to keep them around. They were fun ways to pass the time and live it up at the height of my fame.

Sometimes I felt guilty, but they were also fully aware of my reputation and what they were getting into. They wanted their fifteen minutes and a photo in a tabloid with my arms wrapped around them. There were mutual benefits. Why mess with something if it's working?

Now though, I want more than quick satisfaction and

surface-level relationships. I want something with substance. Someone I can have real conversations with and take out on a date. I'd even go out in public with Cailin. Somehow, I feel that she puts me at ease. I want to experience things with her. Is that crazy? I've never even met her in person. Maybe I've been secluded in my mansion for so long that I'm losing my mind.

I'm eager to see the press release from Cailin. I feel like she really understands me and knows the direction I want to go with this tour. It might take her a while to draft something, so I should be productive too and write a song.

I grab a bottle of water and head into my songwriting room. I sink into the red velvet couch and pick up my notebook and pen. I could try strumming the guitar and coming up with a melody first, but I want to write lyrics.

For a moment, I pause and reflect back on how far I've actually come. When the band first formed, we paid our dues by touring on a bus and playing high schools. We didn't know if anyone would take us seriously, because we were just a bunch of kids ourselves. Slowly we started to play clubs, opening for more popular acts. Eventually, we released our first single and it placed at number three on the charts before claiming the number one spot a week later. We got our big break when a radio station asked us to perform at their holiday concert. After that, things took off.

We recorded our first album and released it in America. This is when the real work began. Our days were jam-packed from morning to night with radio station interviews, photo shoots, and appearances at teen magazine offices. I counted the number of times in one week that a reporter asked my favorite color or favorite food. It happened just about every interview. When we weren't promoting the group, the guys and I were holed up in a hotel room seeking connection with friends and family back home. Although we had each other, we got lonely and began to miss our old lives.

We had to adjust even more during our first European tour.

When we arrived at the airport, we were greeted by a swarm of fans holding posters with our names.

"Jax! Over here!"

"I love you, Mario!"

"I baked your favorite cookies, Oliver!"

"Ridge, can we take a picture?"

"Jack! Jack! Jack!"

A team of security had to hold them back. Because this was our first time there, the fans had been long-awaiting our arrival. That moment is one of my favorite memories.

"We made it," Ridge said as we stepped into the crowd to pose for photos. "This is it."

"This is insane," Jack said. "Someone just threw a teddy bear at me."

"I wish someone threw a teddy bear at me," Mario said as he adjusted his shirt after a fan grabbed it and tried to pull it off his body.

Little did we know there was much more to come. Fans camped outside our hotel overnight and even booked rooms on the floor we were staying, just to be close. We were basically hostages in our hotel rooms because we couldn't go anywhere without a fan nearby.

Once, someone even tried to sneak into our suite dressed as a hotel maid. Luckily, our security caught her before she had a chance to enter. "I swear, I'm with housekeeping," she said to our security guard. "I'll clean their room. Let me prove it to you."

We knew that we were nothing without our fans, so we embraced them as much as possible while also trying to maintain our personal space. As I got older, so did the girls who approached me. By the time I was twenty-one, they were offering me shots and sexual innuendos.

"You should see what else I can do with my mouth," one fan told me. It worked.

How could I pass up beautiful women flirting with me?

There was nothing else to do on tour, so I figured I might as well enjoy myself. "How about we go somewhere more private and you can show me?" I said.

It's been a wild ride since then. After years of back-to-back touring and recording albums, we were burned out and decided to go on a hiatus.

"I don't know if I can do another tour right now," Mario said. He was the first to break.

"I don't know if another tour right now even makes sense," Jack said. "The radio is playing all these grunge bands. They're knocking pop acts out of rotation."

"I agree with Jack," said Ridge. "We really don't fit in right now. I'm starting to feel embarrassed."

"Maybe it's time we gracefully bow out before we fade away," Oliver said.

We all agreed this was a strategic pause, not a breakup. We all needed it. Over the past year or so, I've started to miss performing. But I also have wanted more for myself. I got inspired to create the life I want, making music that's true to me and finding a woman to grow by my side. This new solo album is filling one of those voids. But there's still a deep hole in my life, and that can only be filled by a companion. Not just any girl, though. I'm looking for the woman who will be mine forever.

I know it's wrong to pursue Cailin, but something inside of me can't let this go. I just know she is different. I have her number and I'm going to use it, regardless of the consequences. Maybe the media is right and I am addicted to women. I should jot these thoughts down as lyrics.

Trash the Dress Online Chat

Ariel: I think I've been eating my emotions. So not ready for summer.

Rachel: Don't make the same mistake I did. I got married because I didn't think I could do any better. You are amazing just the way you are.

Cora: What I would give to eat anything besides 99 cent nuggets.

14

CAILIN MCCALL ACCUSED OF TEARIN' UP
ETHAN'S HEART

CAILIN

WAITING for the critique of my first press release at a new job, for a new client, is nerve-wracking. It's even more tortuous because I happen to have a massive crush on this particular client. These are different feelings than when I was a teenager singing along to 5 Leo Hearts songs pressed up against the front row barricades at their concerts. I now feel like I have a backstage pass into the world of Jax Slater, and I never want to have that door close.

I need to impress Jax and his team on a professional level. The rush this work gives me is exhilarating. I also can't help but admit that it's not just the work that excites me. It's also the possibility that I could form some sort of friendship with Jax. He may be a music legend, but I'm seeing him for who he is behind the music and I want a closer glimpse. This job should have come with a warning: panties may get wet.

It takes about a half hour until Harry emails me back with some edits. Overall, he's very pleased with the release. Phew! He just had some minor tweaks from a manager's standpoint and that's cool. I keep nervously checking my email, waiting for a response from Jax. What if he hates it? I put my heart into this, in more ways than one.

I get up to make myself some lunch and realize I need to properly shop for food. So instead, I head into town on a mission to get my favorite sandwich. It's been years since I've sunken my teeth into that portabello mushroom slathered in spinach artichoke dip and gooey cheese between a freshly baked roll. My stomach starts growling at the thought.

Inside the Italian specialty deli, I'm paying the cashier when someone sneaks up from behind me and puts his arm on my shoulder. I turn around to find Ethan.

"Ethan. What are you doing here?"

"Same as you, I suppose. Getting lunch. Want to grab a table?"

I'm not sure what to do here, because I'd love to sit and have lunch with a friend to pass the time and stop agonizing about how Jax will respond to the press release. But I also crossed a line with Ethan the other day and now he's not technically just a friend. We are sort of...involved. In a messy way. At the time, I thought making out with Ethan was a leap towards an exciting post-divorce life. But now, things are different. I'm leaving for tour, with someone who is occupying more space in my brain than he should.

"Great minds," I tell Ethan. I step out from under his arm. "I'm really sorry I haven't texted you back. I've been meaning to get in touch. It's just that things have been hectic."

"It's cool, hun," Ethan says. "We have plenty of time to catch up. So, what is this new job that has you so occupied?"

I wince at the sound of the word '*hun.*' I'm not his sweetheart, for sure. I hope he's not getting attached already. Or again. This is so hard to navigate.

"Actually, I really can't share too many of the details. I had to sign an NDA. But I'll be making an announcement soon." The cashier can't ring me up fast enough.

"That's mysterious. I guess I'll just have to wait for you. I can handle that. I don't like it, but I can handle it."

Ethan touches his hand to my face and I take his hand in mine and lower it. He's not picking up my subtle clues. I begin to walk outside the door now that Ethan and I have both paid for our sandwiches. Ethan follows as I tell him, "I know this may seem like bad timing, but I did want you to know, because I do care about our friendship."

Ethan cuts me off. "I think after the other night, we're a little more than friends."

"We kissed, which I certainly don't do with my friends," I say. "But I just don't want to jump ahead to anything, which I hope you understand. I maybe got caught up in the moment, or I did want it to happen, but it doesn't matter anymore. Things have changed." I look down at my food for a second to avoid eye contact, but then find the guts to look up.

Ethan's face is dropping and I can see his defensive side emerge. "I don't get it, Cailin. What are you saying? Things are over before they basically even started? I thought this was our chance to reconnect."

"I'm sorry, Ethan." I hate breaking up and this isn't even a breakup. But I'm coming across as the one who was wrong. "It's just that this new job is going to demand a lot of my time and attention. And I need to focus without distraction. I hope you'll understand. It will all make sense once I can explain more."

"Well," Ethan says, "I guess I got you wrong."

"Got me wrong? What's that supposed to mean?"

"I didn't think you would act like a summer girl. I thought you were serious."

"You're accusing me of the exact opposite of what I'm doing, Ethan. I'm being honest and letting you know that while I enjoyed the night at your house, some things have recently happened in my life and I'm going to focus on them. I'm purposely not leading you on for anything that's not going to happen. I would think you would appreciate that."

With that, I turn on my heels and storm off to my car. I replay the conversation in my head and consider calling Gemma. She won't believe what just happened. But I can't really confide in her either. I can't tell her about Jax until the NDA is lifted. I need to make this announcement.

Back at home, I finish my lunch, brew a new cup of coffee, and begin drafting the social media post. I have enough feedback from Harry on the press release to draft a sample post for Jax. I send it over to the team. A few minutes later, I see a text across my phone. It's from Jax. He texted me. All this time I've been waiting for an email from him, but I forgot he also has my cell.

Jax: F*ing brilliant.

I take it he likes what he read. All the anger I had over the confrontation with Ethan dissipates from my body.

Me: The press release or the social post?

Jax: You.

Trash the Dress Online Chat

Cailin: I'm having forbidden thoughts about someone...

Alexandra: Do tell. I need some excitement beyond a new episode of Bluey in my life.

Leila: Is he married?

15

CAILIN MCCALL BREAKS THE NEWS AFTER SIGNING NDA

CAILIN

YOU. It's one tiny, three-letter word. Yet, it's been consuming my mind for the past twenty-four hours. There are so many ways this word has paved a path in my life. Collin asked, "Will you marry me?" That question gave me control. My boss said, "You are fired." That statement took away my power. Then Jax Slater, the biggest player alive, who by some miraculous twist of fate knows I exist, just texted me the most direct, intense, hottest use of the word ever. My body reacted immediately. But my mind didn't know how to process it. So, I didn't say anything. Jax either thinks I'm playing it totally cool, or if he was for some insane reason actually flirting with me, he might think I'm not interested.

How did I get here? I'm just a girl trying to move on after her life fell apart and suddenly I'm trying to decode text messages from the famous boy band bad boy who was on the 125 posters taped to my bedroom walls when I was a teenager.

After the press materials received final approval, I got the green light to announce Jax's new album and tour. The media response was as predicted: every national TV show and celebrity gossip site has been reporting the news and reaching out for backstage interviews on tour. It's a lot to handle as the publicist in charge of coordinating it all, but I get a chill down my spine with every email I open, reading each reporter's name, one more impressive than the next.

The biggest thrill, though, was posting my new job announcement on social media and shouting from the rooftop that I'm going on tour. Literally. I found access to the roof of my apartment building, and despite my fear of heights and accidentally getting locked up there, went up and filmed a selfie video of myself announcing the news. Okay, I did text Gemma to tell her I was going up there to film, just in case I got stuck.

Gemma calls me immediately. "Stop it. This is the secret you've been keeping? How could you even keep this Earth-shattering news to yourself for so long? I need every single detail, obviously. And daily text updates once you're on tour. And photos. Not just the ones you post on social. I want the full experience. Are you dying? I would be dying."

When Gemma finally stops to take a breath, I fill her in on everything I've been dying to spill. Even the part about the slightly flirty text that I didn't respond to.

Gemma doesn't approve of my letting that go. "You should have typed something back. Like, even a blushing emoji. Anything."

"Gemma, I'm his publicist. I need to keep this professional. Besides, it's hard to decipher on a text if he was flirting or just really happy with the work I'm doing. I can't let my teenage crush derail me from a really great career opportunity." No matter how much that one word, "you," sent a rush of warmth through my body, hitting spots that really should not be radiating during a client interaction.

"I get it. So, will you stop by and see me before you leave for tour? I want to send you off with some new clothes from the boutique. My gift, congratulating you on your new job."

"I'll definitely come and say goodbye. I have to visit my mom, too."

"Speaking of making your rounds, what about Ethan?" Gemma asks.

"After what happened, I am not even going to share this news with him. He doesn't deserve any decency from me. He can read it on social media if he wants."

"I agree. Just wondering, in case I run into him."

Gemma and I hang up and I spend the next few hours working. By the end of the day, all the emails cluttering my inbox have been read and filed accordingly. I feel like it's safe to disconnect. I grab my phone and sit on my couch for a few minutes to decompress.

There's a bunch of new social media notifications. Everyone is commenting on my video post. New followers are flooding in from the media, and obviously 5 Leo Hearts' fans. Wow, I feel almost influential overnight. I scan through the list of accounts and one notification stops me in my tracks: **Jax Slater started following you.**

I spend the rest of the week running errands, packing, and getting ready for tour. When I said goodbye to my mom, she lectured me on being safe and gave me a female safety alarm keychain. She's happy for me, but she's also a mom worried about her daughter going on tour, so I get it. Gemma gave me so many clothes that I basically have a new wardrobe. I'm set for the bus, show nights, and gosh, even bedtime, because she threw in silk pajamas. I told her no one wears silk pajamas on tour and that I am not impressing anyone because I'll have a bus to myself. She just winked.

We're getting down to the wire now and everyone is in a tizzy, but I never expected Jax to randomly text me.

Jax: Need your opinion.

Me: Go for it.

I move to my couch, nervously pull a blanket on me, and grab a pillow for emotional support. Just the thought of Jax wanting—no, needing—my opinion, gets me giddy. As I settle in, Jax sends me a bunch of photos of him in different outfits. This is not what I was expecting. Also, Jax Slater is sending me mirror selfies. Is this real life?

Jax: Packing outfits for the stage. Harry wanted me to use my old stylist, but I don't want to look like a boy band guy. I want to look like me. So, I went shopping the other day.

He's texting me about clothes. I can handle this. It's part of my job.

Me: I am sort of an expert in clothes. What makes you feel the most confident?

Jax: Definitely pieces that are more laid back and casual, but I think my fans are expecting my outlandish costumes. I don't want to disappoint them.

Me: I think just seeing you up on stage will get them going.

I immediately regret typing that message and stomp my feet on the couch. In an effort to redeem myself, I text him the options I think will look great, which are tight black jeans that hug his backside. Or, at least I imagine they do.

Jax: Thanks, Cailin. I trust your opinion so I'm going with it.

Me: Happy to be of service.

This is where I expect the conversation to end. Except, I see three little dots blinking across the message box. It looks like Jax keeps typing and deleting his message. Finally, he hits send.

Jax: Hope you know what you're getting yourself into going on tour.

I'm not sure what Jax means by this, so I opt to keep it light-hearted.

Me: I am fully prepared with my favorite snacks, so I feel I can accomplish anything that comes my way.

Jax: Is that so? Sweet or salty?

Me: Trick question. A mix of both. What about you?

Are we really having this conversation?

Jax: Spicy, but I also like the taste of sweet things…

He certainly knows how to heat things up. There he goes, borderline crossing boundaries. Is he flirting with me again? This must be his personality. No wonder he has this reputation. But I can't let it get romantic between us as much as I want to fall for his lines. So, I don't reply.

Of course, Jax keeps this going.

Jax: I also like to stream movies on the bus ride between cities. A few hours of my favorite action flicks pass the time. It can get lonely.

Jax is good. Real good at being bad. I, however, am really good at being the good girl. And he will not break me. I ignore his little innuendo.

> Me: Action movies cannot compete with Notting Hill, Love Actually, or The Holiday.

> Jax: I guess we'll just have to settle this on the road.

I know I'm swaying near the edge of what's appropriate behavior right now. Back and forth, between my heart and my head. Each reply back, I feel myself slipping closer off the cliff. This is risky business. I need to get back on solid ground.

> Me: If I'm doing my job as well as I plan, you'll be so busy doing interviews you won't have time to watch movies. You're so hot right now.

> Jax: Are you saying I'm hot?

> Me: I mean, hot... like trending.

> Jax: Oh. Got it. I'm not hot, hot.

> Me: I didn't say that.

> Jax: So, you do think I'm hot.

> Me: Do you ask all your team members if they think you're hot?

> Jax: I'm sorry if I overstepped. I got caught up for a second. You're really easy to talk to.

Now, he's breaking open. I'm trying so hard to hold back, but how can I when my favorite pop star is definitely flirting with me? I hold my breath as I type my response.

Me: It's OK. I like talking to you, too. You're not what I expected.

I exhale. That felt good.

Jax: What did you expect?

Me: Not someone so down to Earth, I guess.

Jax: There's a lot about me people don't see from afar, I suppose.

Me: I'm seeing that. I guess I have a lot to learn. So I can pitch you with fresh angles, of course.

Jax: Lucky for you we'll have plenty of time to get to know each other these next few weeks.

I should start filing for unemployment now.

Trash the Dress Online Chat

Alexandra: Should I be stalking his new girlfriend on social? No. Am I? Yes.

Cailin: Make sure you go all the way to the beginning of her feed to get the dirt!

Leanne: The worst is when you find out she's actually someone you would befriend.

16

THERE'S RISKY BUSINESS BETWEEN CAILIN MCCALL AND JAX SLATER

JAX

I CROSSED the line with Cailin. There I go back to my old ways. It's like I can't be in the presence of an attractive female without flirting in her direction. In my defense, after a while of our text message chat, I forgot we had a business relationship. And to be fair, Cailin is flirting back, despite her attempts to ignore my hints.

Cailin: I do look forward to getting to know you, Jax.

Me: Does that mean you'll watch a movie on my bus one night?

Cailin: I'm part of the crew right? I wouldn't want to miss out on anything fun.

Me: I'm thinking this would be more of a private viewing. I'd be lying if I said I didn't find you sexy as hell the first time I saw you on video chat. You're cute when you blush.

Cailin: You definitely make me blush.

> Me: So, you do think I'm hot.

> Cailin: OK, you win.

Wow, it feels really good to get back to not only talking to a woman, but talking to one who is intelligent, intriguing, and takes me on a little chase. I'm learning that there's more to Cailin than her looks. She has substance. I didn't intend to come right out and confess that I think she's hot. What's that saying about how a tiger can't change its stripes? I can't turn off my prowling instincts when I'm turned on by someone. Apparently, she doesn't mind.

Then, she hits me with reality.

> Cailin: Hey, Jax? Can we keep this convo between us? I probably should not have said that. It's totally unprofessional. I don't know what came over me. I'm serious about my job. I just got caught up...

> Me: I get it. I can tell you're not a groupie. I think that's why I'm starting to like you.

Cailin is obviously a little nervous. I hope I didn't come on too strong or scare her off. I know this is a new job for her. She might just totally reject me, so I should prepare myself for a very awkward tour before it even starts. Way to go, Jax. Great start to building your credibility.

I need an outsider's perspective to see how bad this really is, so I call Ridge. He is always my go-to when I need to get in check. Ridge grew up with me, knows everything about my past, and has seen me at my lowest, as well as my best. I know he'll guide me on the best course of action. Ridge will let me know if I'm letting lust take over, or if he agrees that I should throw caution to the wind and glide full force through these obstacles and sweep Cailin off her feet.

"I need some advice," I tell Ridge once he answers the phone. "Got a minute?"

"Yeah, just one second," Ridge tells me while he lets Kelly know he's stepping out. Kelly yells to me from the other end of the phone. Maybe I should actually talk to her instead of Ridge. A woman's perspective might be more beneficial to me right now.

"Actually, can you put me on speaker? I want to get Kelly's opinion."

"This must have to do with a woman," Ridge says.

"Oh, is there a woman?" I can tell from Kelly's voice that she is giving Ridge a look and they are having a subliminal conversation about how great it is that I am getting out of my funk.

"Kinda. I mean, yes, she's a woman. But it's complicated."

"Of course it is," Ridge says. "Women are complex creatures."

Just then, Ridge winces, "Ouch!"

I laugh because I know Kelly probably whacked him in his stomach, which is tight, but not steel like mine. Ridge has been slacking on his workouts a little since he got engaged, then married. Now that he's in the honeymoon phase and off tour, it's safe to say that he is blissfully not concerned with his abs.

"So, what's going on?" Kelly asks. I know she lives for this drama. Kelly likes to live in an elite world and get the juicy scoop before everyone else. This way, once word starts to spread, she can say it's old news and she already knew about it weeks ago. That keeps her at the top of her social chain and her friends stick to her like glue, so they too can be at the forefront of their self-important circle. All that said, Kelly isn't a total LA girl. She does have a lot of down-to-earth qualities, and I know that's something Ridge really admired about her since the day they randomly met at a party.

"I met someone who I really want to get to know better and I'm not sure if I came on too strong," I say.

"You're Jax Slater. I think people expect you to come on strong." Ridge makes a good point.

"There's one problem. She's my new publicist." I wait in silence for a lecture.

"Okay, I see the problem," Ridge says. He leaves it at that and doesn't rant about this being a bad idea. That's a good sign.

"You've got a thing for your publicist?" Kelly asks.

"I know it's not ideal. I've only met her on video chat and we flirted on text."

"Did she reciprocate?"

"Yes, Kelly. Definitely."

"Then she's into you. But I can see her job being a problem."

Ridge jumps in, "You said you haven't met her yet. How do you know?"

"I can't explain it. I just feel like she's different than any girl I've ever met."

Never before has texting someone given me such delight, knowing that the woman typing those words might just be the woman I've been waiting to meet. The one who has goals, appreciates the simple things in life, and doesn't care that I'm famous. The one who gets my blood pumping as soon as I see her picture.

"This is good," Kelly says. "It's the first time I feel like you can say you're honestly over what happened with Maxine. Genuine interest in another woman is a big step."

"Yeah, man. We were all a little worried about you," Ridge says. "Remember when after you and Maxine broke up and you had hundreds of girls mail you letters? And some girls even threw bras with their phone numbers written in them over the front gates of your house? You didn't even look at them. We seriously talked as a group about having an intervention."

"I know I was at an all-time low, but that seems a bit drastic. I loved Maxine and it takes time to bounce back from something like that."

Ridge transitions before we have a debate. "You know, Oliver took some of those letters."

"Some of the bras, too," Kelly says.

"He definitely made a few phone calls," Ridge says.

"And look where that got him. Nowhere. He's still single," I say.

"But now you have a girl you're interested in," Kelly says, circling back to the reason for this call.

"Definitely interested. Now what do I do?"

I rest my head in my hands and put the phone on speaker. I'm really hoping they give me advice I can use. I've been out of the game for so long and I don't want to do anything to mess up my chance with Cailin. It's important that I strategize. The player is retired. I've quit playing games. My heart is open, as long as she'll love me.

"I say wait until you meet her in person and see if you even like her. This might just be a new fascination or something. Like you realized you want to get back out there and she's the first girl you've met." I see what Ridge means, but that's not the case.

"I'm telling you, the reason I want to get back out there is because of Cailin."

Kelly jumps in to offer a mega romantic outlook. "This is really sweet. Listen, Jax. If this girl woke you from your deep slump and you think she's something special, then you must pursue her. This is like running down the streets to catch a cab and high-tailing it to the airport before her plane takes off kind of stuff. You can't let this go. You'll regret not trying."

"You're right, Kelly. I can't let her go before I even have a chance. I deserve to give this a shot."

I thank Kelly and Ridge for their advice and hang up knowing exactly what I need to do. I might not be in the situation where I have to chase Cailin down at the airport to stop her from leaving. However, she's flying into LA very soon and I can make a grand gesture to let her know my intentions.

Trash the Dress Online Chat

Harper: Can we please talk about Cailin's post about going on tour with JAX SLATER? DETAILS!!

Alexandra: OMG WHAT?!

Melissa: Please tell me this is the forbidden man?

17

JAX SLATER SWEEPS CAILIN MCCALL OFF HER FEET WITH SURPRISE GESTURE

CAILIN

IF LOVE IS all around airports like that hit movie claims, it seems to have missed Los Angeles. Or at least me. I could really use some love right now. Cupid, where are you? Hit me with your best shot. Spike that arrow with some magical beauty elixir. Cailin at 5 a.m. after an overnight flight is a sight for sore eyes. And I feel just as bad as I'm guessing I look.

The tour starts in LA, which is where Jax currently resides, so everyone who isn't local had to fly into town. I roll my suitcase down the long airport hallway and look for the nearest bathroom. I need to do something with myself before I meet Jax for the first time in person, and I'm really wishing I prepared a little more for such a major milestone. I try taking my hair out of the bun, but that doesn't help. My hair is dented in all the wrong places. Back up it goes. I use the bathroom and swish some mouthwash. Now my mouth is as fresh as my mind.

After I wash my hands and apply an organic coconut and vanilla scented hand lotion, I pull out my makeup bag and quickly apply cream-based blush on the apples of my cheeks for a natural dewy 'I didn't try too hard' look. A few swipes of mascara, puffs of powder, and a slick of clear lip gloss later, I feel almost human. This will have to do.

I head out to the airport exit and look for the person from my car service reservation. To my surprise, when I arrive, there are two men holding signs with my name on them.

"Are you Cailin McCall?" one of them asks. They clearly have noticed they are both waiting for me.

"Yes, I am. The one and only. As in, I only booked one of you, so I'm a bit confused right now." I put down my luggage, which is already weighing on my shoulders.

"Allow me to explain," says the driver wearing an all-black suit and black gloves. "Mr. Slater sent me to pick you up. I have specific instructions to escort you to his location."

"Oh, that's nice of him." I wonder if he surprised all his crew members with drivers. "I guess I won't be needing you to take me to my destination," I tell the other driver, who is dressed in jeans and a T-shirt. "I'll be taking this service, but I will pay you for your time."

The driver nods and I give him my debit card to scan.

"You're not some psycho planning to kidnap me, are you?" I ask the other driver. "I'm going to snap your photo and text it to Jax." I do exactly that.

Jax replies back immediately.

> Jax: Ah, great. You met Stan.

> Me: If you assure me that Stan is not a serial killer, I will get in the car with him and let him take me to the tour buses.

> Jax: Just trust me. He's not taking you to the tour buses.

> Me: What do you mean? We all have to meet up in an hour there.

> Jax: I told everyone I'm running late and to
> push things back an hour. That something
> important came up.

Stan is staring at me as I text. So I tell him I trust him, hand over my bags, and climb in the backseat of the car while I continue texting Jax.

> Me: I see. Pulling the old pop star running
> late trick. May I ask where Stan is
> taking me?

> Jax: My house.

His house. Well, now I'm really awake. Talk about a shot of adrenaline. I was not prepared for this at all. Why is Jax Slater sending a car service to bring me to his house? I'm so grateful I mouth-washed, but now I am regretting that I did not reapply deodorant. This is not how I imagined meeting one of the world's biggest pop stars—and my new client—for the first time. I take out my scented lotion and lather it on my arms and neck. Hope Stan likes the scent of the tropics.

> Me: Your house?

> Jax: I didn't want the first time we meet to
> be in front of a bunch of people. Don't worry,
> Stan will drive you separately to the meet-up
> location so no one will suspect a thing. I'll
> show up a few minutes later in another car
> with my bodyguard.

> Me: Of course you have a bodyguard. Will
> this bodyguard be present when I arrive?

> Jax: No one will be blocking my body when
> you arrive.

Before I fully process what's happening, Stan pulls the black SUV up to the biggest house I've ever laid eyes on. He puts a code into the gate and proceeds to drive up a very lengthy driveway. Eventually, we arrive in front of a fountain. Stan steps out of the car, opens my door, and tells me that he'll be waiting here while I'm inside.

My legs feel like liquid as I slowly approach the door. I'm nervous like Angela Chase was as she watched Jordan Catalano walk over to her, right before he took her hand and led her down the hallway in My So-Called Life. I know something big is going to happen, but I'm not sure what's in store. I knock on the door and Jax quickly opens it. He's wearing a pair of blue jeans and I think it's one of the pairs he sent me a picture of, that I said I liked. His plain light green shirt is hugging his chest and showing off his bulging arm muscles. They're decorated with more tattoos than I remember.

He holds a steady face, bites his lower lip, and motions for me to come inside before closing the door.

"Thanks for the ride." In person, his eyes are a deep blue and I'm already drowning in his love, but I can't show that one bit.

Jax takes my hands in his and says, "Thanks for trusting me." I'm mortified that my hands are sweaty and still trying to wrap my brain around this, but yet, I feel like my hands have found a cozy, new, protective home.

We awkwardly stand facing each other in silence for a moment, eyes locked and soaking in every detail of the other. Jax stands about six feet three inches tall. He's about a foot taller than me and I make a mental note to book a chiropractor appointment, because for the next month, I plan on never taking my eyes off Jax. His face is worth the neck pain. We both smile and I begin to laugh, breaking the silence.

"This is a big surprise, Jax. I cannot even believe I am standing here, and that you sent a car service to get me and bring me to your house. Why did you bring me here?"

"I wanted to meet you in private," Jax says. "This might sound weird, but stay with me. You know how some couples do that first look thing at weddings? I only know this because, you know, I was a groomsman in Ridge's. They did that. An intimate moment between the couple that takes place for only them. The wedding is the show, for everyone else. But that moment, it's just the two of them."

I stumble on my words. "You wanted to create a special moment to meet me?" Me. Cailin McCall. The good girl who says the wildest thing she's ever done is go to the store without makeup.

Jax looks deep into my eyes and asks, "Can I hug you?"

Goosebumps spread across my arms as I reply, "I would love to give you a hug." Is that allowed? Can a publicist hug their client? I never really had a client want to hug me before. Maybe this is just normal in the music industry. I still do not believe it's possible that Jax is like, interested, interested in me. He just likes to flirt. But I am not going to pass up a hug.

Jax sweeps me into his arms and squeezes me tight until I feel breathless. I never in a million years would think that my head would be on Jax Slater's chest. I must savor this moment. I bury my face into his chest because, why not? My head lands over his heart and I can feel quick beats. His pulse, I can tell, is racing as fast as mine. I take a deep breath and take in his woodsy, aromatic cologne. There are hints of lemon and maybe some pepper. Whatever the ingredients, it must have pheromones because I'm immediately feeling wild.

"Damn, you smell good girl," Jax says. I made the right decision to bathe myself in scented lotion.

"But you're pretty short." Apparently Jax has a humorous side. I wonder what else I don't know about him.

"You're pretty tall." I, on the other hand, state the obvious when I am at a loss for words. "So, what now?"

"Now, I'm going to get my suitcase and lock up the house. You're going to head over to the meetup. When I see you in a little bit, I'll shake your hand, and we'll pretend we never met. I'll act like there isn't some undeniable force pulling me to you, apologize for the delay, retreat to my bus, and we can hit the road. Then, I'll figure out how to survive the hour I'm going to be locked away in solitude as we sit in traffic on the way to the venue, trying to remember what you smell like and pretending I don't want to know what you taste like."

Lightheaded and trying to comprehend this tilt-a-whirl I'm coming off, I simply say, "Sounds like a plan." I turn one more time to look at Jax before I walk out and feel his stare burning down the curve of my spine, over my backside, and sliding down my legs. We might have a plan, but can we pull it off so I don't risk my job?

There are five large tour buses lined up in the parking lot. Signs are taped onto the door of each bus. One reads, Jax Slater. Another, Road Crew. Then there are buses for Band, Management, and Publicity. I'm the last of the crew to arrive. Stan helps me with my luggage and I haul it over to meet everyone. Harry greets me immediately. It's nice to have his familiar face because I'm kind of intimidated right now. This is my first tour and these are all seasoned vets. I wonder if Harry knows that I just went to see Jax. Can they tell by looking at me that I'm glowing in a new light? Did his cologne rub off on me and betray our secret? I'm totally dazed and confused.

"Cailin, you made it," Harry says. "How was your flight?"

"Hi, Harry. Great to finally meet you. My flight was fine. Just a little jet-lagged, but nothing a good nap won't cure."

"No worries there. We have about an hour's drive to the venue to load-in and then we'll all check into one of those hotels I promised you, so we can all shower. You'll have some downtime while Jax and the band soundcheck. Here, let me introduce you to everyone."

Harry walks me over to a circle of people conducting multiple conversations. "Everyone, this is Cailin. She's with the PR team. She'll be coordinating all the media for tour."

Everyone cordially waves and greets me. Then Harry introduces them individually. There are a bunch of roadies, who load and set up the equipment. There are members of the backing band for when Jax does his melody tribute to 5 Leo Hearts songs. Hayley, the merch girl, is the only other female. I'm interested to get to know her and hope we'll bond.

Hayley walks over to me and pulls me aside. "Hey, it's just us girls here so we'll need to stick together. The testosterone gets a bit much at times."

Like she read my mind. "I bet. How long have you been doing tours?"

"Since I was eighteen. I started out photographing bands, but soon realized it's easier to get photo passes to shows if you are actually part of the crew. Plus, I needed money. I started touring with punk rock bands and that's how I met Jayce and we've been together since."

"You're dating one of the band members?" I ask slightly relieved. This means Hayley will be off on her own a lot and I'll have space to sneak and see Jax. Even though I should stay away.

"He's all mine. I'll be on the bus with the crew."

"Well that's great that you get to do what you love, with the person you love." It truly sounds like a dream.

"What about you? Are you seeing anyone?"

"Me? Oh no. I'm recently divorced. Just focusing on myself right now."

"Oh, wow." Hayley looks at me with a little remorse.

"No, it's not like that. It was mutual. I'm totally happy and ready to move on. When I meet someone, of course."

"Well, there's no better place to get a divorce out of your system than on a tour. Meet a dude, hookup, and leave him for the next city. Or, maybe one of these guys." Hayley points to the crew.

Hayley doesn't have a bad idea. In fact, if I wasn't in the middle of this surreal courting from the boy band member of my dreams, I would probably do exactly what she's suggesting. I'd live it up a little and enjoy my single status. Each city would bring a different type of man into my orbit. Cowboys, southern gentlemen, athletic types, tech nerds. Wait, backup. No more tech nerds. The point is, I'm set on a different adventure. One that's forbidden.

"Good ideas, really. But I'm just focusing on work while I'm here. Big tour, lots of responsibility. Can't get sidetracked."

"I get it. But I'll be your wing-woman if you want."

Hayley smiles and walks away as a black SUV pulls up. My heart starts to race. It's Jax. The butterflies are back.

Trash the Dress Online Chat

Mae: Anyone hear from Cailin yet? I'm listening to 5 Leo Hearts and dying of jealousy.

Alexandra: Ah, Oliver....

Tori: I liked Cute Boys Band better.

Alexandra: @Tori I don't know if we can be friends anymore.

18

LET THE LIES BEGIN! JAX SLATER KICKS OFF NEW TOUR

CAILIN

Jax steps out of the SUV wearing the same jeans and T-shirt I nestled my face on not too long ago. He's wearing sunglasses now and gosh, he is so sexy. He runs his fingers through his hair and suddenly I'm jealous of his fingers. Everyone claps and begins cheering for Jax.

"What up, everyone!" Jax says. He stops a second longer in my direction before turning his head back to the group. "Sorry I'm late. Got tied up on some last-minute things. Who's ready to do this?"

Jax is pumped and everyone is feeding off his infectious energy. He walks over to high-five all of the crew members. Harry pulls him in for a hug. Hayley and Jax fist bump. Then, it's his turn to greet me.

Harry intervenes. "Jax, this is Cailin."

Jax pulls off his sunglasses and sets eyes onto mine, sending a secret message only we know. My stomach is doing gymnast-worthy flips as he shakes my hand. "Nice to officially meet you, Cailin."

"Nice to meet you, too. I'm looking forward to this."

"Well, now that we're all acquainted, let's hit the road," Harry says. "Cailin, I'll show you to your bus and introduce you to your driver, Ken."

A driver. I forgot my bus would have a driver. Someone who would know my every move. This might make things tricky.

"Hello, ma'am," Ken says.

My fears instantly disappear. Ken is a gentle grandpa, who is obviously keeping himself occupied during retirement.

"Hi Ken. Nice to meet you. Thank you for driving."

"You're in good hands, my dear. I've been on the open roads my whole life. Started driving as a second job to support my family when my kids were younger. Loved seeing the country, so I kept at it. And don't you worry, I bunk with the crew at night. But if you ever need anything, you come knock on our bus, you hear?"

"I will. Thank you, I appreciate it."

"Now let's go get you settled." Ken directs me towards our bus.

My tour bus is a show-stopper. It seriously looks like a luxury hotel room. I should have expected no less from Jax. He can afford to treat his crew well and obviously does. I don't even feel like I'm on a bus. There are couches with plush pillows, a seated dining nook, kitchen area, and my choice of bunk beds that sit behind private curtains. I instantly love the curtains because then I can store all my stuff and my space will still look neat. Even the bathroom is better than I expected. It looks just like a bathroom on a plane. I can deal with that. I'll just miss the shower, but I know we have daily hotel stops.

I sit down between two pillows on the couch and pull up the tour schedule. We're going to Los Angeles, Minneapolis, Chicago, Detroit, Nashville, Atlanta, Raleigh, Baltimore, Philadelphia, Asbury Park, and end in New York City. When I first agreed to go on tour, I was excited to see all these new cities. I figured I'd explore each area on my own, bring my laptop to various restaurants and work. Maybe do a little shopping in-between work. I'd hope to casually run into Jax during my days and make small talk. Now, he's calling my phone.

"Hey." Jax has a deceivingly rough voice over the phone.

"Hey, you." We're so close, yet so far away. I'm yearning to feel the warmth of his body against mine again. Such a brief moment of bliss.

"How are you settling in on the bus?"

"Oh, this shabby thing?" I pat a super soft couch pillow. "Seriously, you are spoiling us. We can rough it on less luxurious buses, but I am not going to complain."

"Hey, you only live once right? Might as well enjoy the ride."

"Wow, that was such a corny pun, Jax. But I'm impressed yet again. You'd make a great writer."

"Well, I am sort of a songwriter, you know."

"True." A man whose words make my heart sing.

"Are you going to be writing any songs while you're cooped up on the bus?"

"I always write when I'm inspired."

"And what inspires you?"

"Secret meetings with a girl I'm not allowed to touch in public."

"Ah, I see. And how do you see these secret meetings working out when we have so many people around us? You have a pretty big crew."

"Don't worry about those guys. Every city stop is like a new party for them. They'll be wasted at night and sleep all day until it's time for work."

"Even Hayley?"

"I did a few shows back in the day with Hayley. She's motivated and a hard worker. She also takes great photos. I have used a lot of her behind-the-scenes shots for my social media."

"She seems really nice. Though she is trying to set me up with some of the band guys."

"Whoa, back up." I can tell that right here is when Jax realizes there might be more than a few kinks we need to smooth out.

"Obviously, that's not going to happen. She just asked me if I was in a relationship and I told her I'm recently divorced." Oops. I let that slip. But it's fine. He needs to know and sooner is better, rather than later.

"Divorced, huh?" Jax takes it pretty well. "Looks like there's a lot about Cailin McCall that I need to learn. Like why someone would ever divorce her."

I'm starting to feel like a broken record. "It was mutual. I don't look at it as a failure, just a life lesson that took a really, really long time to play out." I laugh trying to lighten things up. No one wants to start a new relationship—or whatever this is— by dragging up the past. I just want to address it and move on to what's really important.

"I get it. I was never married, but I came pretty close. And I'm happy I got out of it before I spent any more time on something that wasn't going to work out. People think that being a celebrity, dating is easy and you can get anyone you want. But sometimes even if you're a celebrity, the thing you want most can be out of reach."

"Does that mean you still have feelings for her? I mean, I know we talked about it a little before, but..."

But now I really am crushing on you so I need to know.

"No, absolutely not. Did you listen to track ten?"

I quickly scan my brain but can't recall track ten. I'm losing my talent. "I did indeed listen to track ten, but now I'm going to go back and listen again."

"Good," Jax says. "There's a subliminal message in there if you listen really closely with headphones on while sitting in your underwear."

Now he lost me. "What are you babbling?"

Jax laughs with me. Together, our voices intertwine and create a new melody that I wouldn't mind playing on repeat.

"Nothing. Just thinking of you in nothing but underwear with headphones on, listening to my songs."

"Oh, you're going there. What kind of underwear are you picturing?"

"The kind I can easily slide off."

Trash the Dress Online Chat

Tori: Do you guys have a code word when you go on first dates? Like when a friend calls to check in?

Alexandra: The only first dates I have these days are playdates.

Harper: You can just tell the guy you love him if it's not going well and that will pretty much send them out the door.

19

CAILIN MCCALL TRIES TO FOCUS ON HER JOB, BUT FAILS

CAILIN

JAX HAS me all hot and bothered, and by the end of our conversation, I hang up the phone craving him. But now, I have to snap out of this alternate reality I'm living in and get off the tour bus because we've arrived at the venue. Although it was a short ride, everyone seems eager to stretch their legs. There's a new energy radiating around as we gather together and start working in our respective roles.

I realize this is the first time ever that I'm *with* the boy band. I'm a part of the magic, a member of the team, one of the inside people I used to envy. I have my clipboard with a list of attending media in my hand and make my way to find the head of security so I can submit the guest list. There are a lot of big-name reporters and celebrities coming out tonight, since this is not only the first show of the tour, but also takes place in the Los Angeles market. I'm pretty nervous actually. It's my job to make sure there are no issues with arrival, and everyone who was promised a guest pass makes it to the list. But I triple-checked it and also had an intern on our team look at it, so I know I made every preparation.

Harry finds me. "There you are. How's the guest list coming along?"

I hold up my clipboard with pride and Harry nods in approval.

"Interesting," Harry says.

"What's interesting?" I didn't find any of the requests to be surprising.

"This one." Harry points to a name I'm not familiar with. I figured she is a personal friend or family of someone on the crew because her name was sent over from Carlos. She apparently comes backstage to all the shows.

"Brenda." Harry rubs his forehead. "She's a friend of Chris, the tour drummer. But she's a handful and is always hitting on Jax. I thought we weren't going to grant her access after what happened last tour."

Well, that got my attention. "Oh, I'm so sorry, Harry. My colleague, Carlos, sent me over her name to add her to the list. She sent her request to him."

"It's fine," Harry tells me as we walk. "Neither of you would know. I guess Jax forgot to add a list of people he doesn't want backstage."

"I see. Is that list lengthy?"

"Nah, just the stalkers and groupies who always try to get backstage without winning a contest. Dedicated fans, really. Harmless."

"Got it. Well, no more unwelcome women on my watch, you have my word. I'll run the guest list by you each night."

I hand over the guest list to the front door, turn around, and run smack into Hayley.

"Oh! Sorry, Hayley."

"I'm sorry, too! I didn't see you through all these T-shirts." Hayley is holding a mound of merch.

"Here, let me help you," I say.

"Thanks. I want to set up early so I can head to the hotel

and shower. Are you gonna go over or hang out here 'til the show?"

"Do you see me?" I point to myself in shambles. "I need to get myself together before I meet the pop royalty that's coming out tonight. The guest list made my jaw drop."

"I forgot this is your first tour. I'm so used to it by now. I gave up trying to impress everyone and now just dress how I'm comfortable. I'm selling merch, not designer clothes, ya know?"

"I love that you own it," I tell Hayley. And I mean it. There's an air about her that says she doesn't give a flip about what anyone thinks. She's confident and secure in jeans and a band-shirt, and honestly looks fierce. Go, girl.

We arrive at the merch area and both breathe sighs of relief as we place the T-shirts down. It appears that this is the last of them because Hayley already has a ton of boxes in her area. I pull one of the shirts out of a box and open it up.

"What do these shirts say?" I ask.

"There are a few different ones. One with the tour dates, one for the album, and then some fun ones for the super fans." Hayley points to the white T-shirt in my hand that says, "I Love (heart-shape) Jax Slater." I feel like my secret was just revealed and for a split-second panic.

"Do you?" While I was tuned out, Hayley asked me a question. Oh gosh, was she asking me if I love Jax?

The puzzled look on my face prompts Hayley to repeat her question. "Do you want a shirt? It's yours."

I feel relieved. Yes, I'll take a shirt. And yes, maybe it's true. "Totally. If I can have one of each, I'll be sure to wear them and post pics. I am the publicist after all," I remind both Hayley and myself.

"Go for it." Hayley points to the piles of merch. "I'm gonna finish setting up."

"Thanks," I say. It's a perfect time to casually see what I can find out about Brenda and I decide to take advantage of the opportunity.

"Do you ever have friends come out to the shows? I saw Chris put some names down on the guest list tonight."

"Nah. My friends are too cool to be at a 5 Leo Hearts member show. Don't get me wrong—Jax is awesome. But my friends and I are into punk rock." She points to the skateboard on her T-shirt.

I'm gonna just cut right to it. "Harry was mentioning something about a girl named Brenda on this list."

"Boozy Brenda? She came to every show back in the day and hit on Jax. Like hardcore."

"And what does Jax do?" I'm hoping I don't seem jealous, just curious. I mean, I don't really have a right to be jealous. But I don't like the way the sound of Brenda's name makes me feel.

"He usually brushes her off. But I heard that the last show, when 5 Leo Hearts did a few events for charity, was a little different."

"How so?" I don't like the sound of that either.

"Well, it's basically his job to flirt with the fans, right? So, he had some fun with her, I guess. Like played along for a night. Honestly, he was probably bored."

"What do you mean by played along?" Does Jax still hook up with random girls when he is bored on tour? I didn't get that impression from him. I wonder if I'm his next cure for boredom.

"He just got a little flirty, had his arms around her." Hayley places shirts on the table in front of her. "Not sure if they ever hooked up."

"Oh. I see." That leaves me back to square one.

"If she's on the list, Jax must not care if she comes back."

"Got it." I begin to make my way out from behind the merch area. Jax might not care. But I do. And I'm not sure how I'm supposed to feel about that.

In a huff, I head in the direction of the tour buses, but get side-tracked. I hear an acoustic guitar. Then Jax's voice soars through the air. I follow the sounds to the stage. The arena is empty. It's breathtaking being on the other side of the stage. I'm taken back to my days of concert going, and one special night in particular—the first time Jax saw me, only he doesn't know it.

"Cailin, grab my hand," Gemma yelled over the roar of the crowd. I reached for her but my fingers slipped away each time I got close. Girls dressed in matching homemade "I Love 5 Leo Hearts" shirts kept pushing their way between us, as if crushing us would get them to the stage any faster. They were such amateurs. It must have been their first concert.

"It's time," I yelled to Gemma as my hand finally locked in hers. Gemma pulled me towards her and I took out a few girls in our path as we moved from the center of the crowd to the side. This meant war.

"Everyone, move out of the way," Gemma bellowed. "My friend is going to throw up. Hurry!"

I clasped my hands over my mouth, pretending I was about to hurl. Horrified faces glanced at me and quickly stepped aside, parting the sea of people so Gemma and I had a clear path for a few seconds. We were almost to the front of the stage.

Then we got stuck behind some older girls in high heels. There was no way we were going to be able to see the guys over their heads, let alone take pictures. I snuck my good camera in my bra that night, and we were going to get our picture with the band. We just needed to get to the front row.

I spotted security guards moving the barrier to the right of us. This was our chance. As the masses headed towards the new space that was being opened up, Gemma and I ran hand in hand to the sliver of empty floor space up ahead. We sighed and high-fived. We did it, again.

A spotlight hit the stage and the opening notes of 5 Leo Hearts' new single blasted across the arena. Cheers erupted and all the girls in the front row, including me, threw our hands up towards the stage. The members of 5 Leo Hearts floated down from the ceiling to the stage.

My heart skipped a beat as I took in their coordinating

outfits. Jax was wearing a shirt with black fishnet and I could see his chest glistening underneath. It was obvious he slathered on oil before getting dressed, and I wondered what it would be like to slide my hands over his tight pecs.

The guys landed safely on stage, clipped off their harnesses, and made their way over to the front row. It was time to whip out my camera and sneak a photo before security saw and yelled at me, or even worse, took my camera. But I knew if I took out my camera, then I wouldn't be able to throw my hand up and have the possibility of Jax touching it when he ran his hands across everyone lined up in the front row. I would miss the chance to experience the spark of his touch. It was such a dilemma.

"Get your camera," Gemma said. She nudged me in the ribs.

I shoved my hand down my bra and fidgeted to grab my camera. That's when it happened. Jax stepped in front of me, his gorgeous body towering over mine. He looked down just as I looked up at him, with my hand awkwardly cupping my left breast. I was mortified. And I was missing the ultimate photo op.

"Cailin!" Gemma said. She nudged me again. "You just missed the perfect moment."

But she was wrong. The perfect moment had just happened and has been preserved in my memory. Jax Slater winked at me.

Now, I'm part of the team that brings this experience to life. That makes millions of girls across the world happy. A few hours in a bubble, where you forget everything else going on in your life and just live the lyrics being sung out on stage. Tonight, Jax is going to vulnerably open his heart to strangers and share details of the past years of his life through chorus and verse. I can only imagine what that feels like.

I move closer and step onto stage right. Jax doesn't see me behind the curtain. His fingers carefully strum the guitar strings while he talks with the sound tech to make sure the acoustics are perfect. He has a lot riding on tonight and so do I.

Things need to be a success and I can't be distracted. I don't want my worry over the Brenda's of the world to impact my role as tour publicist. Or what I'm potentially building with Jax. If it's real. Does he invite all girls to his house for secret meetings and tell them the same story? I hate how insecure this is making me feel.

I'm Cailin McCall and I am owning my new start to life. I need to assure myself that I have nothing to worry about tonight and I won't let Brenda's presence stop me from being the best publicist ever. I step out from behind the curtain and clap my hands as Jax puts down his guitar and begins to walk off the stage. A smile spreads across his face as he notices me and he takes a playful bow.

"You sound incredible," I say. It sounds powerful recorded, but hearing that live gives me chills. Though, I keep that to myself.

Jax walks over to me and looks around to watch as the band members scurry off stage, check their cell phones, and converse. "Thanks. Let's hope the audience feels the same."

"Why wouldn't they?"

"It's just a big departure from what they are used to, so I hope they can appreciate it."

I see that Jax needs a confidence boost. I want him to view himself the way I do. "Listen, your voice is like a standalone instrument. Those lyrics are telling stories they want to hear because they are obsessed with you. Breaking down every verse will make them feel closer to you. Like they have a connection. Or know more about you."

"You seem to know my fans pretty well." I can tell Jax is just waiting for me to spill it.

"Okay. I do know how they think because obviously I was a teenage girl once and listened to, you know, boy bands and stuff."

Jax scans the room to see if we are alone, which indeed it appears we are. He steps closer to me and whispers in my ear. "So..." He lets that word hang between us as his warm breath sends shivers down my spine. "Was I your favorite?"

"As if I would ever tell you that."

"You don't have to tell me." Jax puts his arm around my shoulder and pulls me near. "I already know I'm your type."

My brain is melting at the sudden closeness between us and I can't formulate a witty reply. "How so?"

Jax slides his hand up the side of my face, sweeping a stray strand of hair away from my cheek. He stares intently into my eyes and holds my gaze for what seems like an eternity. I can't blink. I feel like I've been pulled into the ocean and I'm surfing through the waves, further and further offshore. Then he pulls away, leaving me to drown in his love.

"That's how."

And with that, he picks up his guitar and says, "I'm gonna head over to the hotel to shower."

Trash the Dress Online Chat

Cora: I'm writing a Dating Checklist for a future mate. Seriously writing "Not addicted to porn."

Mae: Always check his Internet history when he's not looking!

20

DON'T TELL HR WHAT'S HAPPENING ON JAX SLATER TOUR

CAILIN

THE WARM WATER streams down my face and I let it slide down my body. I'm not sure if a shower has ever felt this good. After a day of travel, it's certainly appreciated. For tonight, Hayley and I are sharing a hotel room to get ready. She's still setting up at the venue so I got to score the room first.

I have my outfit laid out on the bed across the crisp, white comforter. I'm wearing a black fit and flare mini dress with an empire waist. The soft structure and pleating at the waist and shoulder create an oversized fluttering wing shape. The sides have a cut-out detail along my ribs. It's sexy, but not form-fitted, so I'll be comfortable moving around. I'm going to rough it and wear a pair of teal heels.

I apply clean makeup with rosy cheeks and a subtle smokey eye. And because it's LA and I'm feeling extra fancy, I'm going bold with red lips. I style my hair down in messy waves and choose some beaded bracelets as accessories.

"You look gorgeous," Hayley says. The door closes behind her when she walks into the room.

I just finished posting a selfie to social media with the

caption, "First night of tour!" This is certainly a change of pace for my feed, which I usually fill with photos of books I read. You'd think because I lived in NYC that I would have a ton of artsy and interesting photos to share, but the only sights I saw were outside the window of my office. Now though, I'm going to make the most of every city on the tour stop.

I let Hayley know the room is all hers. That news makes her night because she's hoping to get some alone time with Jayce. I guess even couples that aren't in secret romances need to find ways to sneak in alone time on tour.

"Have fun," I tell her. I stumble down the hallway as my oversized quilted nylon tote bag that I use to carry everything slides down my shoulder. I should have waited to put on the heels.

"Need some help?" someone calls from behind.

I turn to see Chris. "Oh, hey Chris. I got it, but thank you."

"Here, let me get that for you." He grabs my bag. "Where to?"

"Just back to the bus, thanks." I was hoping I would run into Jax in the hotel, but now I doubt that's going to happen.

"You got it. How is the tour life treating you so far?"

"So far, so good." We make small talk on our way to the bus and then Chris politely helps me up the stairs in my heels and hands me my bag before dashing inside the hotel. Ken returns shortly and asks me if I'm ready for my ride back to the venue. I figure I should get there early anyway in case there are any issues backstage with the media. I'll have to wait to see Jax.

After Ken parks our bus at the venue parking lot, I begin grabbing my stuff for inside. I slip a leather crossbody bag with an iridescent chain across it over my left shoulder. After I make sure my phone is in my bag, I grab my list of attending media, ready to head out. Just as I am about to open the tour bus door, there's a knock. Must be Harry, checking in I figure.

I'm totally wrong. There, standing in front of me in tight moto blue jeans and a fitted black T-shirt is Jax. The facial scruff that I love is gone and his face is clean shaven. His hair is freshly washed and styled.

"Jax, hi." I'm trying not to let on my excitement.

"I was hoping I would catch you. Can I come in?"

"Um, sure," I say. I'm worried that someone might see him, but I also want this time together more than anything, so I'll take the risk.

"Don't worry. I told Harry I was going to check in with you and get briefed on the interviews I have tonight. He's at the bar having a drink with some brand. He's trying to get me an endorsement."

My shoulders relax. "In that case, great idea." I was planning on finding him inside the venue to go through the list of interviews he has tonight.

"Your interviews start in an hour. First up is the music industry magazine." Jax and I move to the surprisingly comfortable seating area. We sit so that our legs are touching and I try to concentrate. We go over all the logistics and talking points. Jax is a pro, so I'm not concerned and neither is he.

"Thanks, got it. Just one more question," he asks, pressing his knee against me and placing his hand on top of my thigh.

"Shoot." I place my hand on top of his as if it gives me some control over the situation, but let's face it, I just want an excuse to touch him. If he moves his hand elsewhere, I'm going to have a really hard time with restraint.

"Is this sexy little dress for me?"

"This sexy little dress is definitely for me. But I'm glad you appreciate it. Now you better get out of here before anyone gets suspicious." I regrettably push his hand off my leg.

"Come with me."

Jax leads the way as we get off the bus. He steps down the

stairs and turns to take my hand and help me down. Except, he's too late. My long, thin heel gets stuck in the ridge of the step and I slip forward. Jax catches me in his arms and holds me close. If my body didn't go limp before, it is now. How am I supposed to get my footing when I'm shaking like this? In the arms of the man I've dreamed about so many times? I can feel his breath on me and it's captured mine.

We stay that way, with his arms wrapped around me and my head looking up at him. Neither one of us moves. I wonder if Jax is thinking about kissing me, too. His eyes drift to my lips, but his face remains in the same position. He has the opportunity to make a move if he wants to, and I know that against my better judgment, I will reciprocate.

This is the first test for both of us. Can we restrain this attraction between us to focus on our jobs? That's what's really important right now. Jax needs to prove himself as a true artist and I have to establish myself in a new industry. If we kiss now, there's no doubt we are both going to be side-tracked for the remainder of the tour.

Jax is the first to break. He slides his hand down the small of my back and gently helps me get my footing. I'm hardly grounded, though. We both wanted more to come from that moment, and the tension between us is so thick it could fill the air in clouds. I feel silly about being disappointed because I know a kiss between us would be wrong.

"Good catch," I say. "I guess I'm not made for walking in these heels."

"Do you want to go change them?"

"No, I'm good. Just a little rusty."

We're standing between two tour buses, mine and his. They create a private alley, and this moment continues to feel just as dangerous. This isn't over. Neither of us seems to be able to let it pass. My brain is telling me to walk away now. My body, however, is paralyzed.

"Good. Because I like looking at you in them."

Everything goes dark except for Jax, illuminated in front of me. "Are you flirting with your publicist again, Jax? Someone might hear you." I need to remind him of the consequences.

"No one's here but us," he says. Jax puts his hands on my waist and pulls me towards him. There's no space between us. I know what's going to happen and I know it's wrong. I'm about to throw away years of hard work and credibility. I'll get labeled a groupie, lose my job, and maybe even end up feeling like a fool if Jax isn't as serious about me as I am about him. Yet, I can't hold back any longer. I spent too many years not feeling desired. And here is the man of my dreams, with his hands on my body.

"I want to kiss you," Jax tells me as his mouth finally inches closer to mine. His eyes search mine for a sign.

My insides quiver. I can't pull away from the magnetic force Jax has over me, so instead, I release myself to be free in this moment. I put my arms on his broad shoulders and swallow hard, anticipating what comes next. Going against all I know that is right and professional, I slowly lick my lips and move to meet his.

Jax softly brushes his mouth against mine, taking my upper lip between his. Lips that have sung words I've recited to myself for years, dreaming of a feeling like this. But it's even better. Tiny little sparks burst across my lips and scatter across my limbs, down my arms, into my stomach, and travel down my legs, lighting up my dormant body.

He holds our lips together, savoring the seconds as he gently traces my jawline with his fingertips. It's not enough, I press my chest into him and Jax releases his lips only to meet mine again in a deeper, needier collision. Jax leads my mouth with every stroke of his graceful tongue and I follow his command. His method of alternating from slow and sensual to harder, firm movements keeps me on edge.

I'm kissing Jax Slater. My mind is going a million miles a minute. My teenage self is high-fiving me and squealing at the top of her lungs. The professional in me is praying no one sees this public display because that would mean the end of my job. The romantic in me is cherishing every second, soaking in the taste of his minty breath and the smell of his aftershave.

I open my eyes for a split second, to make sure this is real. That's when I realize Jax's eyes are already open, relishing every intimate detail. He lifts my chin so that our eyes are level and nuzzles our noses together before reuniting our lips. His eyes remain locked with mine and I swear by now I can hear my heart beating out of my chest. A whimper escapes me. This is what desire is supposed to feel like, I discover.

Jax softly explores my neck with his mouth and I reciprocate. I want to run my fingers through his hair, but I can't mess it up right before show time. And then, I remember...

"Oh no!" I pull away.

Jax looks startled.

"My red lipstick. It's going to stain you!"

"Oh damn," Jax says. He rubs his lips.

I know just how to fix that. "Here, let's run back into the bus and grab some baby wipes." Who knew baby wipes would have so many uses on this tour? Maybe I should have taken Gemma up on her offer to get me the value-sized pack. I grab his hand and wobbly run in heels back to the bus.

Inside the bus, Jax locks the door while I grab the baby wipes and remove the red smears off his face. Then, he gently takes his fingers and dabs away my smears.

"How do I look?" Jax asks.

"Not a trace. How about me?"

"Not a trace," he says, coming closer. "So, we can finish that kiss."

Before my brain can catch up and yell at me, Jax picks me up in his arms and carries me over to the seating area. He sits down and I straddle him, thanking the fashion icons for creating this loose-fitting, flowy fabric. His arms wrap around my back and I cradle his soft face in my hands, careful not to ruffle his hair. Heat rises between us and I don't want this to end. But doors are going to open soon. And the media is going to start to arrive.

Kissing Jax gives me a big time rush, but I pull back and try to compose myself. "As much as I want to keep kissing you, I have to fix myself before I head to the press room," I say.

Jax keeps us interlocked for one more, slow, soul-sucking minute. "All right, but do me a favor."

"What's that?"

"Throw out that red lipstick. How am I ever going to steal a taste of you when other people are around if you're wearing that?"

I mean, I'm not going to pass up opportunities for secret kisses. "Clear gloss from here on out."

We stand up and exchange a passionate embrace of our lips one more time, before Jax finally pulls himself out the door. I stand on the other side and watch him walk down our secret alley to the venue. He doesn't stop to check his phone to see if anyone texted him or if he has any social media notifications. He's set towards one direction, on a mission to be the pop star everyone knows and loves. Including me.

Trash the Dress Online Chat

Alexandra: Would you rather go on a date with the hottest guy alive and never touch him or go on a date with someone who is totally not your type but get to make out?

Cora: Ok, it's time you call in a babysitter. You need something else to do with your time!

21

CLAWS COME OUT BACKSTAGE DURING JAX SLATER TOUR

JAX

NOW I'VE GONE and done it. But I don't regret it, I decide as I walk through the venue for the night's show. The cement-floored hallway is lined with framed posters of other impressive acts who have played this stage. The air-conditioning is cranking, but nothing can cool me down.

I had to kiss Cailin. Being so close to her and not touching her was torture. She literally fell into my arms and the moment that followed was just right. I've kissed hundreds of women, but no one has made me feel as intense as Cailin.

As I get to my dressing room and begin to stretch my legs, I tell myself that I would not have even cared if someone walked by and saw us, because I needed to feel her against me. Now, I have to get through the rest of the night and pretend it didn't happen. I need to stop thinking with my emotions and get my head on straight.

There are a lot of members of the press coming tonight and I have a lot of interviews. It's been years since I've spoken to the media. This is also the first time I'm doing interviews alone. No pressure. Yeah, right. I'm totally stressing out right now. I feel all my doubt creeping back. I tell myself an affirmation: "I'm capable and prepared. I can do this." I have to. It's too late to run back now. I do a set of jumping jacks, and head into the press room. Fresh bait for the sharks.

***

CAILIN

The interviews come one after the other and Jax charms everyone with his charisma. I talk to each media outlet and make notes on which reporters and hosts I need to follow on their social profiles. Everyone seems super impressed with the new album. A few ask me to take their photo with Jax, but I don't mind playing photographer. It gives me another excuse to stare at him without suspicion.

Harry is with us during the interviews and then suggests that Jax head over to meet guests backstage. A woman catches my eye. She has long, straight, platinum blonde hair and is dressed in demure tones, down to her boots. She looks effortlessly cool. There's no doubt who she is: Brenda.

Brenda, who is talking to Chris, notices Jax enter the room and abruptly leaves Chris hanging mid-sentence. She darts in his direction and corners Jax before anyone else has the chance to get within his orbit.

"Jax." Brenda kisses his cheek. The same cheek I had my hands on just a few hours ago. It's tainted now. "So happy to see you back on tour. I've missed seeing your face."

Jax gives her a hug and thanks her for the compliments. Brenda throws back her head and laughs a little too hard. "Want to do a shot?"

"No, thanks. I have some fans to greet, if you'll excuse me."

"I'll take a rain check," Brenda says.

I can see her eyes watch him walk away and she's loving every second. I want to tell Brenda that she's never going to cash in that rain check because whatever fling they had before is over. But I don't really know what happened between them. And I don't really know if what's happening between me and Jax is more than a fling. So, I do what I would normally do if I was at a client event. I walk up and introduce myself.

"Hi, I'm Cailin," I say. I extend my hand to Brenda. "Jax's tour publicist."

Brenda drops her guard. She clearly wants to get in good with me. "Lovely to meet you, Cailin. I'm Brenda, an old friend of Chris and the band. And Jax, of course."

"That's really nice of you to come out and support Jax on his solo tour."

"I wouldn't miss it," Brenda says. She flips her hair.

I don't doubt it. She was probably counting down the days until she had an excuse to see him in person and maybe try to rekindle whatever went on between them the last time she saw Jax.

"Well, do let me know if you need anything further. You can put all future requests for shows through me. Chris can give you my information. Will you be coming out to any others?" And by that I mean, please don't come to another show, thanks.

"Great to know. Carlos usually hooks me up." She's getting tense.

"Carlos and I work closely, but he's not on this account right now, so please feel free to reach out." I strategically toss my hair off my shoulder.

"Will do. I always have a good time with Jax. Maybe I'll take you up on your offer."

"If there are any more LA shows. Which right now, there are not."

"I'm down to travel if there's a party." Brenda winks at me.

"It was nice meeting you, Brenda."

"Nice meeting you, Caitlin." She stresses the letter 't.'

"Cailin," I correct her before I walk away. I scan the room for celebrity guests to make sure everyone is accommodated, but it doesn't look like any have arrived yet. They probably come late to skip the opening acts. On this tour, the opening act is a young female pop star who recently had a Number One song. I see her standing in the corner talking to one of the reporters who spoke with Jax earlier. I can't imagine being a sixteen-year-old pop star, let alone going on tour with Jax Slater. She's one lucky kid. Her mom is never far from her side, which tells me her family wants to make sure fame doesn't get the best of her.

Jax is doing his thing, making sure he thanks everyone for coming, and obliging to every selfie request. Our eyes meet for a brief moment and he flashes me his perfectly straight, professionally whitened teeth. I don't mind letting everyone have their time with him. Just Brenda. I scan the room and see she's having a drink with Chris. Looks like she's good and occupied.

I grab a sandwich and a bottle of water and sit down by myself to eat before the show starts. As I take a bite and begin to chew, I see Hayley come in and give her a wave. She waves back, grabs some grub, and makes her way to me.

"Hey," she says, sitting beside me. "Thanks for letting me have the room earlier."

"You really don't have to thank me. I totally get wanting to have alone time with your boyfriend." I can tell Hayley and I will have unspoken girl code worked out the rest of the tour.

"So, tell me something."

"Sure." I wipe my mouth with a napkin.

"What happened to your red lipstick?"

"Oh, I, um. I..." I clearly didn't expect her to remember that I had on a bold red lipstick when she saw me at the hotel, and now I don't. I can't even say that it came off as I ate because there's not a red lip print around the rim of my water bottle. Or my napkin.

"You don't have to tell me if you don't want to. But I just happened to notice a tiny smudge of red lipstick on Jax's neck and when I asked him about it, he was equally flustered. I put two and two together. Don't worry, your secret is safe with me. And if you do want to talk about it, I'm here."

I feared this would happen and now someone knows. One notch of my credibility is knocked off my resume. I can't add making out with my client as a professional accomplishment. I guess I'm lucky it's Hayley to find out first, because I might be able to beg her to keep my secret. At the same time, I need to play it cool. The bigger deal I make out of kissing Jax, the more incentive I'm giving Hayley to gossip about it. If she tells Jayce, then it's over. News like this would travel fast. So, I do what I think is best for this situation. I take a sip of my water and simply say, "Thanks. I appreciate it."

Awkward silence fills the air for a moment. Then, I panic. "When did you notice the lipstick, Hayley?"

"Just a few minutes ago when I walked in and said 'hi' to Jax. I saw a red smear on his neck and well, my first thought was that it was lipstick and..."

"Oh no." I put down my sandwich. Forget food. It appears I have an appetite for destruction instead.

"I promise I won't say anything. We can talk more about this later when we're alone. He wiped it off."

"It's actually not you that I'm worried about right now. But Jax did a bunch of media interviews and posed for photos. What if people see it?"

"It really wasn't super noticeable. Besides, if they did see it, no one has seen you with lipstick on tonight except for me and Jax."

"Except for the fact that I posted a selfie hours ago on social media with #jaxslater."

"Ok, let's not panic. You can just take it down."

I pull out my phone and check my social media. My photo already has 200 likes.

"Too late. As a publicist, I know taking down this photo will cause more damage than leaving it up."

As a publicist, I say again to myself. This is it. The end of my new career before it even started. I can see the headlines now. All this time I've been worried about Brenda and what she had going on with Jax. I should have been focused on my own status.

"I'll just monitor the hashtag and online alerts. The first sign of trouble and I'll address it. For now, please keep this between us." My eyes water as I plea to Haley.

"Your secret is safe with me."

Doors are going to open to the general public soon, so I don't really have much of a choice other than to move forward and not dwell on what happened, or predict the disaster to come. Jax will be taking the stage in about an hour. But the real show is going to be watching me figure out how to clean up this mess, save my job, and keep my relationship with Jax a secret.

Trash the Dress Online Chat

Drew: Learning to live as a single person again is so hard. No one gets it, but I know you guys do.

Alexandra: Times three for me as a single mom!

22

JAX SLATER STEPS INTO THE SPOTLIGHT AFTER A DARK DECADE

CAILIN

As everyone scatters out of the backstage area to get to their seats for the show, only crew members remain. I thank the media stragglers for coming and show them to the door, silently praying that they only run really nice stories and edit all lipstick stains out of their photos.

"I'd say so far things are shaping out exactly as we'd hoped," Harry says.

"Things are definitely shaping out," I reply under my breath.

"What's that, Cailin?"

"I was just wondering how Jax feels all the interviews went."

"Yeah, how did they all go?" Harry asks Jax.

"Awesome, really. Cailin managed everything smoothly. I think everyone got the time they needed to get the quotes for their stories. I'm eager to see what the headlines are going to say."

My nerves are getting the best of me. "Me too."

"Well, I'm off to go find Ridge," Harry says. "He just texted me that he's here."

Ridge, Jax's cousin from 5 Leo Hearts. While part of me is super excited to meet Ridge and see them together in the same room, part of me is wondering if now is a good time to mention the lipstick stain to Jax.

"See ya," Jax yells to Harry.

That leaves just Jax and I on one end of the room. Across from us, the others drink beer and converse loudly in their little groups. I'm afraid to have this conversation with Jax. What if he tells me he regrets kissing me and it was one big mistake? The first night of tour might begin in scandal and that's exactly what he's been on a mission to avoid. I'm like the wrecking ball that came in and knocked down all that he was trying to rebuild.

Jax lowers his voice and tells me, "I know what you're thinking. I saw you talking to Hayley. I know she knows. Don't worry. She's not going to say anything."

"I trust Hayley, for as well as I know her. But I'm worried about the media. You took a lot of photos."

"If anything, this might work out in my favor. Think about it. The 'boy band bad boy' has lipstick marks on his neck the opening night of tour for his solo album. The first signs anyone has seen of me romantically linked to a woman in a long time. Although, it's going to put a dent in my plans to shed that image."

"It's going to create a mystery for sure." My pulse slightly slows down.

"Right. And that's only if they notice and focus on it." Jax's voice is calming me in a way that only meditation apps on my phone have done before.

"Okay, so maybe it's not so bad. There's only one tiny thing." I wince having to come forward and talk about posting a selfie.

"What's that?"

"I posted a selfie of me back at the hotel, dressed for the show, with my lipstick on. But I mean, it would take some serious digging for a reporter to link that to me, right?"

"Never underestimate the media."

"That's what I'm worried about. But let's talk about this more later. You need to get ready and I don't want people to wonder why we're deep in conversation."

"All right, but I want to see you in that dress after the show. In private."

And with that, he jets off to go light up thousands of girls' nights and I know I'm in trouble.

Most of the VIP guests and media have floor seats in a private section near the front of the stage for the show. I'm standing on the side of the stage with Harry, who just introduced me to Ridge and his wife, Kelly. He's just as boyishly cute in real life as his photos. Kelly portrays the picture-perfect role of a boy band wife. She's perfectly proportioned, impeccably dressed in a mint designer jumper, has flawless makeup, and her hair is brown with senior-level stylist painted balayage. The rock on her finger is more carats that I can count. I admire her nails, which are gel-manicured in a neutral blush pink.

"So nice to meet you," I say to them both.

"If you can handle working with Jax, we'll have to talk about getting you on board for the 5 Leo Hearts big reunion tour," Ridge tells me.

"I didn't know a tour was in the works, actually. But that sounds great."

"Nothing is official," Kelly says. She puts her arm around her husband. "Ridge is getting the itch to tour now that he sees Jax out on the road."

"Kelly wants me to stay home and make babies," Ridge says, taking her hand in his.

"Not a lie. But I'll support the tour too." She playfully kisses his cheek.

"It must be hard when he travels for long periods at a time," I say.

"It's okay," Kelly says when Ridge steps away. "I usually join him on the road. But sometimes I like to stay home and get our house in order. Now, I want us to focus on the next chapter."

I imagine what it must be like to be married to a pop star. Kelly seems to have dedicated her life to Ridge. She has to trust him on the road when she's not there, even though she knows gorgeous girls will throw themselves at him. It takes a strong woman to have that amount of faith. Their relationship must be rock solid.

Music plays loudly as the crew sets up for Jax. Kelly and I yell in each other's ears as we continue to get acquainted. I wonder if there's a chance we could actually become friends. That is, if things with Jax and I progress. And the media doesn't blow us up tomorrow morning.

"I love your dress," Kelly says. "Has Jax started to flirt with you yet?"

"Thank you. Why would he flirt with me?"

"You're totally his type. I can tell."

I hope she can't see me blushing through the darkness of the room. I just laugh.

"How so?"

"You're cute, slightly edgy. Great fashion sense. So far, from what I can tell, you're career-oriented, so you have your own goals. But I don't think you're so career-oriented that you miss out on the simple joys of life. I mean, he's told Ridge and I a little about you."

"Wow, I didn't know Jax talks about me to anyone."

"He was really impressed with the press release you wrote and how you described his new album. Jax may have the 'bad boy' image to the outside world, but there's a lot more to him and I wish he got that credit."

"I haven't known him very long, but I can see that already," I say. I'm learning a lot about Jax Slater and the more I discover, the deeper I fall. It's one thing to crush on him from afar, when there's literally no chance of ever meeting him or having any of those fantasies come true. It's another thing when those dreams begin to become reality. I have a chance to be one half of a classic love story around how an underdog got her man. But if things work out on the opposite end of the spectrum, I'll be just another girl who let her fantasy take her on a journey that ultimately broke her heart.

The background music stops, along with our conversation, just as everything turns dark and a spotlight hits centerstage. The crowd roars and starts to chant, "Jax! Jax! Jax!" My heart beats to the sound of his name as I watch him walk out on stage with his acoustic guitar. Everyone falls silent. It's like they are in the church of rock 'n' roll and service has just begun.

It's breathtaking to watch Jax perform so closely. There's a part in the show where he does a tribute to his 5 Leo Hearts days and serenades a fan. All the girls in the audience freak out and climb on top of each other, begging to get chosen. By girls, I mean women my age, because they all grew up loving him. I guess they don't feel awkward at all.

When it comes time for the serenade, I notice the woman he pulls up is wearing an engagement ring and wonder if that's intentional. She seems to have forgotten her commitment to her fiancé, however. She sings along to every word and desperately tries to grab his hand as it lingers near her. I always wanted to be that girl. But now, I'm glad I never was. The universe was waiting to send me something better.

After his set, Jax comes out and performs two more songs for an encore. By the time he walks off the stage, he is drenched in sweat and breathless. So am I. Everyone gives him a high-five or a handshake as he makes his way behind the curtain. I stand off to the side and clap. I want to go run up to him and throw my arms around him, swirl across his slippery body with my own.

But I'm his publicist, so I can't. I can—and should—

however, go up to him and congratulate him on a great show. So that's exactly what I do.

What Jax does next, though, I don't expect. He wraps his arms around me in a big bear hug and holds me a few seconds longer, letting me know he wishes it could linger, too. Harry comes up and puts his arms around Jax, rightfully oblivious as he breaks up our embrace.

"Well done, team," Harry tells us. "Night one is a success. Did you see everyone singing along? They freakin' loved it. Even the new songs held their attention."

Harry looks at me and says, "The photo pit was lighting up. Let's see when we can get some shots from the photographers so Jax can make a social media post. Can you work on that?"

"On it," I sign off to Harry. I grab my phone from my purse to check my notifications as I make my way to the post-show meet and greet for VIPs. I find a quiet corner and slip into a chair, eager to relieve my throbbing feet. I vow never to wear heels for the rest of the tour. Unless, maybe New York City since that will also be a special show. But middle America media will get a more laid back version of Cailin McCall. Well, casual in style, anyway. Right now, my nerves are a wreck and I hope that the rest of the tour is less stressful—at least from my own doing.

Gemma texted me a million times asking for updates and photos. Of course, I had to tell her I saw Ridge and I'm sure she went back in time to her teenage self. I open her thread of messages.

Gemma: OMG, Ridge is there! Is he hot?

Gemma: What's his wife like?

Gemma: Did you talk to them?

Gemma: You look super hot in that selfie you posted.

Gemma: How is the show going? I need
details!

Gemma: Photos, please! Anything? A social
story of the show? Your girl is dying over
here.

I haven't even told Gemma anything about Jax yet. Boy, do I have lots to fill her in on. I make a mental note to call her tomorrow when I have some free time on the bus. For now, I need to monitor #jaxslater and also the media to see if anything incriminating is posted. So far, all I see are photos of fans posting pics and clips from the show. A bunch of media I recognize from the pre-show event posted their photos with Jax, but he was positioned looking forward, so the side of his neck is hidden. I think we're out of the woods. I put down my phone and scan the room to see who has made their way back to meet Jax.

And then, it happens. I get a text from Marisol across my phone. Fear runs through the pit of my stomach. I don't want to read it. Yet, I have to know what it says. Not just for my job, but my sanity. I inhale a deep breath and muster up all the courage I have inside my body to click the message. The first text is just a link. Before I click to follow it, I read the text that follows.

Marisol: This is gold. Do you know about this
mystery girl who left those lipstick marks on
Jax? We can leverage this to get him even
more attention. Everyone is going to want to
know who she is. Do some digging! See if
it's a fling or a new relationship we can
announce.

Welp, day one of tour and I just encountered my worst-case scenario.

Trash the Dress Online Chat

Mae: Trying to remind myself that things will get easier. But everyone around me seems to be celebrating getting engaged, having a baby, buying a house. And here I am living with my grandmother.

Cora: I hear ya. I wish I had family to turn to.

23

JAX SLATER IS SET ON ROCKING CAILIN'S WORLD

JAX

WALKING out onto the stage for the first time as a solo artist was just as scary as I predicted. Without Mario, Ridge, Jack, and Oliver on either side of me, all attention was on me for every move or potential mistake. If the fans didn't enjoy the show, I would have no one else to blame. But I tried to push that out of my mind as I stepped onto the stage into the darkness and instead embraced the unknown. As soon as the spotlight turned on and I saw thousands of flashes from cell phone cameras go off, I knew I was going to have a great show. I fed off that energy the entire night.

I opened the show playing one of my new songs and it definitely caught my fans off guard. My bold and unexpected move left them in silence for the entire first song and when I strummed the final chords, a roar erupted from the audience. All the validation I needed happened in that moment. The audience cheered when I played every new song. They sang along to the 5 Leo Hearts anthems. These women nearly beat each other up competing for my attention when I picked a fan from the crowd to serenade.

After my final bow, I threw a towel over my shoulder and walked off the stage as a new man. I did an entire show on my own. I played guitar, sang songs I wrote, and performed them on stage for people. I no longer feel like an imposter. Right now, I feel like I'm an artist. An artist without a hit new single, but an artist nonetheless. Maybe tonight some of the A&R guys from the label will see the songs in a new light and come back and tell me we have a winner.

I take a few minutes to myself in my dressing room to catch my breath and cool down before going to the post-show meet-and-greet. I enter my room, close the door, and sit on the firm couch. As I grab and chug a bottle of water, I can't help but continue to feel proud of myself.

The whole time I was performing, I had one person in mind that I wanted to make sure I did my best to impress. Not the fans, not the media, but Cailin. Feeling her eyes on me from the side of the stage was all I needed to stop worrying about every-one's opinions.

Everything is going well when I speak to the media. I can tell they are genuinely happy for me and interested in what I'm doing now. It feels like everything is on track. But I'm also waiting for everything to derail.

Cailin's lip prints on my neck. God, it felt amazing. I felt her kiss travel through my body. And yes, I wanted to take her to bed right there. Showing restraint isn't easy for me, but I'm doing it because I know things will happen when the time is right. As in, when we're both ready.

That kiss has the potential to stain not only Cailin's reputa-tion as a publicist, but the press surrounding me. I took a lot of photos with fans and reporters before Hayley pointed out the lipstick streaks. Who knows how many more photos are going to get posted? Starting off tour with my bad boy image intact is just what the public expected, and everything I didn't want.

Now, I need to act like nothing is wrong and go meet the fans who purchased the VIP package. These are always my hardcore, longtime dedicated fans. Some of them, I have come to remember because they are quite loyal and come tour after tour, to multiple cities. They've baked me cookies and pies, made me photo collages, bought me teddy bears, and handed me sealed letters. I've gotten messages ranging from how 5 Leo Hearts music has helped them through hard times to marriage proposals. This is my first meet-and-greet in years and I'm curious to see who comes—those fans grown up or a new generation.

There's only one way to find out. It's time to put on my second performance for the night: the pop star who isn't worried about negative feedback.

"Jax," says Harry as he crosses paths with me in the hall. "I was just coming to find you. The meet-and-greet is about to start. Great turnout of sales for that package. We sold out all that we offered."

"Amazing, I'm glad we kept it intimate. I'll be able to talk to them longer and everyone should leave feeling seen."

As I enter the backstage area, everyone freezes with excitement. Then, a round of applause breaks out and a flock of women circle around me. At first glance, it looks like these are longtime 5 Leo Hearts fans. I give each fan a hug and know that I just made their night. I enjoy these little acts of kindness and think it's important to form connections with your fans. Some stars, like Maxine, never liked strangers touching them. Guess I never had that problem.

I search the room and see Cailin with Hayley and some of the band members. That's a good sign. She's not hiding on her bus.

A woman around my age approaches and introduces herself as Melissa. "My best friend and I followed 5 Leo Hearts everywhere. We even started a fan club in our school." She blushes as she admits the level of her fandom.

"That's awesome," I tell her. "Is your friend here with you?"

"No," says Melissa as her face drops. "We didn't stay friends after high school. Life changes and all that. But I have new friends here with me today."

Life changes for sure. Maybe my fans will be as receptive to the new album as I had hoped. Melissa introduces me to her friend, Daria.

"Hi, I'm Daria. This is baby Emery." Daria points to her rounded stomach. "Her first concert. Can we take a photo?"

"Of course." I put my arm around Daria and point to her belly, making sure to give her a photo she will cherish forever.

Melissa and Daria are my tame fans. They're basically down-to-earth girls who understand that I'm simply human. On the other hand, there are fans like Aiden and Maria, who put me on a pedestal.

"Oh my gosh, I can't believe I'm meeting you. You're even hotter in person," Maria says. She's wearing a vintage 5 Leo Hearts T-shirt with a photo of just my face.

"She's single," Aiden quickly adds.

I smile and pretend I didn't hear him. This is when things can get awkward.

"Will you sign my arm?" Maria asks.

As I oblige, she tells me, "I'm going to get a tattoo of your signature."

That's one of the pressures of being a public figure. Fans like Maria put so much faith in me and I fear I'll do something to let them down. Then she'll regret having my signature in permanent ink on her body. Maybe she'll want to get it removed. Or she'll have to cover it up. I hope she at least waits to see the headlines tomorrow before she heads to a tattoo parlor.

"Might just want to take a picture instead," I say.

"Oh, we are definitely taking a picture, too," Maria says. "I need to post it, print it, and frame it. Maybe send it out on my holiday cards this year."

I better give this photo my best smile. At least the lipstick smear is off my neck.

As I wrap up with the fans, I get caught up in conversation with a few other people. I don't see Cailin in the room anymore. She must have gone back to the bus. I need to wrap this up so I can go talk to her in private. I don't care who sees me walking onto her bus.

Trash the Dress Online Chat

Leila: My eggs are going to shrivel up before I find someone to have kids with.

Drew: Considering freezing mine.

24

CAILIN MCCALL FEARS CURTAIN CALL ON
HER CAREER

CAILIN

THE REST of post-show meet-and-greet flew by in an hour. Jax
did his thing socializing with everyone and I spent some time
hanging out with Hayley and the rest of the crew. Back on my
bus, as much as I want Jax to walk in and undress me with his
eyes, I change into an oversize T-shirt and shorts that are comfy
for sleeping on the bunk. It's going to be my first night sleeping
alone on a tour bus and I really don't know what to expect. Ken
was sleeping all day so he is prepared to drive through the night.
We have a long way to Minneapolis. I feel bad that he's going to
be driving all night, but he assured me he's a night owl.

I don't want to text Marisol back so late and I'm not quite
sure how to respond. Instead, I text Gemma to see if she's awake
and able to talk. Of course, she calls me in one second.

"Tell me everything."

"There's a lot to tell, I don't even know where to start," I
say. I sum up everything that happened since I arrived at the
airport as I rest on a bunk bed.

"Wow, that is a lot," Gemma says. "So basically, the pop star
you've crushed on since you were a teenager thinks you 'get

him' and is pulling out all the stops to impress you and get in your pants. And you're loving every second of it, but also paranoid about losing your job and looking unprofessional. But now, your credibility may be on the line because traces of your secret make-out session can potentially be leaked to the media."

"Basically, yes." I pull the covers up to my neck, wishing I could hide under them forever.

"Have you talked to your boss?"

"Not yet. I'm not sure I should tell her that it was me. What if she fires me?"

"That might be a risk you have to take. Own up to what happened and let her know she can trust you to tell the truth. She might be able to help with damage control rather than encouraging that Jax and his mystery girl make headlines."

"That's true." I have to think of this like I am the lead on crisis communication.

"Sometimes doing the right thing is the hard thing," Gemma says. I'm glad she's not just telling me what I want to hear. "It'll be uncomfortable, but you're strong and can handle whatever comes your way."

I sigh because I know she's right. "Thanks, I know what I have to do."

"Okay, now that we have that settled, let's talk about other important matters. How good of a kisser is Jax and how hot is Ridge in person? Is his wife nice?"

Leave it to Gemma to bring the conversation back to her main concerns. "Kissing Jax is very surreal. I spent most of the time in my own head about it, but I also enjoyed it very much, obviously. It's all so new and I am afraid to get too excited, but I also want to imagine being his girlfriend for real, and not just in my dreams. And the fact that it may be a possibility is pretty wild."

"I am just living vicariously through you, bestie. My own love life is coming second to motherhood right now."

"Aw, I know this is a big adjustment for you, but motherhood suits you, and you're an awesome mom. You and Mark will find your groove."

"I know we will and I'm cherishing every second of baby Stella. She's already growing up so fast, it's like she changes every day."

"I can't wait to see her when I get back from tour," I say.

"I feel like that will be an eternity for me. I was just getting used to having you back."

"I'll be back before you know it." Saying that aloud actually makes me pretty sad. If I'm back home with Gemma, then I'm not going to be with Jax. Am I prepared to handle that? I haven't really thought beyond this tour. Everything is happening in a whirlwind.

"I'm so glad we got caught up, but I have to get some sleep before Stella wakes me up in a few hours. Update me tomorrow, Okay? Don't worry. You got this."

I hang up with Gemma and conclude that our conversation confirmed two things. One: I need to fess up to Marisol tomorrow. Two: I am falling for Jax and my heart might get broken.

Just as I get nestled under the covers, there's a knock at my door. I open it expecting to see Jax, but it's Ken, standing in a drizzle of rain.

"Hi dear, sorry to bother you. Just wanted to let you know that Jax and Harry are still hanging inside the venue with some folks, so we won't be hitting the road just yet."

That explains why Jax hasn't snuck over to my bus. I mean, he said he would, so I hoped that would be true.

"Thanks, Ken. Be careful out there tonight."

"Always am, my dear."

I'm in the midst of closing the door when I see Jax walking out to his bus. "Cailin!" Jax waves to me as raindrops lightly land on his face. Harry traps Ken in conversation.

"Hey there," I say very formally to Jax in case anyone is watching.

"Sorry, things ran late inside. I wanted to see you, but I know we have to hit the road to make the next show on time."

"It's totally okay. I think I know what I have to do," I say.

"Actually, so do I," Jax says. "But I don't want to rush talking about it. I'm going to go back on my bus and call you in a little bit, okay?"

"Okay." My apprehensiveness is front and center.

"It's going to be okay, don't worry." The way Jax looks at me assures me it will be. "And Cailin, before I go, I want you to know something."

"What's that?"

"You look even hotter in those little shorts and T-shirt than you did tonight in that dress. And I didn't think that was possible."

"Stop it." I playfully push him away.

"Just sayin'. I'll call you soon!" Jax runs off to his bus and nods to Ken and Harry.

Those four words hold significant power. Jax is saying that he's not going to settle for natural encounters with me. He's intentionally intertwining us and I have become someone he wants in his inner circle. Someone important enough to surpass text messages and get promoted to phone calls. This is now the story of how a 29-year-old boy band fan's teenage dream comes true when she begins working for her favorite member, and although she tries with all her might to remain professional, she ultimately risks it all for love.

True to his word, Jax doesn't waste any time in dialing my number once we're all on our buses and back on the road. I'm still getting used to being alone on a big bus so I really welcome the company, even if it's just the sound of his voice vibrating in my ear.

"Tonight was unbelievable," I tell Jax. "How do you feel?"

"Pretty incredible. And relieved. I was really nervous, but once I got back out there, I got right back in the mode."

"I thought you were amazing, and didn't expect anything less. You're going to make my job pretty easy."

"Speaking of your job," Jax says. I wonder if he regrets kissing me now that he's had time to process. "I'm really glad you're here."

That's what I needed to hear. "Me too. But I have to ask. Is this like, the first tour where you..." I'm not sure where I'm going, but I know what I'm trying to find out. "Like, do you hook up with girls on tour a lot? To pass the time?" There, I just spat it out. Blech.

"I know what you're getting at, so we can just squash that right now," Jax says.

I wish we were having this conversation in person. Or maybe not. Maybe I have more courage to ask these questions over the phone.

"I don't want you to be someone I'm just passing the time with for the duration of this tour. I know it sounds a little crazy. But maybe that's just me. I know maybe from your point of view, seeing me as like a celebrity or whatever, that it might seem like I can get whatever I want. And yes, I can. But I don't want whatever I can get."

"Like the Brendas?"

"Exactly. Like the Brendas. That girl has been all over me for years. I've flirted with her before just for fun, but I'm not interested."

"I appreciate you telling me that. I wasn't sure and it kind of threw me off when I heard her talking about you tonight." Look at me, fully expressing my feelings without fear of what comes next.

"Like I told you before, from the first time I saw you on

video chat, I just felt intrigued and wanted to get to know you better. I know we come from two different worlds, but we're really not that far apart. The more I talk to you, the more I feel I can share with you and that you understand. You're not out to be with me just because of who I am. If anything, I know being with me might cause you more problems. But I can't deny how attracted to you I am and how I want to use this time on tour to get to know you."

"I want to get to know you too, Jax. This whole experience so far has been incredible. I feel swept off my feet, like is this really my life right now? And that scares me because it's almost too good. I could lose my job from the lipstick scandal. And what happens after tour?"

Did I just go there? Oh yes, I did.

"Neither of us knows what the future holds at this point. But I was talking to Harry about the lipstick thing. Don't hate me, hear me out. Harry's like my dad. I never had a dad, so he has stepped up and always been a father figure since he's known me. He's like that with all the 5 Leo Hearts guys, but especially me. He knew right away I'm into you and called me out on it."

"He did?" This is my sign that Jax has legit feelings and I mean something to him.

"When he found out I texted you about the press release, he knew. He said I never text anyone else on the team. Harry usually speaks for me on email."

"So, you usually aren't so hands-on with your PR team?" I just need to confirm for my own confidence.

"Never. This is a little different because it's a solo album and tour. I want to be more involved. But I also wanted more opportunities to talk to you. And once we started talking, things just took off. I forgot I was your client. I just wanted to be myself."

"I'm glad you've had Harry as a male presence in your life. That must have been hard growing up."

"I won't lie. It's where my rebellious mindset began. Never

thinking I was good enough. If I was, maybe my old man would have stuck around, right? But my mom and grandma did the best they could raising me, and my mom gave up everything to help me chase my dreams. We lived with my grandma in this old house, built in the forties. Everything was so outdated. But we had all we needed."

Picturing him as a little boy warms my heart. "I never knew that. I mean, obviously by now you know I followed 5 Leo Hearts a lot. Like, a lot. If we're being vulnerable. But I never read that about you in interviews."

"I knew it. You did have a crush on me back then."

"Fine. Yes. You were my favorite. Now can we please move past this humiliating topic?"

"And now you made out with me."

Look at this ego. He is too much sometimes and I love it. "And left a trail of lipstick on your neck, don't forget."

"It's actually all I've been thinking about."

"Me too. Marisol wants me to find out who the mystery girl is so we can leverage it for PR."

"Of course she does. That's why she's one of the best in the business. She knows how to spin anything into attention for a client. But I'm guessing you're freaking out."

"To say the least. I just started this job. I'm starting in a new industry and I have to prove myself. So far, all I'm showing them is that I cross the line with their biggest clients."

Tears well in my eyes and I feel disappointed in myself. But at the same time, I wish Jax was here to wipe them away and kiss my forehead. It's like professional success is the angel on my shoulder, and love is the devil, provoking me. I'm torn between which one is better for me in the long run. The scary part is that there's no way of knowing and I can't do anything besides trust my instinct.

Jax takes a deep breath. "You have a lot riding on this, but you also proved that you can write press releases and social posts that capture interest. And all the headlines that are coming out are from media you got to attend. Plus, the entire night was flawless. Harry was very impressed. Not one person complained they weren't on the list."

I realize Jax is making very good points. I am doing my job well. And I have to keep it up. "I need to be honest with Marisol. She won't want her company's character to be soured if it comes out that you're with me. It'll be worse if she doesn't know in advance."

"Then I support you in telling Marisol. But after talking to Harry, I think maybe we should also admit the truth to everyone."

"What?" Can Jax be serious right now? But also, he must be serious if he wants to go public with me. So soon? Is he confident in us? A million questions are going through my mind.

"Let me explain. Harry thinks it's good for my image to go public and admit I'm back and thriving. This new album is essentially a stripped-down version of me, and I can show I'm moving on from the breakup with someone who isn't a celebrity. No one needs to pity me anymore. They can cheer me on. Cheer us on."

"And what about my credibility? I'll get labeled as the publicist who dates her clients. And I really love where things are headed with us. But I am not even used to having a conversation about whether there is an 'us' the first time I make out with someone. This is all so sudden. What if you end up not even being able to stand me? Then we're stuck in a fake relationship?"

"I highly doubt I'll end up not being able to stand you. I agree this is all moving fast. But at the same time, I don't want to slow down. All I know is that I want you in my life right now and I want to see where this goes. And I don't mind taking you off the market so all these other guys on tour can stop ogling you. If you'll have me, that is."

"Jax, are you asking me to go public and be your girlfriend? We haven't even had a proper date."

"I'm asking you to take a leap of faith. To—I don't know—live in one of those rom-coms you watch all the time. Let yourself get swept away. Forget about the other things that are holding you back, like your job. We can figure that out. Just focus on how you feel."

I'm well aware of my feelings because they're making a mess of me. I'm nervous about falling so hard and fast. I'm also excited that this is actually a problem in my life right now. There's a part of me that's lonely, too, because I'm missing Jax.

Jax continues, "It's not optimal that we're riding down a highway in separate buses right now. But I promise you I'm going to ask you on a proper date tomorrow as soon as we stop in the next city. I'll even deal with going out in public for you."

"Jax Slater, you are one big surprise after another. I'm going to call Marisol first thing in the morning and pray she doesn't fire me."

"Call me after you talk to her. I'm totally beat, but I'm going to think about you as I fall asleep."

"Good night, Jax."

"Sweet dreams, Cailin."

I hang up the phone in a daze. It's late and I'm exhausted. I can't help but wonder if I'm dreaming. Or am I about to go public and be in a relationship with Jax Slater?

I toss and turn for what seems like forever and I can't fall asleep. It's raining hard outside, but not even the pounding rain can silence my brain. The wind captures my full attention. Just as I wonder if I should give Ken a call to make sure he's okay driving up there, our bus comes to a screeching halt. I grip the side of my bunk, fearful of falling off, just as I feel a crash. The sound of glass shattering confirms my fears. There's been an accident.

Trash the Dress Online Chat

Georgia Rose: Just got back from my solo adventure abroad! Ladies, I kissed strangers in Italy, jumped off cliffs into the Ligurian Sea, went to an opera. It was amazing.

Cora: Ok, if you can do that, I can drive across America!

Alexandra: Speaking of...I wonder how Cailin is doing on tour. Anyone hear from her?

25

CAILIN MCCALL'S DREAM NIGHT COMES TO A SCREECHING HALT

CAILIN

I JUMP out from my bunk in a state of shock. Shards of glass are everywhere. Heavy rain is pouring into the bus, carried by harsh wind. My first thought is to go to check on Ken and then call 911, but first I need to put on my shoes. I use my cell phone to light my way to my sneakers and then carefully slip them on to navigate around the glass.

I don't know if it's safe to run out onto the highway, but I need to make sure Ken isn't injured. I pull a hoodie over my head and my body begins to shake in fear as I dodge raindrops and wind. Finally, I make it around to the front of the bus. A truck is pulled over on the side of the road ahead of us. It must have side-swiped us.

I see Ken holding his head, but as soon as he sees me, he signals a thumbs up. "Ken!" I yell over the roar of the storm. "Are you okay? I'm calling 911!"

"Already called," Ken reports calmly, as he leans out of the window. "Go back inside where you're safe."

"Just sit there and don't move. You might need medical attention."

This is not what I signed up for when I agreed to go on tour. I didn't even think about storms or accidents on the road. But even if I had thought about them, I know I wouldn't have let fear of a potential situation stop me from pursuing the opportunity of a lifetime. Which brings me back to standing on the highway in the middle of a torrential downpour.

The truck driver remains in his vehicle so I assume he's okay. Authorities have been notified and I can't risk walking over there and getting hit. Ken assures me he's okay, so I agree to go back onto the bus. I wonder if the rest of our buses are ahead of us or behind us.

On the bus, I pace back and forth, unsure of where it's safe to step or sit. Then my phone rings. It's Jax. "Cailin, are you okay? We were riding behind you and just pulled over. I'm coming to you. Don't move."

"I'm all right," I manage to stutter. I want to break down and cry at the sound of his voice. "Ken is okay, too."

Sirens blaze as cops and an ambulance arrive. I walk outside, where Jax and his driver meet me at my door. His driver goes to attend to Ken and speak with the cops. While Ken is getting examined by the first responders, Jax pulls me in tight and kisses my forehead.

"I was scared as hell when I saw this was your bus. I don't know what I would have done if this had been worse. I was the one who demanded we drive on buses instead of flying between shows. I didn't consider our safety, or the higher risk of accidents. I was just thinking of myself."

Jax regretfully drops his head and stares at the ground.

I lift his chin. "It's not your fault. No one could have predicted this."

As we lock eyes, I break down. I don't want to cry in front of Jax, but I'm overwhelmed with emotion right now. I almost died. One minute, I was lying down to go to sleep, and the next, something totally unexpected put my life at risk. Something I couldn't prepare for if I tried. And it had the potential to impact my life forever. Not just my life, but the lives of everyone who cares about me. I'm reminded that our time here is so precious.

And on top of that, now the man I am falling for is telling me he was worried about me, which means I'm already important to him. If this incident has shown me anything, it's that I'm not going to run from anything good. I need to see where this goes with Jax, even if that means risking my career.

Rain drenches us as Jax runs his fingers through my tangled hair and I ugly cry into his chest. After a few moments, I pull myself back and look up at Jax. He wipes the tears that have been streaming down my cheeks with his wet hands. Then he tenderly kisses my lips. I don't know if anyone saw and I don't care.

"Let's go get you checked out just to be safe. Then we'll get your things. You're staying on my bus the rest of the tour." He takes my hand and we begin to carefully walk along the side of the road.

"I don't want to invade your personal space. I can stay with Hayley. Or Harry."

"Hayley's bus is maxed out. Harry would drive you insane, and you're not going to bunk with a man you hardly know. Besides, I want you with me."

My chest swells. "I want to be with you, too."

Jax continues to hold my hand, not caring who sees, as we reach the paramedics. Ken is cleared, but because of his age, they are extra cautious and want to transport him to a local hospital to get fully examined by a doctor. From there, it's decided that the bus is totaled, thanks to broken mirrors and windows, and that Ken will fly home. Jax and I both wish him well and tell him to call us after he finishes at the hospital. Jax texts Harry so he can call Ken's wife and let her know what's going on.

After I give my statement to the police and everyone agrees I am in good physical condition with no injuries, Jax and I gather my belongings. His driver, whose name I learn is Diego, helps us load my stuff onto Jax's bus. By this time, the rain has let down a lot and it's safe for Diego to get back on the road.

Jax and I are both soaked and water is dripping off our bodies, forming puddles on the floor of the bus. His gray sweatpants and white T-shirt cling to him. I can't help but think of an old music video from another boy band. When the video begins, the group members are each shot on camera dancing in the street as they tell the girl they are singing to that she needs to stop playing games. Then, as that group's bad boy begins his solo verse, rain starts to pour down on them. Magically, their outfits change into open button-down shirts so you can see their slick chests. Every inch of their bodies is soaked and they push water off their faces to continue singing.

Now, I'm in my own traumatic version of a boy band video. Except we're out of the rain. My teeth are chattering and I'm not sure if it's from the cold or my nerves. Jax grabs a towel and uses it to squeeze water out of my hair.

"Thanks," I tell him through shivers of all sorts. "Where can I change out of these clothes?"

Jax points to the bedroom. "Are you sure? You need to get changed too?"

"Ladies first." Jax pulls my suitcase into the bedroom area and then grabs his own change of clothes.

I get changed, detangle my hair, and open up the door. At this point, I am way past the anxiety of Jax seeing me in any state but my best. I'm just grateful to be alive and here with him. Jax quickly changes in the bathroom and then joins me. He takes my hand and walks me over to the bed, pulling me next to him as he sits down.

"How are you feeling?"

"Honestly, I'm fine. Just shaken up. I'm really glad you were near. My hero," I say. I take initiative and kiss him for the first time. Remnants of my vanilla lip balm transfer between us as our mouths move in symphony for a few passionate minutes.

When we come up for air, we nestle into each other's arms. Jax pulls the covers over us and holds me. The touch of his hands on my body lets me know that he's here for me. He's saying nothing at all, yet it's all loud and clear. Just like another song that one of my favorite Irish boy band members sang on the soundtrack from a rom-com movie that I adore. I fall asleep as the little spoon.

Trash the Dress Online Chat

Alexandra: My vow of celibacy is going to go out the window if I keep scrolling dating apps.

Tori: Swipe right.

26

AFTER BUS ACCIDENT JAX SLATER BEGS
PLEASE, DON'T GO GIRL

JAX

THE MEET-AND-GREET TOOK LONGER than I expected. Every time I tried to leave, someone else grabbed me. The reps from my label waited until the end of the night to introduce themselves. There were four of them. The two A&R reps are named Sean and Alicia. I wonder which one of them is hating all my songs. They're both new to me.

The head of the label, Brad, and I go way back to when he signed 5 Leo Hearts. I remember the first time we walked into the label's office. We flew from Orlando to Los Angeles with our parents, because we were so young we needed guardians. My mom and Aunt Lucy, Ridge's mom, attended everything. Mario's dad came, while his mom stayed at home with his younger siblings. He's a lawyer, so it made sense to have someone with legal expertise on our team. Oliver's parents both traveled with us, which I always envied. Jack was already eighteen, so he didn't need a guardian, but his mom still came for support.

When we walked into the huge lobby of the label the day of our contract signing, I felt an invigorating energy. People were bustling, music filled the air. An assistant ushered us to a conference room like we were royalty.

"Enjoy some food." The assistant pointed to the conference table. It was filled with trays of sandwiches and non-alcoholic sparkling cider.

"Whoa, there's a cake with our name on it," Mario said. "This is awesome."

"First, let's seal this deal," Brad said.

Photographers snapped away as we signed our contract. We posed for photos, shaking hands with Brad. Those were later published in the music industry trades, accompanying interviews with Harry about how he discovered us and secured our deal. Everything moved at lighting speed from that moment forward.

I'm fortunate that over a decade later, Brad still supports me.

"We want to sign you for the release of your solo album," Brad said. "It's about time one of you guys breaks out and I'm glad it's you."

"I won't let you down, Brad."

But I fear that I am. The A&R team keeps pushing for a hit single. I've written so many songs, and I don't know what else I can possibly write to give them what they're looking for, but I'm not about to give up. There *will* be a hit single released around this tour, even if it's not on the actual album.

The marketing rep, a guy named Juice, told me tonight that once we get the single, we'll make a video and reel for social media. "As it goes viral, we can release a digital single." I've never released a digital single. Back in my day, bands charted album sales. I'm grateful to be a part of this new era of the music industry, but I need to prove that I can keep up with the pace other artists have set.

After I met all the new folks at my label, I was finally able to get back out to the buses. But by that time, we had to hit the road. Unfortunately, I had to settle for talking to Cailin on the phone. At least I got to see her for a hot minute. And I do mean hot minute. One look at those little shorts was all it took. Luckily no one was around to witness my desire.

But then the accident happened and everything changed. Ending the first night of tour with Cailin in my bed was something I thought about and pushed out of my mind. I never expected it to happen like this. I didn't realize how bad the storm was until after I got off the phone with her. I texted Harry and he put out a group text to all the drivers, suggesting we pull over. But of course, that wasn't the smartest idea because the drivers aren't reading their texts while they are on the road navigating a storm.

I peeked out the window to get a glimpse of what was happening outside when I noticed up ahead one of our buses pulled over along the side of the road. I identified it as Cailin's when I looked at the license plate. I have the license plate for all of our buses stored on my phone in case of an emergency. Never thought I'd actually need to pull up that note.

I quickly called Diego—who thankfully answered his phone on Bluetooth—and told him to pull over. In that instant, when I thought something might have happened to Cailin, I realized how much I care about her already. I would never have been able to live with myself if she got hurt, or something worse. She's already dealing with enough, thanks to the lipstick scandal. My neck and her lips. My bus. I'm already causing her pain. All I wanted to do was make sure she was safe and hold her in my arms.

And now, she's fast asleep with her back against my chest. Tonight isn't about my physical needs, and that's a first. It's about Cailin's emotional needs, growing our relationship through trust, and offering her security. I want to do this for Cailin. She needs to know that whatever comes our way, we can overcome the obstacles. In my world, there will be plenty of roadblocks. I hope tonight's events didn't scare her away from this life on the road. It's her first tour and it's not off to the best start for Cailin.

As I rest my head on my pillow, I'm not going to deny that it's torture being this close to her, with so little clothing and thin sheets between us. Now that she's staying on my bus, which I hope is for the rest of the tour, I hope that things will continue to progress for us. I've never felt this way about a woman before and I think that's why I'm going full speed ahead. I've had my fill of women, and no one made me want to keep them around. Cailin, though, I don't want to let her go. And I'm at the point in my life where I don't want to just see my bandmates and fans start their families. I want my own.

Cailin is everything I could want in a partner. At least from what I see so far. That's why I need to use this time to get to know her completely. And I need to break out of my fears and show her the man I can be, too. I already feel more confident just having performed and met all my fans. I want to take her out in public and not let my worries about what people will think or say stop me. With Cailin by my side, I know I can do it. No, not just do it. Actually enjoy it.

But first, I need to get through my temptation to wake up Cailin and start making passionate love to her. For the first time on this bus, I'm regretting that I don't have access to a cold shower.

Trash the Dress Online Chat

Alexandra: Tomorrow would be the anniversary of when we got engaged and I am starting to have feelings of regret again.

Cora: Have you made your Good Riddance list yet? All the reasons why your marriage wasn't working. Do this so you can go back and read it at times like this!

27

CAILIN MCCALL WAKES UP IN BED WITH
JAX SLATER

CAILIN

I WAKE up with my head lying on Jax's chest and his arms around me. He's already awake.

"Good morning." Jax softly greets my cheek with his lips.

I hope I don't have morning breath. This is the first time I'm waking up in bed with a man who has yet to see me naked. This is also the first time I'm waking up in bed with an international pop star. But more importantly, it's the first morning I'm waking up in the arms of Jax, the man who made me feel eternally safe last night after I had a terrifying experience. My heart is filled with gratitude.

"How long have you been up watching me sleep?" I sit up and rub my eyes.

"Long enough to discover that you crinkle your nose when you dream." Jax sits up and bops my nose with his index finger.

"And how do you know I was dreaming?" I yawn.

"I can only guess by the peaceful look on your face. You're pretty when you sleep." He brushes his hand against my cheek.

"I am actually horrified thinking of what I must look like right now after going to bed with soaking wet hair." I look around the small bedroom area half thankful there are no mirrors and half wishing I could see my messy appearance.

"I quite enjoy seeing you wake up with tousled hair, but I can't help but wish I was the one who worked it out of place."

I jolt back to reality, flashing back to the accident last night. "How's Ken?"

"Harry sent a text. He's all good. Already back at home. He got an early morning flight home. Short, quick one."

"Good. I was worried about him. He's such a nice man. I hope his wife wasn't too worried." I lean back in his arms. Now that one concern is off my mind, I move onto the next. Headlines. Morning news. I need to call Marisol.

"Do you know what time it is? Or what city we're even in?"

"I think we're somewhere in Colorado. Halfway to Minneapolis." He pulls up a location tracker on his phone.

"Colorado. I'm so excited. It's so breathtaking in photos."

"I already have the greatest view," Jax says.

My life has taken an interesting turn. One minute, I'm signing divorce papers and wondering if I'll ever find true love, and the next, I'm lying in bed on a tour bus, waking up in the arms of one of the sexiest men alive—according to magazines and me.

"Are we caught up to the rest of the crew?" I ask.

"We should be. Diego is probably on the crew bus sleeping off the night drive. Everyone's probably anxious to hear about last night." Jax brings up a good point.

"Do they know I'm on your bus now?"

"I'm sure Harry told them. He hasn't called me yet. He's probably giving us some space." Jax stretches both his arms. Turns out I have a great view, too.

"Speaking of figuring things out, I need to call Marisol."

"How about this," Jax says. "We'll get dressed. I'll go out and touch base with Harry and the rest of the crew. You can have some privacy and call Marisol."

Jax and I begin to sit up. I motion to fix my T-shirt that's sliding down my shoulder. But before I can reach it, Jax notices and gently presses his smooth lips against my shoulder bone. I wish I could imprint that feeling. Jax is totally unaware of the effect the littlest touch from him has over my body. "Then, we're going out exploring. I still owe you a proper first date."

"Nice try, giving me something to look forward to while I work up the nerve to confess everything I've done wrong to my boss."

"You got this. And no matter what Marisol says, you got me."

"Even if she fires me?" I'm only partially joking.

"She's not going to fire you. Trust me. I'm one of her highest paying clients and she needs to keep me happy."

"That somehow just makes me feel worse, but thanks for trying."

Before Jax walks out of the room, he tells me, "No matter what happens with Marisol, I plan on holding you every night and waking up on this bus with you next to me the rest of this tour."

Relief. That sums it up. I don't look as horrible as I imagined as I survey myself in the bathroom mirror. I appreciate that Jax gave me space to get ready alone. The smell of his cologne lingers in the air and I don't mind at all. As I fix myself, I wonder how the conversation outside is going, but I need to focus on my own dialogue. Once I muster up the courage, I dial Marisol's number.

"Cailin, I'm so glad you're okay," Marisol says. She doesn't even say hello. Maybe the accident will help me get some sympathy points.

"I'm sorry I didn't call you sooner, Marisol. A lot has been going on, but I can assure you everything is on track with the media." I can't sit still, so I pace the length of the bus.

"I'm not concerned about the media at all. Jax is making all the headlines and social media is going crazy about the show last night. I'm seeing rave reviews. You're doing a great job. I hope the events last night don't deter you from wanting to continue managing press the rest of the tour."

"Not at all. I definitely want to continue the rest of the tour. That is, if you'll have me. I need to be honest with you." I stop pacing and take a seat. Here goes nothing. I need to come clean. This is so hard to do, but I'm a grown woman and I know this is better for both brands all around.

"First, I want to tell you how honored I am to come on board with your company and have your team welcome me with open arms. I appreciate that you put so much faith in me and have the confidence that I can manage such a demanding account my first week on the job." I pause for air.

"Your past experience speaks for itself, Cailin. Imani could not talk you up enough. I trust her, and after speaking with you I knew you would be a great fit for our company. Is something bothering you?" Marisol's tone changes to concern.

"I got your text about exploiting the mystery woman behind the lipstick stain."

"Does Jax want to keep that private? I don't want to do anything that will make him uncomfortable. But it can be good for his image if we can bring him back into the spotlight with a new love interest on top of the album and tour." I would agree with Marisol if it wasn't me.

"Actually, Jax is okay with revealing his new love interest." Here it comes. The moment everything I worked so hard for is going to explode. Goodbye public relations career.

"That's great!" Marisol says. "Then I don't see the issue."

"The problem is that revealing the woman might reflect poorly on our company." I'm stalling, but I need to just spit it out. "It's me."

Marisol pauses to digest this startling news. I seem to have this effect on people.

"I see. I see." Marisol's lack of immediate reaction has me so stressed, I wouldn't be surprised if my hair starts to fall out.

"I know this reflects very poorly on me and I can assure you I didn't set out on tour with these intentions. Things just happened and I take complete accountability for putting your reputation on the line with mine. I take my career so seriously and I know I just ruined this amazing opportunity you gave me." I wish she could see the remorse on my face.

I'm shaking at this point. I let myself down and I let Marisol down. I deserve whatever is coming my way.

"I appreciate your honesty, Cailin. I'm sure admitting the truth wasn't easy for you, but this also proves what a good publicist you are because you got ahead of the crisis so we can plan for damage control. You said Jax wants to go public?"

I fill Marisol in on Harry's theory. She agrees it can be good for Jax.

"The issue now is figuring out how this might impact our PR firm," Marisol says. "And how we're going to reveal you as the mystery woman. What press do we have lined up for the next show?"

My chest deflates as I let go of the breath I didn't know I was holding. "Does this mean I'm not fired?" How can this be? I'm not going to argue with it.

"I'm going to tell you something, Cailin. When I was around your age, I fell in love with my coworker. I feared I would lose my job, just as you're fearing right now. We kept it a secret for a year. It was hard on both of us and the guilt ate me alive. I hated lying to our colleagues, who became close friends. We had to pretend we weren't a couple every time we went out and I always had to dodge questions about why I wasn't dating anyone. It was very stressful on me."

"Wow, thank you for sharing that. What happened? If you don't mind me asking."

"We got engaged and the company we worked for fired us

because it was against company policy for two employees to date."

"I'm sorry." Marisol understands what I'm going through because she has been in my shoes. Things are actually working out in my favor.

"Don't be. That's how we started this company."

"Your husband is your partner? That's amazing. I didn't know."

"He's more in the background these days, handling financials while I am client facing," Marisol says. "But the point is, we can't let work stand in the way of love. Jobs come and go. But true love only comes around once. If you and Jax feel like you need to explore this, then you owe it to yourselves."

Wow, I did not expect this. Marisol is proving to be my mentor in more ways than one. "I cannot thank you enough for being so understanding. I promise I won't let you down."

"Now, we need a plan," Marisol says. "I want to leave everyone in suspense a little longer as to who you are. For now, let's release a statement from Jax that confirms he's in a relationship. Why don't you talk to him and then touch base with me later? I'll connect with Harry as well."

"I will. Thank you again. So much."

"We'll speak soon, Cailin."

"Bye, Marisol."

I did not expect to end the call on a positive note. I really thought I was going to get fired and would be hanging my head in shame as I packed my bags. Instead of writing copy for a social media post announcing my departure from the tour, I am fighting back the urge to run around, scream, and jump on the bed like a kid on Christmas morning. I was courageous and honest and the universe rewarded my actions. I feel like the weight of the world has been lifted off my shoulders. I'm free to date Jax Slater—which still blows my mind to even say—and I get to keep my job. Just as I am running my hands across my face in relief, Jax walks onto the bus holding two cups of coffee.

"Uh, oh. Bad call?" he asks me with concern as he places the coffee cups on the table.

"Unbelievably great call, actually," I say and then stand up to meet him. "I still have a job and Marisol agrees we can go public."

Jax twirls me in his arms and plants a big, wet kiss on my face. The scent of hazelnut coffee beans lingers in the air as he playfully slaps my backside and tells me, "That's amazing. See, I told you it would all work out."

"We still have some details to consider, like how we want to handle the fact that I'm the mystery woman. But Marisol wants to start by having you release a statement to the media. I'll draft a few options for you today and we can go over them before we send along, to get her thoughts."

Jax shakes his head. "No need. I already know my statement."

"Which is?"

"I've unapologetically fallen for someone who brings a new energy to my life."

Trash the Dress Online Chat

Harper: Can someone remind me what the upside of divorce is again? Having a rough day.

Julie: Divorce gave me the opportunity to explore my feelings for women.

28

JAX SLATER AND CAILIN MCCALL FOLLOW
THEIR PASSIONS

JAX

I WAS SO worried about what Marisol would say to Cailin. I had various speeches prepared in my head in case she got fired or tried to end things with me. Luckily, I didn't have to use them. Cailin grabbed my face and planted her lips on mine as soon as she heard the statement that I want to release.

"I never would have drafted a quote like that," she says.

"That's because you don't know how I really feel, or realize how much you're changing my life," I say.

When Cailin told me that I need to release a statement, I wanted to come right out and say 'I'm in love.' Because I am. I love her. My heart is one hundred percent filled with love for this woman. It's never too soon. When you know, you know. Which I now understand.

I want her to know, too. I want to shock the world and tell everyone that I have moved out of my post-breakup slump. I'm no longer mourning my relationship with Maxine. In fact, I'm more disgusted with myself for putting up with her for so long. But it took meeting Cailin to realize what I really want in a woman.

I decided to say I 'unapologetically' fell for her because I don't care that a relationship like ours can be frowned upon. I know it can be looked at as a press stunt for attention. I know it's going to bring trouble for Cailin at work. I know people are going to say that she's just another one of my conquests. None of that is going to stop me because I also know the truth. Hopefully, Cailin feels the same way.

As Cailin and I continue to explore each other's bodies, I think about how I understand now when people say you can't choose who you love. It just happens. Love is a force beyond your control. Looking back, I think I chose to care about Maxine because the media fawned over us together. Two pop icons make quite the headlines. It felt good to get that attention. Maxine and I both thrived from the praise we got every time we landed a cover story. We had chemistry. I had love for her, but it wasn't pure, true love. Not like this. I put up with certain things against my better judgment and then it all came crashing down.

I felt lost and was angry with myself. I hid as a way to face what happened. After a while of that, I lost interest in dating. I was so over the games of Hollywood. I just wanted to feel normal. And staying home allowed me to feel like myself, not Jax from 5 Leo Hearts.

Then, I met Cailin. Just one look at her, and I knew everything was going to change. In just a short time, she has brought a new confidence and excitement into my life. I want to experience things with her, no matter who is around. She makes me feel better than I ever have in all my years. She fills an emptiness. Cailin gives me something to look forward to and offers me encouragement spend support. She's dedicated and humble. I want her to be mine forever.

At this point, Cailin and I are on top of each other, fully clothed, but I feel my completely naked soul. I sit up and break away from Cailin. I need to capture this.

"Is everything okay?" she asks. I get up and grab a notebook and pen.

"I just got inspired," I tell her. I open my notebook and begin writing lyrics that just flow out of me like a dam that has been holding back flood water for years.

"Well, don't let me stop you from your creative process." Cailin grabs a book and settles on the couch. I appreciate this. She isn't demanding my attention, like so many other people. She's giving me some space and taking advantage of time to herself to indulge in her own passions.

As I write, I pour my heart and soul into each verse. I think about the first time I saw her on video chat, the moment I gave her a hug at my house, our first kiss, and everything that's led up to this point. The chorus is a future stadium anthem. I know it. This is the single.

I just need to write the music, record it, and send it off to A&R. If this is not the song, then I don't know what else I can do to please these people. This song is me at my most vulnerable. I explored fears, feelings, and dreams I have never admitted to myself. I wrapped them up on a summary of how Cailin has made me a better man. How I will never apologize for loving her, because by loving her, I've also learned to fully love myself. But I don't want her to know yet. I want to sing the full song to her once it's ready.

I have a guitar melody in my head, but I'll focus on the music another day. That burst of inspiration has drained all my creativity and I want to come back to the music when I'm fresh. Right now, I need to replenish my body. I need my greatest source of energy. I need Cailin.

"Hey," I say. I close my notebook and stash it in my backpack.

Cailin looks up from her book and sets her gold-flecked eyes on mine as her response.

"Do you want to stop reading about fictional characters in passionate love scenes and make our own?"

Cailin throws her book across the bus. The bookmark floats through the air and lands a few feet away from her novel. She doesn't seem to even notice. Her gaze is set hungrily on me. Then, Cailin playfully pounces on me. Completely unexpected and I love it. I've yet to see this dominant side. She straddles me and just when I think she's coming in for the kill, she slides her fingers under my armpit.

"I can't take it!" I wail under shrieks of laughter.

Cailin keeps tickling me, but I'm not letting her get away with it. I thrust forward with my hips and reposition us so that she's beneath me and I'm straddling her. I give us both a few seconds to catch our breaths. In between gasps for air and laughs, I manage to distract Cailin enough to sneak my hands under her feet.

"Oh my gosh, you got me. You got me!" she says. "Truce! Let's make a truce!"

I love this spur of the moment child-like play. It's just what we've needed to lighten things up. We're dealing with some heavy situations, but we can't let those topics consume all of our interactions. But the next time I straddle Cailin, we're going to have a different round of fun.

Trash the Dress Online Chat

Alexandra: Should I sell my wedding ring or save it for my kids one day?

    Tori: How big of a rock is it?

29

JAX SLATER SPOTTED GETTING COZY AT
CAFÉ WITH MYSTERY WOMAN

CAILIN

I'VE BEEN on a few different types of first dates. I've made the mistake of letting friends set me up on a blind date in college, only to get stood up, and end up meeting another guy who asked to buy me dinner. I've met a guy I connected with online and then had him duck out after an hour to go meet his next date. I've gone to the movies, mini golf, and hung out with groups of friends on other first dates. But this is my first date with a man I've crushed on for decades, already made out with, and is technically my boss.

Jax holds my hand as we venture out to explore the town we've stopped in for a few hours. The brisk morning air hits my face and makes me feel alive. I still have my job, I'm walking through a town where I've never been, and I'm on my first official date with Jax. I'm rising like the summer sun. I wonder if people are going to notice him and come up and ask for autographs. But since it's still morning in a small town, I think we're safe.

"This is nice," I say.

"Not a bad start for our first date. But I need to find somewhere to take you to dine." Jax surveys the signs outside each establishment.

"Maybe we can find an app to point us in the right direction," I say.

"That would take away half the fun of this adventure," Jax says. "We need to find the best or worst place so we can look back on it and tell stories."

"Are you planning ways to create memories with me, Jax?"

"I don't think I'll ever forget anything we've been through so far." Jax speaks on behalf of both of us.

"You can say that again." I stop mid-stride and look at Jax. "Hey, what do you eat for breakfast? Are you a big fan of the first meal of the day?" I realize I don't know these basic things about him, but I want to know them all.

"When I'm home, I usually have a black coffee and a protein shake to start the day. Then, after my morning workout, I go big." We continue walking. There's silence except for our voices and a few birds chirping.

"Like a morning feast?"

"Eggs, yogurt, fruit." Gotta start my day right, you know. What about you?"

"I drink my coffee black too. Not many people do."

"I totally pictured you as a fancy latte girl."

"Oh, don't be mistaken. My afternoon coffees are quite fancy when I get out on the town."

"I knew it."

"Isn't it funny? There's so much we don't know about each other. Yet, I feel really close to you."

"I know what you mean," Jax says. He stops to brush the morning scruff of his upper lip against my cheek. "So much I need to learn about my girlfriend."

"You know, I didn't officially accept your girlfriend offer." I like teasing Jax. It's my new favorite activity.

"I consider you agreeing to eventually go public with me as

your acceptance." Jax slips his arm around my waist, like it has always belonged there.

"Have you ever had a normal girlfriend before? Someone who wasn't famous?"

"Since I became famous? No. That's why you're so refreshing. You care about things besides vanity issues. If anything, you're quite the opposite. You'd rather keep things private, when others will do anything for attention."

"So, I'll be your first?"

"Does that mean you're agreeing to be my girlfriend?"

We pause our steps and I turn to look Jax in the eyes. "Yes, Jax. I'll be your girlfriend. Do I get to wear your varsity jacket, too?"

"You're something, else."

Smiles break across both our faces and without worrying if anyone is watching, Jax gives me the most romantic kiss. I feel like I'm in a movie scene where there has just been a big declaration of love and everyone in the audience is swooning. Except in the movie, our big moment would not be interrupted by my stomach growling.

"I have to feed my girl." Jax points to a café across the street. "Let's check this place out."

We dash across the street to the café. As soon as we open the door, we're greeted by swirls of cinnamon and coffee floating through the air. Mismatched velvet couches and wooden side tables with scattered newspapers and magazines draw me near. I'm instantly feeling cozy and famished.

A few baristas shoot each other looks when they see Jax approach the counter. It's obvious they are subliminally freaking out because Jax Slater is at their coffee shop.

Jax must be used to this because he turns up his charm. I don't know what he is saying about having anxiety when going out in public. I've seen zero evidence. "Good morning, ladies. Can you tell us the best items on the menu?" In between words,

Jax holds my hand. One of the baristas stares at me. Guess I'll have to get used to this.

The barista with long, blue braids in her hair and chocolate stains on her apron shares her favorite pastries and drinks with us and we decide to go for it all. Jax and I sit next to each other on a small purple couch against a corner wall. The table beside us has the morning paper open to the Help Wanted ads and a section has been carefully torn off the corner. Our thighs are pressed together and Jax rests his arm around my shoulders as we lean back and wait for our order.

"What's your hometown like?" Jax asks me.

"It's the best. I grew up in a small lake community and spent my summers swimming. Our neighborhood was full of kids, so we were always outside playing and running back and forth to each other's houses. Our parents were all friends. It's just the childhood I would want for my kids."

"That sounds really special. I grew up in Florida, as you probably know. But things were a little different for me growing up with a single mom. I guess we got left out of a lot of things that groups of families did together. But she had her own support system and we were happy."

"And you had your grandma, right?"

"My grandma was the best. She watched me after school while my mom worked. And she took me to the beach every weekend so I could surf."

"Do you still surf?"

"Occasionally, but it's harder in LA. I can't go anywhere, even the ocean, without paparazzi. Kinda ruins the zen of it all."

"That must be really hard. Do you like living there though?"

"I bought my place there because I thought I was going to be with Maxine forever and she would never leave LA. But since the breakup, I'm just stuck in this big empty house. I feel like I've been living in a fish bowl, on display for everyone to watch.

I spend most of my time writing songs, which is why I decided to make a solo album."

"Seems like you're not stuck on LA as home then?"

"I'm open to new beginnings," Jax says. He puts his hand on my thigh and heat surges up my leg. Just as he leans towards me, our food arrives.

As we devour our food, Jax and I continue conversing about all the things couples usually discuss on a first date. And then, also the things divorced women unfortunately have to discuss on a first date. Men are naturally curious about the marriage, why it ended, how we feel now, and if we still speak to our ex.

I make a mental note to post about this in the Trash the Dress Group. Gosh, everyone is going to freak out once they hear this news. I want to interact with my tribe, but I also will need to keep the details of my relationship private. Luckily, I know that group of women are trusted confidants. They share intimate details of their lives and everyone respects each other's secrets.

Jax and I discover we are aligned in so many values and goals, despite having two drastically different lives. We also balance each other out in the ways we are opposites. I know he has a rebellious streak and I'm wholesome, so I can ground him when needed. He's already made me more adventurous, just by the fact that I am out on tour and putting myself in the public eye.

I sip the last of my coffee and tell Jax, "I have a really important question. One topic we didn't cover. Do you like dogs?"

"Digging deep, now. I thought you were going to ask me if I want kids."

"Another very good question. Kids are a deal-breaker for me. As in, I want them." I have dreamed of being a mother my whole life. I realize right now, if Jax and I aren't on the same page with a timeline for when we would hypothetically want to start a family, that we might be over before we even start. But it's better to know upfront, I guess. I'd rather not drag out a relationship and delay heartbreak, fall in love with him, and then have to end things because I'm ready to start a family and he's not. I recall Jax telling me he broke up with Maxine because she didn't want kids, so I think I'm safe.

"I can picture you being a great mom. How do you see that fitting into your career?" He takes a sip of his coffee, his lips forming the perfect O.

"I never thought it would impact my career. Things have changed a little. I definitely don't see myself leaving a family to be a tour publicist, or anything like that. I want to be a hands-on parent, but also still maintain a career doing something I love. Luckily, I have a lot of areas I can explore."

"What if your kids came on tour with you?" Jax is obviously asking me if I could see myself having kids with him. I have to give him credit. He clearly has intentions with me and right now this conversation seems larger than life, but he is ensuring that we are both clear on what we want so neither of us end up crying a river.

"If the father of my children were, oh, a popular musician who toured frequently, I think it would be fun to hit the road as a family and tour the world before the kids start school. I would just have to figure out what to do with the dogs."

"I didn't realize you have dogs," Jax says.

"Not yet, but I want one." I pick off pieces of my banana nut muffin and pray that Jax is not a cat guy. "That's why I wanted to know if you like dogs. Another deal-breaker basically."

"Bring on all the deal-breakers, because I swear, you're not going to find one. I'm telling you, we are going to work. We already do. I love dogs. The bigger the better."

"Me too." Whoo! Jax is not Collin. Praise Cupid. Thank you for sending me someone who shares my love of dogs.

"I grew up with a chocolate lab, named Bear," Jax tells me. "That dog was my best friend. Whenever I felt lonely or was upset because my mom was having a rough day, Bear knew. He would curl up next to me and just be there."

My heart aches to think of Jax having a sad childhood. But thinking of him comforted by a dog just warms my heart to the point where it might burst.

"I had a golden retriever growing up. Sunny. I always snuck her on the beach at the lake to go swimming. My mom said the lake water wasn't good for dogs, but Sunny loved to swim, so I couldn't deny her that joy."

"Cailin breaking the rules? I'm shocked."

"So, you love dogs. And kids. I know you mentioned you wanted them before…"

His eyes light up, the brightest blue I've seen them. "I can't wait to be a dad. Some of the guys in the band already have kids and I see how it's changed their lives. Ridge is on his way there. Kelly is gonna be knocked up this year if things go her way. And I want that for myself too. Life is short. Like I said before, I lived a full life. I've traveled the world, experienced more than one person can dream. But the most important things are the simple ones. And I want to come home to my own family."

"I feel the same way. I'm at the point in my life where I've had enough to know what I don't want and I am just ready for what I deserve."

"That's why I feel like we hit it off so well. I can tell that about you. And in case you haven't realized, when I know what I want, I go for it."

"Oh, I totally realized." I playfully push his chest and Jax gently catches my wrists to pull me towards his chest.

"Do you know what I want now?" he asks, as he locks our lips in a simmering kiss.

"I know I want to get out of here," I say.

"You read my mind."

We walk up to the register to pay, and the baristas stop playing it cool and finally ask for a photo with Jax. One of them hands me her cell phone. I note that this is the first of many times I will probably get asked to take a picture of Jax with his fans in public. I don't mind that one bit because I see a part of myself in each of these girls. I'm just the lucky one who gets to live the dream. And I hope I never have to wake up.

Jax and I stroll on the sidewalk with our fingers weaved together. That's when I realize that I have not even taken a photo with him yet. My teenage self is severely disappointed.

"Thank you for the perfect first date," I tell Jax. "But I have a request for one more first. I want to remember this moment." I reach to grab my phone out of my sling bag with my other arm and snap a photo of our hands melded together.

"Send that to me," Jax says.

I text the photo to him and he takes out his phone. I watch as Jax saves the picture and then opens up his social media account. He posts the photo of our hands with the statement he gave me earlier.

"It's official," he says. "I just confirmed to the world that I have a girlfriend."

Trash the Dress Online Chat

Cailin: Highly recommend career changes.
　Cora: Would need a career first.

30

JAX SLATER REVEALS NEW RELATIONSHIP

CAILIN

MY FIRST DUTY as the girlfriend of Jax Slater is to learn how to manage interruptions. I have not yet had time to fully process the fact that I am now dating pop music royalty, however, the public only needs one second to register Jax from across the street before fans come rushing our way. By now, word has gotten out that Jax is in town and crowds have begun to form around us as we explore the city. Some people respect his privacy, but many think nothing of tapping him on the arms as we stroll and asking for a photo. I'm always the designated photographer, which I suppose is my second duty in my new role as Jax Slater's girlfriend. I don't mind at all though, because it really makes my official job as his social media manager a lot easier when I'm helping to create content with his fans.

Jax is so cordial and always makes sure he acknowledges everyone. He is so nice that I can see the bad boy reputation vanishing before the end of tour. Maybe that's not such a horrible thing. While Jax chats, I give him some space and text Marisol to let her know that Jax went rogue and made a post.

Thankfully, she approves and understands that I didn't get a chance to run it by her first.

Imani also reached out and sent me a ton of emojis, which means she is happy for me and approves. I know if there was anything going on behind my back she would tell me, so everything must be good in the office. I'm so glad she's not mad at me or accusing me of potentially ruining her credibility. That could definitely have happened if things didn't work out in my favor.

Gemma also texted me. She obviously saw the photo Jax posted and is requesting every detail. I realize Gemma is the only one from back home who knows the truth. I need to tell my mom before we announce that I'm dating Jax. She will be thrilled and surely brag to all the new kids on the block, as well as longtime neighbors. She'll finally have a one-up over her friend's kids because her daughter moved on from boys to men.

I check my work email and the tabloids have already started to reach out asking for details on the woman in Jax's life. They work quickly. They must have interns monitoring the accounts of all major celebs so they can be first to report any updates. This increases the pressure for me to reveal myself. Since I've already been seen in public with Jax today, clearly making out without abandon, it makes sense that I do so sooner rather than later. I text Marisol and she agrees.

Jax manages to escape his devoted fans after granting everyone a photo. We head down the street to a nearby park that one kind lady told us we could visit and enjoy some privacy. She was right. We find a bench hidden among a bunch of trees and sit down. Jax pulls up his phone and starts reading the comments on the photo. There's already one million "likes." The comments however, aren't all kind.

A few of my favorites from the haters are:

"Back off, Jax is mine."

"Is this the lipstick stain girl?"

"As if he is going to be faithful to someone! He belongs with Maxine. This is just a rebound."

"I'm sure he already moved on from lipstick girl. He's a rock star. He's living it up on the road."

"No Jax! I'm your number one fan. Please consider dating me. Click my profile."

"God, your hand is so hot."

"This is one lucky girl. I wish I was your girlfriend."

We crack up as Jax reads the comments aloud. "They already hate me," I wheeze. "I'm going to have online groups dedicated to commenting on my life."

"Or," Jax says, "they might love you. We might get our own hashtag. You never know."

"Maybe I should just come forward. But instead of a social media post, how do you feel about doing an exclusive interview with a media outlet? There are so many requests coming in, we can leverage this for a cover story." I may have red hearts bouncing from my eyes, but my mind can still do its job.

"I'm not going to turn down the opportunity for a cover story," Jax says. "But they're going to dig deep. How do you feel about me telling the world that I seduced you after meeting you on a video conference?"

"Ha! Is that what you did?"

"I'll make it clear that I am the one who initiated this and you were staying professional. But eventually, you couldn't resist my charm."

"I wouldn't say it was your *charm* that won me over, though you were very persistent and charming in your pursuit."

"We'll have some time to go over the details," Jax says. "Let's do it."

With that, I'll gratefully bid my privacy adieu. "Okay, I'll tell Marisol we're going to grant an exclusive cover story and discuss which outlet we should offer it to first. Then, we're going to have to book morning shows. TV is going to want to do a feature segment. We'll request that you perform one song after the interview."

"You're so cute. I love how your mind is so focused on being the publicist. Don't forget, this is going to change your life."

As if I can forget what's happening. For now, I'm trying not to think about it. I don't want my friendships to change. I don't want people to stop me at the grocery store and tell me how much they love or hate Jax and I together. I don't even know where I'll be grocery shopping after this tour. What happens? Do I go back home and go back to my life and try to do this long distance with Jax? Does he plan to stay in LA? Would he move to New York? Do I even want to move back to the City? Would Jax ever live in a small town? Can a retriever live on a tour bus?

"Are you okay?" Jax asks. The expression on my face must have given me away.

I shake it off and try to focus on just savoring the present. "Yeah, I'm fine. I was just getting lost in thought. Nothing important. I think this will be a positive step forward for you and that makes me happy. Yes, it's going to change my life, but I hope for the better. And you know, once we go public, it makes it really hard for you to break up with me because then everyone will say we faked it for the press."

Jax puts his phone in his pocket and grabs my hands in his. His oceanic eyes splash into mine as he says, "Cailin, we haven't known each other for very long, but I know how you make me feel. And I know that feeling is unlike anything I have felt before. I'm falling in love with you."

I'm stunned. My body feels like it's going into shock—he has a way of doing this to me, apparently—but I can feel Jax grip my hands in his so I know I'm conscious. His hands are sweaty. He's nervous. I am too. I know exactly what he's describing because I feel the same way. I pull my hands away from his and put one hand on each of his cheeks, matching his gaze. I love that I can just touch his face whenever I want.

"I'm falling in love with you, too," I tell Jax. "And if this was a reality TV show, I would give you an end of date rose. But this is my real life and all I can give you is my heart and trust that you will never break it."

"I promise you this, I will never do something to intentionally break your heart or make your beautiful eyes cry."

Jax seals his promise with our lips and I give myself to him completely in that moment. I can feel my soul seep out of my body, meet his in the space between us, and form one being. This is more than just a kiss. In this moment, we're committing ourselves to each other. I'm giving him all that I am and praying that this relationship becomes everything I hope it will.

I just told Jax Slater that I'm falling in love with him. But wait, back up. Jax Slater just said he's falling in love with *me*. I can see the headlines. **Opposites Attract: Bad Boy Pop Star Falls for Girl Next Door.** Heck, I'll be the one pitching this story, let's be honest.

If I had to go through an unhappy marriage and years of jobs I hate to end up here, then it was all worth it. Every day I worked late and came home exhausted. Every night I cried myself to sleep because I was sleeping next to a man who lost interest in my body. The humiliation of getting fired. The fear of the future when I moved back home. All the years of feeling like I was meant for more, but just not sure how to get there, were all worth it. I manifested a better life and it came true beyond my wildest dreams.

I hear a biker ride past us and remember we're in a very public place. When I'm with Jax, I feel like the rest of the world stops. But I'm going to have to stay aware of the fact that I'm in a very public relationship now and all eyes are going to be on both of us. Right now, this small-town is practice. This is just a warm-up for what's to come after I reveal my identity to the press. It's going to get real, very quickly. We're fortunate that no one is hiding in a bush snapping our photo.

"We should get going back to the buses," Jax says. He pulls his phone from his pocket and checks the time. "We're going to have to hit the road soon."

"I'm glad we got some time alone to really talk." My hand gravitates to his on its own.

"I'm glad you finally agreed to be my girlfriend."

"You know, you basically had me from the moment you said 'hello' to me on video chat," I say.

"All I had to do was say your name? You mean I didn't have to send a car to the airport to pick you up, or meet you in secret to prove that I wanted you?"

"I love that you did all that. No one has ever gone so out of their way to make me feel so special before." The sun's rays are strengthening and the heat is starting to hit. I put on my sunglasses, happy I opted for my tortoise-shell frames today.

"Get used to it. You ain't seen nothing yet." Jax slides his black aviator frames over his nose. I didn't think he could look any sexier, but he has proved me wrong.

"You know you don't have to do anything outlandish to make me happy, right? I'm content just spending time with you."

"That's why you're so amazing. And exactly why I am going to spoil you. And you're going to let me because it makes me happy."

"I can't argue with that," I say. It's about time I have a man who wants to treat me like a queen. I've spent too long being the breadwinner, carrying the load of the relationship for someone who didn't pull their weight or acknowledge my worth. This is going to be different and I can't wait. Sunglasses or not, nothing is going to dim my light moving forward.

Trash the Dress Online Chat

Rory: I'm worried my son is going to resent me for divorcing his father.

Alexandra: I worry all the time that the twins will blame me for cheating and ending the marriage.

31

CAILIN MCCALL SEES JAX SLATER WHEN THE LIGHTS GO OUT

JAX

LOVE SUDDENLY HAS A NEW MEANING. Up until recently, love has meant heartbreak and yearning for something I couldn't have. Love was an obsession that fans had for me. But after this morning with Cailin, I know what falling in love means. I want to know what makes her happy and sad. I want to know how fast her heart beats when she's nervous or excited. I want to watch her nervously pick at a muffin during breakfast. I even want to know what makes her mad. Because no matter what, I want to be there for every moment and create new ones with Cailin.

It might have been risky to say it aloud, but it just felt right to tell Cailin I am falling in love with her. I'm not going to play it cool because I only have a few weeks on tour with her, and I want to ensure that when this is over, she's going to still be a part of my life. And I think she feels the same way. I'm one step closer to changing public perception, but yet, the only thing that I care about is what Cailin thinks about me.

I've never had a girl give me a run for my money. Women are usually falling at my feet, but not Cailin. She really made me work to get her to agree to be my girlfriend. I know a big part of that is because she's worried about her job and her reputation. So I have to do my best to make sure that in all my interviews moving forward, I stress that she's a professional. I'll protect her however I can. I don't want Cailin to have to deal with the dark side of the media or to know how the words they print can have you questioning your own character.

By the time we get back to the tour buses, everyone is outside waiting for roll call so we can hit the road. When they see us, my crew begins to clap and cheer. They must have seen the social media post.

"I knew it," Jayce says.

"I didn't say anything!" Hayley yells to Cailin. She gives her two thumbs up. I must admit, the approval feels nice.

"You knew?" Jayce says to Hayley.

"Girl code," Hayley says.

"What about girlfriend code?" Jayce says.

"Sisters before misters," Hayley says.

"I really like her," Cailin whispers to me. It must be near 98 degrees outside now, but that's not why she glistens.

Harry walks over and pats me on the back. "I'm thrilled. Marisol has filled me in on everything. It's great to see you so happy."

Chris walks out from the bus. "What's all the commotion?"

"Jax and Cailin are dating," Hayley says.

"No way. Nice, man," Chris says. He nods at me. "I guess we'll have to break it to Manny that Cailin is off the market."

I'm surprised to hear that Manny, the tour bass player, was ever interested in Cailin. He has barely spoken two words to her as far as I have seen. And I never take my eyes off her.

"I told you I had to make it official before someone on the crew tried to get with you." I speak softly into her ear and brush her hair away.

"As if he stood a chance." My neck tingles when Cailin whispers back.

"Okay you, two! Save the sexy talk for your bus," Hayley says.

Some of the guys pull me aside in conversation and I see Cailin and Hayley gravitate towards each other. I haven't felt this happy in a while. I hope the next time we are all celebrating together it's because one of my new songs tops the charts. It's still in the back of my mind that the pressure is on and I need to prove myself, not only in love, but also in music.

CAILIN

"I heard about the accident," Hayley says when she pulls me aside. "That is freaking scary as hell."

"It was terrifying. Thankfully Ken is okay and Jax pulled up after."

Hayley puts her hand across her heart. "In all my years on tour, the worst we have ever encountered is a broken-down tire. I did hear about something similar happening to that band of three brothers from Tulsa who sing that song about, um, bopping or something, though. Anyway, it really made me think about life. And if something ever happened to me, do I want to go out as a merch girl? Or do I want something more for myself? To get my photography business going?"

I understand where Hayley is coming from. Shaking my head, I tell her, "Sometimes it takes a traumatic event to find the courage to change your life."

Hayley nods in agreement. "It has me thinking about a lot. Even dating Jayce. It's all fun, but I don't see him settling down. He wants to live on the road forever and drink beer every night. There's more to life than a party."

My mouth drops open in a gasp, "Are you thinking of breaking up with him?"

Hayley crinkles her face and scrunches her mouth. "I don't

know. I have a lot to think about, but I hope to have a clear answer about that by the end of this tour. Take today for example, I could have been out with my camera, photographing this amazing place. But instead, Jayce and the guys wanted to hang out in a bar, shooting darts." Her sighs tell me more.

As we all disperse to our buses, Jax and I find our way back to each other and walk in sync back to our bus. Our little home. I wish we could place a welcome mat outside the door. I'd get one that says, "Home is wherever you are."

Once inside, I throw my bag down on the table and kick off my shoes. It's nice to be back to our private sanctuary. I realize that for the first time since we've become an official couple, Jax and I are alone on the tour bus. We have hours until our next stop and that leaves plenty of time for us to get better acquainted with each other. That makes me equal parts excited and nervous. Anything can happen. And I want it all.

Jax slowly takes off his shoes and jacket. I can't help but stare at his toned and tattooed biceps. The only thing that distracts me is watching him neatly place his shoes in a corner, oblivious to the fact that it's a complete turn on. But back to those arms. I picture my mouth moving along each detailed work of art lining his skin, because now, as his official girlfriend, I can technically use my mouth anywhere I want on Jax. My yearning for him is almost too much to handle. It's been suppressed far too long. I ache for him.

Jax walks over to me and I know he is thinking the same. "I've been waiting to get you all to myself in private." He runs his hands through my hair. His wide pupils meet mine and hold my gaze as I fall deep into his stare. I want to move my hands to hold his, but my mind has forgotten how to interact with my body. I'm powerless to this feeling that's radiating between us. Somehow, I'm able to formulate the words I've been trying to get out.

"What exactly did you have in mind?" My stomach feels like it's about to go down a forty foot drop on a roller coaster ride that I was afraid to board, but too scared to miss out on. I know what Jax has on his mind because it's the same thing that I can't stop replaying in my own head. We've both had enough of the secrecy, the stolen moments, and the conversations about our reputations. In this moment, we are not the pop star and his publicist. We're two people with a hunger for more of each other who have nothing holding us back.

This is the moment.

Jax takes my shaking hand and leads me to the bedroom. Even though we're the only people on the bus, he closes the door.

Trash the Dress Online Chat

Sara: Greetings from Egypt. I'm newly divorced.

Sydney: Me too! Anyone else going through recovery and divorce?

32

JAX SLATER SAYS NO ONE ELSE COMES CLOSE TO CAILIN MCCALL

CAILIN

OUR LEGS ARE TANGLED and I'm too blissful to move. I'm lying in bed naked with Jax Slater. Something I've dreamed about for over a decade. But this was beyond my most intense fantasy. It may have been the first time Jax had a chance to ravage my body, but there was no fumbling. He took me to o-town and I'll never be the same.

"That was incredible," Jax says as he leans his head into his pillow.

This pleasure has made up for years of being in a marriage where we had sex out of obligation. I forgot how incredible sex can be with someone you're attracted to inside and out. Collin and I had that when we started dating, but it quickly fizzled. Today alone, Jax and I saw our relationship progress leaps and bounds. From candid conversation to intimate moments, I feel like he knows me better than Collin ever did. Jax cares to ask questions and digs deep into my desires and dreams. And that is the most attractive thing about him. Though, his six-pack abs are a close second.

I trace his tattoos with my fingers, savoring the moment

that I'm seeing them up close. For years, I stared at them on posters that lined my walls. Each one reveals a part of Jax. And I want to know the meaning behind every drop of ink.

"What's your favorite tattoo?"

Jax moans. "That's a tough one. I've collected them through all different times in my life. The most recent one is on my back." He sits up and it's the first time I realize I'm looking at the tattoos on his back. "See over on my left shoulder? The skeleton key?"

I see it all right. Goosebumps chill my arms. "You have a skeleton key tattoo?"

His voice reveals concern as he asks, "Is that bad? It's a tribute to my grandma. I got it when she passed away. Remember I told you her house was old? All the doors had skeleton key locks on them. It drove me crazy because I could never lock my door and have privacy. But when I reflect back on that house and growing up, that always reminds me of my grandma."

"I actually love it." I hold up my inner wrist that is usually decorated in bracelets. "I just got a skeleton keyhole."

"No way," Jax says. He takes my wrist and strokes the tattoo. I'm branded by his touch.

"It symbolizes all the diaries I kept growing up and I got it as a reminder to always chase my dreams."

"You're extraordinary." Jax raises his eyes to meet mine as light peeks through the curtain shade.

"This is pretty amazing. I feel like everything is just oddly falling into place. Do you believe in fate?" I start to massage his shoulders, taking full advantage of the opportunity to run my hands up and down his back.

"Fate? I don't know. I just play the cards I'm dealt," Jax says while he stretches his neck from side to side.

"Well, I do. I believe we can manifest what we want, and this right here, is the universe sending us a sign." How else can I justify what is happening in my life right now? I lean my face forward and rest it on his shoulder from behind.

"What's it saying?" Jax asks me.

"Maybe that we are a perfect fit?" Dare I be optimistic?

"Oh, we definitely fit perfectly," Jax says, pulling me back in front of him and onto his lap. I can feel his excitement throbbing against me.

There's no way we're getting out of bed anytime soon.

JAX

Cailin and I pull ourselves out of the bed to get some water and food. I'm in dire need of hydration. I've never spent so long in bed, tenderly exploring someone and making sure her needs are met. I have a desire to deeply fulfill Cailin.

"I didn't realize how starving I am," Cailin says. We manage to make our way to the kitchenette area. Cailin cuts the sandwich rolls and visions of her hands a few minutes earlier dance in my mind.

"We worked up quite the appetite." The moments before I took Cailin in the bedroom, I felt like I was about to burst. Yet, all the built-up tension was worth it because being with Cailin, I felt like I transcended to another level of the universe. This deep love, this unexplainable passion to become a part of her, is something I didn't think existed because I never felt it with anyone. But it does exist. And it was worth pushing back my impulses.

"No more of that, or we are never going to get it together." I love how Cailin pushes me away in an attempt to be serious. She can't keep a straight face.

"I can't help it. I can't keep my hands off you." She's wearing my T-shirt. It's the first time a woman has worn my clothes and I find it sexy as hell. Maxine prepared her post-sex outfit next to the bed.

"Let's at least try long enough to make our sandwiches. Deal?" Cailin doesn't hide the fact that she is enjoying my shirtless torso.

"Deal." I make coffee to get my mind off of what I really want to do next.

"Just what I need," Cailin tells me, inhaling the coffee aroma. "We need to start making ourselves presentable. We're going to hit the next town soon, right?"

I nod.

"I can't wait to use the hotel shower," she says. "I also haven't checked my work email in a few hours. I think it's a weekday. I've totally lost track of time at this point."

"I've lost track of everything that doesn't have to do with you." That says a lot because I need to stay focused on my tour, the album I'm about to release, and the hit song that's not on it because I have yet to record one.

Cailin has already pulled up her email on her phone. "Guess what? We have a confirmed phone interview for you tonight before the show with none other than the number one weekly newsstand magazine."

"Get out. The cover story?" I put down my mug, splashing a drop of coffee on the table. I try to play it cool, but I'm so relieved to have a cover story secured. This means I'm still relevant.

"The cover story." Cailin shows me her phone. "They are going to send a photographer to tomorrow's show."

I give Cailin an appreciative kiss that won't lure us back to bed and tell her, "Good job, publicist."

"It was a pretty easy pitch," Cailin says. "Everyone wants to know how this story is going to play out." So do I and I can't help but have that thought linger in my mind.

CAILIN

I reply back to the reporter and shoot Marisol an email to let her know that everything is going according to plan. With Jax coming clean by saying he made the first move, it will take some of the heat off me, and Marisol's firm will keep its credibility. The reporter will probably ask Marisol for a quote to confirm that she's okay with her employee dating one of her biggest clients.

We eat and go over the details for the interview. I prep Jax on some questions he should be prepared to answer as we make ourselves presentable. My hair has been pulled into a messy bun and I can't wait to wash it and wear it down. Jax puts on a pair of jeans and a vintage looking T-shirt with strategic rips in it. He probably paid $100 for those rips that I can do myself with scissors. But it's $100 well spent. This shirt clings to his body, which is still damp from sweat. Traces of our passion embedded in his threads.

We discuss that there's nothing to fake or cover up here, so he's just going to have to be honest with whatever is thrown his way. We just have to hope that the questions are genuine and the reporter doesn't dig for a controversial hook. Once that's settled, Jax gets cozy on the couch and starts strumming his acoustic guitar. This is another milestone for us— the first time we're just hanging out and he has the opportunity to play for me.

"I wrote some lyrics the other day and I think I just got inspired with a melody I want to get down," he says.

"It sounds beautiful." I could listen to him play the guitar forever. A swoon-worthy melody fills the air while his calloused fingertips strum along. Jax doesn't look up as he plays, rather he is fixated on getting out what's floating around in his head. I don't mind, though, because it's my own private symphony that I don't have to share with anyone else.

"Just like the woman who inspired it. The song is about being unapologetically in love."

"Like the statement you made to the media."

"Also, how I'm feeling."

Jax starts singing a chorus and my heart begins to melt. I've never had a man do something so romantic for me. And here is the man of my literal dreams, sitting in front of me, writing a song about loving me. That's when it hits me and a teardrop escapes my eye. By the time it slowly falls down my cheek and lands on my shirt, Jax has raised his head in my direction.

"I hope those are happy tears." He puts down his guitar and moves closer to me to wipe the corners of my eyes.

"I love it," I tell Jax. And then something comes over me. I don't want to hide it or play it cool. I'm so deep into this right now, there's no escaping it. I'm diving in headfirst. I can't let fear of heartbreak or any of these too-good-to-be-true intrusive thoughts invade my mind. I've already hit rock bottom earlier this year and look where it brought me? Beyond anything I could ever imagine for myself. I'm going to tell Jax how I feel.

"I'm completely in love with you, Cailin." Jax beat me to it.

"I love you too, Jax," I say, my mouth breaking out into the biggest grin. The unexplainable feeling that envelops me when Jax pulls me into a passionate embrace can only be summed up as relief and ecstasy. He's showing me how I am supposed to be loved.

"Is this really happening?"

"Oh, it's happening," Jax says. "Tonight, after I do this interview, the whole world is going to know that I love you."

The whole world. Those words ring in my head as I nuzzle my face against the man who has the potential to be mine forever, or crack my heart open and be documented as my biggest mistake. Things seem too easy, too perfect, and I can't help but wait for my wake-up call.

Trash the Dress Online Chat

Harper: Reminder to always get everything in writing.

Cora: And screenshot text messages! Email them to yourself and friends.

33

JAX

I CAN'T SHAKE the feeling that something is bothering Cailin. When I told her that after my interview tonight the world would know I love her, I'm pretty sure I felt her shoulders tense. Revealing that I'm in love will be positive for me, but I know this is all new territory for Cailin. She's going to have to deal with a lot of change in her life. That's why this interview I'm going to do will be the most important conversation of my life.

Since Cailin stopped to chat with Hayley, I had some time alone in the hotel room. By the time Cailin arrives back to the room, I'm standing in my towel. I see her reflection sneak up behind me as I wipe steam off the mirror.

"Your shower was way too quick. Why don't you join me and we can make sure you didn't miss any spots?"

With that, Cailin drops my towel and I'm at her mercy. I draw her to me and start removing her clothes before we step into the tub.

Every time I think we're done, we go another round. Neither one of us is ready for this session to end. But finally, I can't take it anymore. I give in to Cailin's demands that I do the interview in private. She says that she doesn't want her presence to influence my responses. I argue that there's nothing I'm going to say that I wouldn't want her to hear—I want her to know everything. But she insists that there's a conflict since she's not just my publicist, but also the focus of this interview, so she shouldn't be in the room when I discuss our relationship. I think she's just nervous, but I agree to do the interview alone while she goes to catch up with Haley.

Ultimately, it's probably better that Cailin isn't here right now to see me sweat. Turns out, I'm the one who is carefully crafting each sentence that comes out of my mouth. I feel like I'm having to defend Cailin, and I don't really like where this conversation is going, so I need to redirect the reporter.

"It does put her in a compromising situation with her job and we have talked about that in-depth," I tell the reporter. "She is lucky to have the support of her team and it's really important to me that she is portrayed in a positive light in this story. Make it clear that this is not some arrangement for publicity or to enhance her career. This is something unexpected that happened and we really are only focused on growing our relationship. I hope we can have everyone's support."

This reporter is digging deep into everything, trying to find the drama. But I am going to stand up for Cailin like she deserves. Next, the reporter asks me why Cailin is the one who got me to 'settle down again' instead of going back to my womanizing ways.

"I love how she doesn't let life knock her down," I say. "She's fierce in pursuit of her dreams and has goals. She doesn't care about being in the spotlight, but she doesn't mind that my life is in the public eye. She appreciates the little things in life. And she sees me beyond my career. But most importantly, I don't want to spend a day without her now that I have her in my life."

My mind drifts to all the things I love about this woman. I savor the moment each time she snuggles up against me. I love the way she still blushes when she gets nervous. Heck, I think it's cute that I still make her a little nervous. I notice how she bites her lip when she's deep in thought. And how her nail polish is perfectly painted or completely removed, but never chipped. I adore her at night when she gets changed and takes out her contacts. She has a new sexiness to her when she wears her wide-framed black glasses. I love how she leans against me and reads a book while I strum the guitar. But I keep that to myself.

CAILIN

Jax wanted me to stay with him while he did the interview, but I wanted to give him his privacy. The last thing he needs is to feel that because I'm his publicist and his girlfriend, that I'll always be lingering around during interviews. He needs to know that I trust him and I'm not going to micro-manage his interviews. Besides, I've been wanting to check in with Hayley and also have to tell her that she can have our hotel room to herself.

"You're the best," Hayley says. "I can totally use a bath to just sit and think about my life. I miss baths."

"I thought you might like the time with Jayce, too."

"It will be good to have some alone time with him, I agree." Hayley's mood has shifted since we first met. There is definitely trouble in paradise. I don't like seeing my friend so bummed. I need to think of something to cheer her up.

"How about tonight we all do dinner? Definitely the four of us, and anyone else who wants to tag along is welcome. I'm sure Jax won't mind. He just has an interview to do."

Her frown turns upwards. "That could be fun. I'll check to see what's around here. Let me know what time Jax can be ready."

"Perfect," I tell Hayley before I let her go enjoy her bath.

While I have some time to myself, I decide to call my mom and Gemma and update them on what's going on. Gemma is over the moon jealous. My mom is happy for me, but also being cautious because she's afraid my heart might get broken. However, that is not going to stop her from bragging to all her friends, and she asked when the magazine cover with Jax will hit newsstands so she can make sure she's first to get one.

As I tiptoe back into the room, Jax is just finishing up the interview. He doesn't hear me come in and I don't want to interrupt, so I stand quietly by the door and listen to his response. And I'd be lying if I said I didn't want to secretly listen to what he's saying about me.

When Jax said he doesn't want to spend a day without me, my heart almost bursts like a confetti cannon. That statement is basically more romantic than the vows Collin said to me during our wedding. Not that I constantly compare the relationship. But how can I not acknowledge that this right here is what love is supposed to be like? And I'm so happy I was brave enough to end my marriage, even though I was comfortable in it, because I opened myself up to this relationship. I could be missing all this if I stayed married. I would be home right now, eating dinner with Collin while he ignored me and scrolled on his cell phone. Instead, I'm on tour, at a hotel, listening to a man who is crazy about me confess his feelings without caring about opinions. Jax wraps up his interview and I move to join him sitting on the bed.

"What you said about me was really sweet. How did the rest of the interview go?"

"I didn't hear you come in." Jax puts his arm around me. "The reporter was tough. She dug deep trying to get a scoop, but there's no dirt. Just the truth."

Now, we just have to hope the truth makes the headlines, I think, as we leave the hotel and head to the venue.

After soundcheck, Hayley, Jayce, Harry, Chris, and some other crew members join Jax and I at a local hot-spot for dinner. I can see why the community loves this place. Generational photos of the owner's family line the walls. The menu boasts family recipes. Everyone on staff is welcoming and it's evident they all take pride in their jobs.

As predicted, all heads turn as we enter. I can feel everyone's eyes, especially on me. In a few days, once the cover story hits newsstands, the mystery will be revealed to curious onlookers. I try to act like I'm used to being part of a pop entourage.

Hayley sits on a plush chair to my left and Jax to my right. I learn Jax is a sucker for a good special and orders a sample of every dish from the calamari to the truffle pasta. I'm a sucker for him.

The guys are in a total boy zone—involved in their own conversation about the latest social media memes and comedy shows on TV—but Jax keeps his hand on my thigh, stroking my leg as he speaks.

"How was your bath?" I ask Hayley.

"Glorious. I got to thinking about a lot."

We speak low so no one can hear us. "What did you discover?" Jax rubs his hand further up my leg, but I try to stay focused on my conversation.

"I need to give Jayce an ultimatum. He needs to grow up a bit or I'm out."

"I think it's definitely worth having a conversation with him about how you're feeling. If there's one thing I have learned from following the posts in my divorce support group, it's that a relationship can't last without honest communication." I gently tap Jax's hand and lead it back down my leg.

I also want to encourage Hayley to pursue her goals. "What about your dreams? Did you think about what you want to do with your career?"

"A little. I think this is going to be my last tour as a merch girl. I need to take some time, go back home, and see where it leads me." Hayley wipes the condensation off her glass with her thumb, circling it repeatedly in a nervous motion.

"So that will impact Jayce, too. Do you live together?"

"We split time between my house and his. He's in Florida, so it's nicer for us to be there in the winter."

"It sounds like you two have a lot to talk about. Why don't you try to get some alone time tomorrow when we make our next stop? Maybe a nice lunch or something?"

"That's a really good idea. I need to peel him away from the guys. And the beer." Hayley darts her eyes in Jayce's direction.

Someone is clinking a spoon to a glass to get everyone's attention. Harry stands up and says, "I'd like to make a toast since this is our first official tour family dinner. To Jax, and his new album, and this dedicated crew. We couldn't do it all without you."

Everyone cheers and raises their glass. I hold up a glass of sparkling water and Jax notices I'm not drinking. Time for me to make another big reveal.

I lean towards his ear and tell Jax, "I actually don't drink." This could be the moment he decides I'm too much of a good girl. Usually, I just find it annoying when I meet new people and have to explain or justify that I don't drink. No one makes a big deal if you don't smoke or do drugs. It's just expected that everyone drinks alcohol. I've always been the outcast holding on strong to my beliefs of maintaining a sober lifestyle and I'm proud of it. But I don't know how important it is for Jax to have a girlfriend who fits in with social norms.

"Somehow, that doesn't surprise me," Jax says. "Another refreshing thing about you."

Wow. It's so nice not to have a guy pressure me to drink. Or ask if I want just a sip from his glass. Jax just respects me and my decisions.

I hope that Hayley can get that same support from Jayce. As our appetizers come out, I notice them sharing food off each other's plates. There's definite chemistry. But I hope she doesn't have to learn the hard way that chemistry isn't enough to sustain a relationship.

Harry takes out his cell phone and snaps a few photos of the group as we're all laughing. I want to freeze this moment in time, but I also can't wait to see what the future will bring. First though, we need to get through tonight's show and the photo-shoot. Because as soon as those headlines come, I am pretty sure that my privacy will be a thing of the past.

Trash the Dress Online Chat

Cailin: Everything is about to change. Eeek!
Alexandra: Living vicariously through you!

34

JAX SLATER CONFIRMS HE'S 'UNAPOLOGETICALLY IN LOVE' WITH HIS PUBLICIST

CAILIN

THE NEXT FEW shows come and go in a beat. One of my favorite memories so far is the night I wore my yellow sundress and Jax walked off the stage, guitar in hand, and softly kissed my forehead. He stayed that way, with his arms around me, even though he had people waiting for his attention. He made sure I felt important. And I could not help the silly grin on my face as I soaked in the moment. Even thinking about it now makes me smile, as I rest in my favorite nook on the bus.

Thankfully, tour is moving along well. Jax and I spend an equal amount of time between the sheets as we do out exploring the sights. When he's in soundcheck, Hayley and I have some girl time. We've been getting really close. She's like my Gemma of the road, always there with advice, and I feel like I can tell her anything on my mind. Things seem to be getting better for her and Jayce too, after they had a big sit down.

I scroll my phone to catch up on social media. I've been making time to talk to the girls in my Trash the Dress support group, too. I've been getting close with a few of them. Recently, a member, Cora, had to flee an unhealthy situation, and a bunch of the girls chipped in to get her a hotel room for a few days. This is such an amazing community of women helping complete strangers on the internet. I'm really grateful to be a part of it. It makes me want to do more to help women. I'm not sure what, but it's something I'm thinking about as a future goal.

Today is a big day. The cover story on Jax comes out. We're going to go into town to pick up some copies, but I know it's going to run online first. So I keep refreshing the browser on my laptop and checking my emails, hoping for a link from the reporter or an alert that it's been published online.

"Finally! Jax, the story is posted online. Come see, hurry."

I click on the link as Jax runs over. It's the homepage feature. The headline reads **"Jax Slater Confirms He's 'Unapologetically in Love' with His Publicist."** There's a photo of him from the shoot he did under the headline. I'm in awe. First, Jax is so handsome I can't stop staring. On top of that, I landed this cover story. It's my first big accomplishment as a music publicist, and it just so happens to be national news about my boyfriend.

"Oh my gosh." This is really happening. I pinch myself.

"Scroll so we can see what the rest of the article says." Jax is so adorable. I know he's trying to play it cool, but he can't fool me.

We read the article and are ultimately happy with the piece. They of course did some digging on my Instagram and published old photos of mine. And yes, the lipstick photo from the first night of tour is one of them. This is it. My face is everywhere. I should just turn off my phone now.

"There's no going back." My words are meant to tease him, but my eyes are telling him I'm in this for the long haul and I hope he is too.

"The only place I'm going with you is forward. And maybe to bed. Do we have time for…"

I cut him off. "No way. We are going out to buy this on the newsstand. Go grab your sunglasses." I stand up, ready to bolt.

"As if that is going to hide my identity." Jax rolls his eyes at me.

"Ok, we can send Harry." I say.

"Let's definitely send Harry," Jax says. "I have other plans for us to celebrate."

* * *

JAX

After Cailin and I had our own cover story celebration, we go into town. I know we sent Harry to get copies of the magazine, but I want to see them for myself on the newsstand, too. It makes it all real.

One part of me feels that the news might be so fresh that no one will bother us yet if we're out in public together. That part of me, as I find out, was indeed wrong. Cailin and I walk down the street and I notice passersby stop to watch us and then whip out their cell phones to take photos of us.

"So, it begins," I say.

"I'll consider it practice for the paparazzi," she tells me. Even though we're both shielded behind our pairs of black sunglasses, I can tell her eyes are wide open and aware of every-thing. I hope it doesn't start to make her uncomfortable.

Cailin must sense my worry because the next thing she asks me is, "How is your anxiety?"

I simply squeeze her hand three times. I originally started this secret handshake of sorts to tell her "I love you." But it's evolved into a secret language we've seemed to have developed for when we're out in public. We let each other know that we got this, we're here for each other, and that no matter where we are, it's all about the two of us. My three squeezes let her know

I'm fine. And this time, I believe it. I haven't even needed to use affirmations in a while.

We get to the convenience store and head straight for the magazine aisle. There it is, my reflection looking back at me. The publication chose a cover photo of me taken backstage. They set up background and some lighting and at the time, I doubted how the photo was going to come out. But the closer I look at the photo, the more I approve.

The last time I was on a magazine cover, I was standing next to Maxine on a red carpet. Before that, I was with my band-mates. I've never had a solo feature on a cover. I don't count the tabloids that blew up a photo of my face and ran a front cover blurb like **"Is Jax Slater Addicted to Women?"** This cover is me, raw and real. No makeup artist. No clothes chosen by a stylist. No fake smiles. I'm actually not even smiling. I look rather serious and that sets the tone for the story.

Cailin naturally snaps a photo of the magazine on the newsstand because she is now in publicist mode. She transitions between Cailin my girlfriend and Cailin my publicist rather easily. But I can tell when she's in work mode and when she's in play mode. I'm getting better at reading her cues. I know that as much as I want to take advantage of alone time on the bus with her, that she still has a job to do. And I think the space we give each other is appreciated on both ends.

I just hope that she's not going to need more space as the media starts to laser focus on her, because that is inevitable. Even with this feature story, the tabloids are going to dig into her past and maybe bring up things she won't be happy to have public. As we head back to the buses, I remind myself that Cailin is strong enough to take it and I hope she proves me right.

CAILIN

As expected, my phone is blowing up. Girls I haven't talked to in a year, and people who never even reached out to see if I'm okay since my divorce, are among my incoming texts. It's interesting to see how some people only care about you when they think it's cool to be associated with you.

I do make a post to my Trash the Dress girls because I want them to hear it from me. Everyone is genuinely happy and excited. A few of them even ask me if I can introduce them to Oliver since he is the remaining single 5 Leo Hearts member. I keep that in the back of my mind.

My mom texts me a photo of her in the grocery store holding the magazine. I'm embarrassed for her. Gosh, I hope the tabloids never approach her for gossip because she will be the first to spill the beans.

Jax did a post about the article and I'm eager to read the comments. Again, most people are really happy for him. And some are disappointed. For instance:

"Team #MaxineandJax." Okay, I didn't even know that was a thing, but now I cringe thinking about it. I wonder what Maxine thinks.

"This gives me hope that real girls can find love with their dream guys."

"Totally loving the #popstarandpublicist." Oh, look at that one, maybe we will have a trendy couple hashtag now.

I want to make a post. It will be my first public post with Jax, announcing myself as his girlfriend. So far, I've only been posting photos of the places we're exploring, pics with Hayley and the crew, and Jax performing. Now, I can actually post a photo with Jax. Part of me wants to keep my photos private. But another part of me is really excited to share this news.

I choose a selfie of us on the bus together. We took it one night when we had an action movie marathon, per Jax's request and my compromise, and snacked on the sweet and salty mixes we discussed on our first text chain. I'm not dressed up or in makeup. This is authentic, and that's what I want to hone in on

—the fact that we're just like every other couple and our relationship is real. I post the photo with simply a heart emoji caption and tag Jax.

As I'm finishing up, Jax comes back onto the bus. He popped out to catch up with Harry when we got back from the store. It's time for us to drive to the hotel and get ready for another show. We have plans tonight to all go out as a crew to a club in town. This is totally not my thing, but everyone is pretty excited about a DJ that's spinning.

"I just thought of something I don't know about you," Jax tells me, giving me a kiss. "When is your birthday?"

"That's so funny. I didn't think to ask your birthday because I know you're a Leo. And I'm not gonna lie, I have known your birthday is July 25th for years."

Jax laughs at me and I share, "My birthday is March 30th. I'm an Aries and we are a perfect astrological match, in case you were wondering."

"I was not wondering, but now I know you're obsessed with horoscopes. What else do you know about our signs?"

"We're both fire signs, Leos are terrific in bed—this you have proven—and oh, yes, the erogenous zone of the Leo is their spine."

"My spine, eh? I'm not sure about that. Maybe you should test that out."

I pull Jax down to me and start massaging his back.

"Okay, I see what you mean," Jax says, relaxing into my palms.

"Hey, your birthday is coming up soon." I work my hands on his shoulders.

"Soon. After tour ends. I planned it that way." He groans, signaling his pleasure. Turns out he's not the only one with magic hands.

"So how are we going to celebrate?" I kiss his left shoulder blade.

"I actually haven't thought about that. But now I guess I

have a lot to celebrate. Let's go somewhere. I want to take you on a trip."

"That sounds amazing. But I just started my job and I don't know how vacation time works." I sigh as my hands travel down his back.

"Oh right," Jax says. **Newsflash: Jax Slater Adjusts to Life Dating a Civilian.**

"Normal girl," I remind him.

"You are far from ordinary. I wonder what you would be working on after this tour."

I haven't thought about actually having to leave him and go on a tour with another band. Part of me has been purposely blocking the looming timeline from my train of thought.

He notices the pensive look on my face and motions to return the massage. "Hey, if this is your dream job, then we can work around it."

"I don't know if it's my dream job. Working with you is a dream. But I don't think I want to tour with other bands. I don't want to leave you, especially right away. This job, like I said before, just fell into my lap at a time when I needed it."

"You're always talking about manifesting and the universe and fate. Maybe this job was just supposed to lead you to me."

"And now I found you and I can just move on? That would be nice, but I have bills to pay and an apartment I just bought. I need to have a plan, I guess. Not to mention, I just went public as a music publicist. What does that say about me if I quit after the tour?"

"Who cares what they think? Do you know how much criticism I've had to deal with in my life? You just have to do what's best for you. Do what you want and what makes you happy. You can't live your life for others."

"You're right," I say.

"You'll figure it out and I'll support you. Literally, you can quit your job and move in with me. Sell your place."

"I really appreciate that, but I can't rely on you. I need to pave my own way, alongside you."

"What about coming to spend time with me in LA after the tour? You can still work remotely, right?"

"I can." Jax's hands feel so amazing on me that I would agree to just about anything.

"Are you worried about something?"

"No, I just set up my whole apartment and I'm proud that I did it on my own." I thought I would have more time to discover myself as a single woman before I found love again. But I don't mind that I skipped a few steps.

"I can come stay with you." He wraps his arms around me from behind and hugs my back to his chest.

"Jax, you would not survive in small town USA."

"Why not? I wasn't born into luxury. I have humble roots just like you. I actually prefer the simple life."

"Well, for one thing, you're used to living in a palace by the beach and this is a small one bedroom condo. No at-home gym or pool."

"You have a lake, right?"

"Yes, but what happens during the winter months?"

"I'm trying to find solutions for us. I'm sure your local sports gym has a pool. Are you trying to find excuses that this won't work?"

"No, not at all. I'm just worried my world isn't good enough for what you're used to every day." I trail off realizing how silly that sounds. "But I know I'm wrong because all I've learned about you is that you are not the stereotypical pop star. And I think we will have an amazing time wherever we are, together."

"We don't have to solve anything right now," Jax says. He moves next to me and I lean my head on his shoulder. We sit in silence for the remainder of the ride.

Trash the Dress Online Chat

Cailin: So, I have a boyfriend...
Alexandra: This is the greatest post-divorce comeback ever.

35

COUPLE ELOPES ON JAX SLATER TOUR—
CELL PHONE PICS ARE PROOF

CAILIN

HAYLEY and I push through the crowded club to make our way to the women's restroom. Our crew is hooked up in the VIP area, but we still have to trek to the bathrooms. The floor is sticky from spilled drinks and there's a distinct smell of sweat drifting across the dance floor. I'm pretty sure some guy grazed my backside on purpose as I walk past him and his friend, even though he apologizes over the roar of the music.

"I don't actually have to pee," Hayley says.

"You mean I just walked all this way in heels for nothing?" What form of unnecessary torture is this?

She holds up her hand, and a glistening gem glares back at me. I grab it.

"What is this? Are you engaged?"

"Jayce asked me earlier today. We want to keep it on the DL because, well, this moment is about you and Jax. But I had to tell you."

I give her a hug. "This is incredible! I'm so happy for you. Does this mean you guys worked everything out? How did he pop the question?" I am very aware that I sound like Gemma right now.

"We went out to lunch, like you suggested, and we had a serious conversation. I told him things weren't working for me and I needed him to shape up or ship out. He told me he doesn't want to lose me. I thought that was it."

"And then?"

"We finished our lunch and I felt like we found some solid ground. Honestly, I would be happy with that. But on our way back to the bus, we passed a ring shop and Jayce pulled me inside and told me to pick one. I couldn't believe it. But it showed me he was serious about everything we talked about and he said there was no time like the present to prove his intentions. We even applied and picked up a marriage license in town."

"To say I'm surprised is an understatement. I am so happy for you." I grab her hand and get a closer look at the round sapphire on her ring finger. Leave it to Hayley to choose a ring that goes against tradition. "Honestly, I want you to bask in this moment. Don't keep it a secret."

"Are you sure? I don't mind waiting to share the news with everyone, really."

"Of course I'm sure. Unless you're still feeling this out. Are you? Not sure?"

Hayley sighs and says, "No, this is a good thing. I want it. It's time that we get married."

"Hayley, as a card-carrying member of young, divorced women of the world, I want to make sure you aren't settling. You can't marry someone hoping they will change. You can't have any doubt. You have to be aligned with your goals."

"I know, I know. I'm just tired of being in a stagnant place in my life. I want to move forward with something." A group of women enter the restroom and we motion past them out the door.

"I support your decision," I tell her as we make our way

back to the guys. "But I'm also here if you change your mind or need to talk it through."

We walk through a foggy mist that's covering the dance floor. Pushing past all the moving bodies, we finally make our way back to the VIP area. To my slight annoyance, we find waitresses all over the guys. One is trying very hard to flirt with Jax. I clear my throat. Apparently, she didn't get the memo he's taken. But she will now.

"Hi, babe," I say. I kiss his lips and take my rightful throne, on his lap. That move makes me feel like a lioness. Like I've come into my power. The wait staff retreat to their corners like prey running scared.

"Look at you, getting jealous," Jax says.

"I'm not jealous. Just claiming what's mine. Speaking of which, Hayley and Jayce have some news to share." I direct our attention to my friend.

"We're engaged!" Hayley's gem catches the spotlights above and emits a rainbow around our group.

"No way, dude. Congrats," Jax says. The guys all high-five and congratulate Hayley and Jayce.

"When's the wedding?" Chris asks. He's that guy—the one who asks the awkward questions that no one wants to answer and is totally oblivious about his behavior.

"Give me a year or two to pawn off planning to my sister," Hayley says.

"Not a fan of wedding planning, I take it?" I personally loved planning my wedding. Every detail from the seating cards to the bridal party gifts. It's sad that those pictures can never see the light of day again.

"No way," Hayley says. "Can you even picture me in a white dress? Can a bride get married in black?"

"This is my future wife," Jayce says. He shakes his head, but it's clear he adores Hayley because she's not like everyone else.

"Why don't you guys just skip the wedding?" Chris says.

"Like elope?" Hayley's eyes open wide at the idea.

"Heck, I'd marry her right now to prove to her I'm devoted," Jayce says.

"I can make that happen," Chris says. "I'm ordained. Married my brother and his wife a few years ago. Internet approved marriage officiant right here." He points to himself with both thumbs.

"Get out," Jax says. "I can't picture you studying and passing a test."

"Just offering up my services. Take 'em or leave 'em."

Hayley and Jayce look at each other as if they are seriously considering the offer. I wish I could pull her aside to share some words of wisdom. She was just talking about her uncertainty towards getting engaged a few minutes ago. She can't rush into a marriage. It would be a mistake. But instead, I shoot her a supportive glance, letting her know I am there for her no matter what. Sometimes, we need to make our own mistakes. It's the only way to move forward to where we belong.

"I mean, I'll do it if you want to." Jayce looks to Hayley for the final decision.

Hayley twists the ring on her finger, contemplating this major life decision for a total of five seconds. "Let's do it."

I look at Jax, who knows nothing about what's really going on, and is thoroughly enjoying the spectacle happening before him. Hayley's going to get married wearing a black T-shirt that says Fearless, and ripped black jeans. How romantic. At least Jayce's all black outfit completes the color scheme.

"We don't have rings." I point it out to buy Hayley some time. She doesn't pick up what I'm throwing down.

"We don't need them," Hayley says. "We can get matching tattoos tomorrow. I'll check the reviews of the best artists in the area."

"Oh, great idea," I mutter under my breath. "At least let me give you something borrowed." I take my ivory knotted hairband off and place it on her head.

"Thank you, it's perfect."

"Okay, gather round," Chris says. The live DJ finally paused for a break. "No need to drag things out. Jayce, you love Hayley. Do you want her to be your wife?"

Jayce and Hayley stand across from each other, holding hands. Jayce drops his hand to take a swig of beer and then promptly brings his hand back together with Hayley's. He doesn't notice her roll her eyes. "Yeah, I do," Jayce says.

"Hayley, do you take Jayce to be your husband?"

Hayley pauses for a second and looks at me, before saying, "Yes, I do."

"Then I now pronounce you husband and wife. We'll fill out the paperwork tomorrow morning. You can make out while we watch." Chris takes a bow.

Jayce and Hayley seal the deal while everyone claps. Jax pulls me in for a kiss. This wedding may not be my version of perfect, but it does seem pretty perfect for Hayley and Jayce. If she's gonna walk on sunshine from now on, then that's all that matters. I grab my phone and snap a few photos for the newly-weds. No matter how this turns out, the event deserves to be documented.

Jayce and Hayley head off to the bar and the rest of the crew disperse across the dance floor, presumably looking to fish for their hookups for the night.

"You want to get out of here?" Jax asks me.

"Is it rude to leave a wedding reception before cake?"

"Being that there's no cake, I'd say no." Jax pulls me towards the door. We get outside and breathe in the cool summer night. A crescent moon shines down from the sky, illu-minating a few stars. Jax notices the goosebumps on my shoul-ders and puts his arms around me as we walk down the dimly lit street.

"That was interesting," he says.

"Very rock 'n' roll." I don't want to comment any further because I'm not sure I should mention how I feel about Hayley's choice. I'm not one to judge others. But having recently come out of a divorce and hearing the stories of others in my support group, I want to help a friend who might be getting married for the wrong reason.

"Do you know something I don't know?" Jax is onto me.

"I just hope they aren't rushing into it, that's all. Between you and me, Hayley was having her doubts earlier this week. She gave Jayce an ultimatum and that's when he proposed." I bite my lower lip, not able to hold in my worry.

Adding a guy's perspective, Jax says, "Maybe he needed that wake-up call. That he didn't want to lose the most important thing in his life."

"Maybe. I hope so."

"Sometimes when you know, you just know. And then what's the sense of waiting?"

I get the sense Jax is talking about us. I definitely know how I feel about Jax and that equally thrills and terrifies me. I remind myself that there doesn't have to be drama with every relationship. I can accept something good in my life because that's what I deserve. Hell, I manifested it. And I'm going to enjoy every second.

Jax pulls out his phone and makes a call to Harry, who stayed back tonight to go to dinner with some friends he had in town. "Book a private jet. Cailin and I are gonna fly to the next show."

"What?" I ask in dismay as Jax hangs up the phone.

"I promised to spoil you with surprises. If you can't take off work to go on vacation with me, then we're going to turn our everyday life into adventures."

"I'd say just being on tour is an adventure, but you continue to sweep me off my feet." Once again, I pinch myself to make sure this is real life and not a fairy tale.

"About 35,000 feet. And that's not all I have in store. Just you wait and see."

Trash the Dress Online Chat

Mae: Cailin's dreamy escapades inspired me to reach out to my high school sweetheart. He's recently divorced. Maybe we have a second chance at romance?

Cailin: I love this! Yes! Keep us updated.

36

JAX SLATER AND CAILIN MCCALL TAKE OFF AND HIT TURBULENCE

CAILIN

"OK, this is definitely the best flight of my life," I say to Jax.

Besides the fact that we're flying on a private plane with couches and a TV, we're being waited on hand and foot by attendants who also offered to give us couples massages. The massage oil seeps into my skin and the scent of lavender fills the plane. Jax is enjoying his massage so much he just mumbles a reply. It's been way too long since I've treated myself to any spa-like luxuries. Actually, it's probably been since my wedding years ago. I was always too consumed with work to focus on this level of self-care. That's what happens when you're working hard to support two people. Jax is showing me how to slow down and indulge, and it's something that I'm not going to resist.

After our massages, we cuddle next to each other and snack on a platter of cheese, crackers, strawberries, and nuts. Touring on a bus was fun, but honestly, I could get used to this.

"Where do you want to go next?" Jax asks. He grabs a slice of strawberry and feeds it to me.

"Any tropical island will suffice," I say.

"I'm serious though. I know you want to see how things play out with your job, but let's assume we figure that out and you're free to travel. I want to take you somewhere romantic, where it's just us and we don't have to think about interviews or hiding from paparazzi."

"Is there anywhere you haven't been on all your travels?" I can't decide between eating cheddar or asiago cheese right now and he's asking me about islands.

"I have one place in mind. I was always saving it for something really special, like a honeymoon or something."

"Oh... like with Maxine?" I don't know why I said that out loud, but it's what I was thinking.

"Okay, Ms. 'I was married before.'" He's right. Sometimes I can be insecure, especially with this man who seems too good to be true.

"I just want to go someplace that you imagine for me and you only."

"One day, I'm going to tell you to just pack your bags and surprise you. You'll see."

"I look forward to all of your surprises, Jax."

"I'll surprise you every day if you live with me." There he goes again, saying something that seems unreal.

"Move in with you? With all my stuff?" I nervously shove the cheddar in my mouth.

"I've been thinking a lot about our options. I can sell my place and we can start fresh wherever we want. I know you don't need or want my financial support, but I can and will cover everything until you figure out what you want to do next. At least consider it."

"Hmm, let me think about it? Do I want to move in with my insanely hot, amazing boyfriend who treats me like royalty? I mean, I don't see how I can pass that up." It's a big step, but I want it.

"Is that a 'yes'?"

"That's 'yes', for sure." I can't hide my smile.

Jax pumps his fists in the air, victorious yet again. "Yes! I am slowly breaking you down."

"The question is, though, where would we live?" I don't know why I can't let myself enjoy the moment without thinking of potential problems. I'm used to being in crisis mode now.

"That would be the million-dollar question. But while we figure it out, maybe we can do a tour of our own. You can spend a few weeks in LA with me, and I can check out where you're from."

I cut in, "Meet my family and friends."

"And we can even go back to Florida. I'd love to show you where I grew up. Man, I haven't been there since I was a kid."

"You never took anyone, I mean, like Maxine, back there? Sorry to keep bringing her up. Just curious. Since you were with her for so long."

"Never. I don't think she would even have been interested, now looking back. There would be no cameras following us around to show for it, so it wouldn't have been worth it for her. And I never thought of it, to be honest. That must mean something, right?"

"She didn't completely have all of you, did she?" I run my fingers through his hair. His locks are getting longer and I love it when it's naturally messy.

"I thought she did, until I met you."

We've both been having revelations about love and relationships. "Not to keep bringing up the past, but I have learned a lot about myself just by being with you and I realized that what I thought was good or right, really wasn't at all."

"This little adventure we'll embark on will be for us to really learn everything about each other. Because I want to know it all, Cailin. And I want you to know me completely. This is real for me."

"This is real for me too."

"What I'm trying to say, is...."

Just then, the flight attendants come in and clear our food.

"Can we get you anything else, Mr. Slater?" the one with the short blonde hair asks.

"No, thank you. Everything was delicious."

"Wonderful," says the other, with bouncing dark curls falling out of her bun. "Then we can move onto the next portion of your flight."

"The next portion?" I am stumped as to what else Jax could have planned for us on this plane ride.

The flight attendant motions for us to take a seat on the couch and she turns on the big screen monitor. "Mr. Slater has selected a movie for you to view."

"Please, no more action flicks," I say.

"Relax," Jax says, pulling a blanket over us. "It's one of your rom-coms. I looked them up online and picked the one that sounded the least cheesy."

Stop the press. **Jax Slater Trades Action Flix For Rom-Com.**

"O-M-G, I am super excited. Which one did you choose? It doesn't matter because I am going to make you watch them all eventually."

"I don't doubt that, and I deserve it after all the movies you sat through for me. Compromise and all that couple stuff, right?"

"Okay, enough talking. Press play."

As the opening credits come across the screen, I realize Jax picked my favorite movie. It's set in England and ironically features a washed-up pop star.

Being with Jax makes me feel even higher than the 35,000 feet we're flying in the sky. Everything is perfect. I rest my head on Jax's shoulder and wrap my arms around his stomach. The plane is hitting a little bit of turbulence, but I know together, we're set for a smooth ride. Or, at least I hope we are.

Trash the Dress Online Chat

Tori: Would you rather your ex be the last man you ever kiss or kiss a literal fish?

Harper: Literally the same feeling, so...

37

CRASH LANDING FOR CAILIN MCCALL AND JAX SLATER

CAILIN

As soon as the plane lands, Jax and I turn on our phones. As much as we want to disconnect, we still need to be available to the world right now. We have to head to the hotel to shower, then get back on the bus to the venue for soundcheck. Somewhere along the line, I need to respond to my work emails. It's important that I show I'm not checked out now that I'm dating Jax. I need to prove that I can manage being his girlfriend and publicist.

We're still on the plane waiting for the okay to exit as my phone loads. My cell is blowing up with notifications. It was only on airplane mode a few hours. Yikes. I realize my phone is not the only one sounding like it's going haywire. Jax's phone is also blowing up. Something happened. I don't have any clue what could be going on, but I'm suddenly anxious. We look at each other and then at our phones. After what seems like an eternity, my text messages load. I scan them before I click on any message.

Gemma: WTF is going on?

Hayley: Are you OK? Are you still on tour?

Mom: Honey, come home. I'll get you at the airport.

Imani: I'm investigating this, don't worry.

Marisol: I'll take you off the account.
Call me.

"Jax, something is going on." My hands are shaking and my entire body goes weak. These messages don't foreshadow good news. My mom, my boss, and my friends all know something and I'm in the dark.

"Shit." Jax throws down his phone.

I pull up the message from Gemma and click the link. It leads me to an online tabloid site. The headline: **Woman Reveals "I'm Pregnant With Jax Slater's Baby."**

I feel like I've been hit by a semi-truck. My brain can't even comprehend that sentence. "I'm Pregnant with Jax Slater's Baby." I read it five times before I scroll down to read the article. Apparently, some woman is claiming she was dating Jax before tour started and is pregnant with his love child.

Jax never mentioned dating anyone before tour started. We had all these conversations, about our past, dating, and honesty. He outright lied to me. I should have known better, but I thought he had changed. So much for clearing up his bad boy reputation. I break down in tears and look at Jax who is sitting with his face in his hands.

"None of this was real to you, was it? I was just another fling. I bet you have been laughing at how gullible I've been, falling for this act."

"Cailin, let me explain."

"There's nothing to explain, Jax. I'm a fool. You played me."

"It's not what you think."

"It's not what I think? Some woman is pregnant with your child. Pretty sure that didn't happen without you."

Jax walks over and tries to reach for me. I push him away. "Don't touch me. Stay away from me. You disgust me!"

"Cailin, I love you. Would you please just calm down and listen to me?"

"I'm done listening to all the bull you're going to feed me. I'm done. I'm leaving." I don't even grab my suitcase. I leave everything behind. I don't want reminders of anything to do with this tour. I just need air. I need to get out of here, away from Jax. Away from the scene that shattered my heart. I run down the parking lot of the private airport and straight into the town. Jax calls after me and starts to follow, but I have enough of a head start that I lose him.

My head is pounding, my heart is aching, and I'm out of breath. I collapse onto a bench about ten minutes later. I'm near a café. Thank you, my guardian angels. I walk inside to rest and call a car service. I need to get to the nearest commercial airport to fly back to New Jersey. Never before have I ever been so grateful for my fanny pack. I didn't even think to make sure I had my wallet before I ran out, but it was with me the whole time. At least I can rely on fashion to remain loyal.

A server approaches me a minute after I slump into a two-seater table. "Can I get you anything?"

"N-no. Not right now, thank you."

"Are you okay, ma'am?" I don't like how she's looking at me closely with doubt.

"Yes, thank you. I ran here, gotta get in my daily steps, that's all. I'm chill. Like iced tea."

"Are you sure you wouldn't like me to call someone for you?" She is clearly not buying my lines.

"Already did." I check my phone. Where is that driver? I need to get out of here before Jax starts a search party. I realize I must look in shambles. I open up the camera app and put it in selfie mode to check my appearance. No wonder why the server is asking if I am all right. I've been betrayed by black mascara stains, revealing the path of my tears. My cheeks are bright red and my eyes are still flooding over, further spilling dark puddles.

I go into the bathroom and splash cold water on my face. The water is freezing, yet I feel no pain. Nothing can feel worse than the pit of my heart right now, which is numb. I was blindsided and now I am broken.

Every day, I loved Jax more and more. I risked my job, my career, and even my privacy. I thought I'll be loving him forever. I am so disappointed in myself for being so foolish. I never grew up from the teenage girl who dreamed of marrying her favorite boy band member. I got caught up in a fantasy that was never going to last. I believed I had his heart. He was too romantic, too perfect, too forward from the start. I was blinded by my infatuation, looking through foggy rose-colored glasses and ignoring the warning signs. I thought my tragic trait was ignoring red flags, but maybe I trust too easily. Or it's that I believe in love.

I always viewed myself as a strong woman. Heck, I left a marriage that was not serving me. But I strayed from the post-divorce goals I set for myself. I took a job that was beneath me when maybe I should have waited for another Vice President level position. I let my crush on a stranger in a poster dictate my next move.

And now, I'll be the subject of countless media headlines. I bet they already started. I can picture them: **Is Jax Slater Still Dating Cailin McCall?**, **Baby Breakup: Jax And Cailin** **McCall It Quits**, and **Jax Slater Proposes To Baby Mama.** Those are just the first that come to mind.

The thought of Jax moving on with another woman makes me sick. If he's the standup guy I think he is, he will want to be present in his child's life. He'll be a great dad. A great husband, even if he doesn't love her. He will ensure she wants for nothing.

Meanwhile, I'm here breathing in the remnants of his scent on my sweatshirt. Thinking of the sound of his kisses. The way his eyes squeeze together when he laughs. How he made me feel protected after the accident and encourages my career. How his fingers twirled my hair. The way he loved me. Or I thought he did.

Another famous boy band's song creeps into my mind as I move outside to wait for the rideshare. It's about being hit by the truth and subliminally tells me that I am doing the right thing by leaving and saying bye-bye. The music video for that song features the band members as marionette puppets. I wonder if I was just a puppet in Jax's game to clear up his reputation. He was pulling my strings all along and I didn't realize.

I replay the same thought in my head—it was all a lie. One beautiful lie. Does he just throw out *I love you's* to everyone he dates? Flirt with everyone to sleep with them? Gosh, Harry must have thought I'm such a naïve girl. Just another one of Jax's conquests, but at least I was the one who got a paycheck. And Hayley. Why didn't she warn me? I thought we were close.

Finally, the car service arrives. I open the back door and dash inside. "To the airport, please. As fast as you can," I direct the driver as I buckle my seat belt.

While the driver sets off, I pull up the nearest airport on my phone. I wish the location Jax's jet landed had outgoing flights for the public. On my phone's browser, I search airlines and book the first flight back home. It leaves in two hours. That should give me just enough time to arrive and go through security. Of course, I have no luggage so that helps.

I remember that I left my laptop on the plane with all my stuff. Great. I'll ask Marisol to coordinate with Harry and have all my personal items sent back to my place. It's not like I'll need my computer for work anymore. I'm done with Jax Slater. I'll look for a new job once my laptop arrives.

I reply to Marisol's text and fill her in and she says she'll get my belongings shipped back ASAP. I tell her we'll touch base later, after I'm done traveling. Then, I text my mom to tell her I'm coming home. I know she'll want me to go stay at her house. She'll have an uplifting speech ready about how you can never trust men. Then she'll worry about what to tell all her friends.

As for my own friends, I reply to Imani with a few emojis and signal I'll talk to her when I'm ready. I ask Gemma to meet me at my apartment later today. If anyone will understand the depths of my pain, it's Gemma.

My phone starts to ring and I wonder who else could possibly have the guts to reach out to me right now.

It's Jax.

I reject the call and block his number.

Trash the Dress Online Chat

Lizzie: I decided I could have worked my butt off to make my marriage work but in the end, marriage is two-sided and I didn't fail at anything.

Alexandra: Yes!

38

CAILIN

Jax is looking at me with a strong stance. He's confident in his action and doesn't even blink when I brush past him over to the cashier to pay for my water. Of course, he can't blink because the Jax Slater in front of me is just an image on the cover of a magazine at the gift shop. Turns out I can't get Jax out of my head, or my line of sight. I make a face at the magazine and the cashier asks, "Do I know you from somewhere? You look so familiar."

"I get that a lot. Must have one of those faces." I collect my change and quickly put on my sunglasses even though I'm indoors. If people start to recognize me, this could be very bad. None of my training in crisis communications covered how to hide in the airport when you've become a public figure overnight. The last thing I need is strangers snapping photos of me and selling them to the tabloids so they can report **Heartbroken Cailin McCall Spotted Solo At Airport**.

I board the plane and take my economy seat, a world away from the luxury accommodations I enjoyed earlier today. My seat is near the back of the plane and I'm squished between a plump man in a business suit and an elderly lady. The man, thankfully, puts headphones on and watches a movie on the screen in front of him, and the woman is knitting a potholder. I'm grateful I don't have to make small talk. However, my mind is immediately transported back to the jet with Jax, when I was cuddled on his lap watching a romance bloom on screen. Real love, I conclude, only exists in the movies.

I sink into my seat, grateful that I'm not sitting next to the gabby woman across the aisle. She's been talking to her friend about everything from her dry skin to orthopedic foot inserts. The woman takes a stack of magazines out of her carry-on bag and just when I think the rest of the passengers and I will be spared any more stories, she starts talking about celebrities. I lean over to get a closer look at what she's reading, only to discover it's a weekly gossip rag.

"Did you hear that Jax Slater knocked up some fan?" she says to her friend. "That poor girl he was dating. I really feel bad for her. I had a feeling he didn't change. Everyone made a big deal about him finding love, but once a player, always a player."

"I've been following that story," her friend says. "Such a shame. These celebrities are all messed up. And with his past, who knows how many secret kids he's fathered."

I make all efforts to shield myself from their view, but I can't hide from my hurt feelings. This is just one conversation of millions, I'm sure, where people are dissecting my relationship with Jax. I can't blame them for the small talk. Celebrity drama can be entertaining and I've been guilty of doing the same, but now this is my life. I can't just turn the page on this story.

This is going to be a very uncomfortable flight. I close my eyes and try to sleep for the next few hours, but I'm in a nightmare whether I'm awake or not. I wonder what Jax is doing. Did he call his baby mama? Is he happy? Does he know the shape of my heart is forever changed? Or is he more worried about how the guest list for tonight's show is being handled?

Maybe he's smart enough to check my laptop. After all, he's

sharp enough to devise a plan to seduce me while he has a secret baby mama. However, I will give him credit for one thing. He probably didn't know. Otherwise it wouldn't make sense as to why he publicly declared his love for me.

I stumble off the plane and find my mom and Gemma waiting for me. They group hug me and I unleash the floodgates. Words can't relay how I feel.

"He's a jerk, honey," mom says, just as I expected.

"To heck with pop stars," Gemma says.

"I just want to go home," I say. I pull away and begin to walk away from the terminal.

"Wait, don't we need to go get your bags?" mom asks.

"I left them." But I'm carrying a lot of baggage.

"You left your clothes?" Gemma is gasping, thinking of all the clothes from her store rotting away in my suitcase. "The pajamas made from imported silk?"

"Don't worry, Gemma. Marisol will get my stuff shipped back to me. I don't even have my laptop."

"Well, what does Jax have to say about this mess?" My mom is outraged.

"He didn't say anything. He said he wanted to explain. But I didn't want to hear it. I'm done. I ran off the plane, all the way to a café and called a car."

"Wait, you were on a plane?" Gemma needs the rest of the details. "Where did you go?"

"Long story. He took me on a private jet to get to the next show."

"Wow. That's impressive. So, you didn't see the news when it broke?"

"No, we were in the air. Getting a couple's massage and watching my favorite movie like everything was right in the world. I should have known love doesn't come so easy."

"There's something missing," my mom says. "It doesn't make sense that he made all this fuss about you."

"He didn't know he knocked up some chick, I'm sure,"

Gemma says. "I do feel like he had to have some legit feelings for you if he spoke to the media about you, Cailin. Do you want to give him an opportunity to explain?"

"Nope. I've already been played as a silly girl. I'm not going to give him the chance to grovel. It's over. He's having a child with another woman. There's no room for me in that equation."

We get into the car and my mom begins driving home. A 5 Leo Hearts song comes on the radio. Gemma quickly switches the station from the passenger seat. "Those songs certainly all seem like shams now, don't they?"

Everything feels like it was just in my imagination. I knew it was all too good to be true, but I let myself get swept away. Loving Jax was like going to paradise only to find out there's a hurricane.

"We will get through this, honey," Mom says. "Why don't you stay with me tonight?"

"No, thanks Mom. I need to go home and just have some time to myself. But if you can go to the store and get me some food, that would help. I don't want to be seen in public right now."

My mom nods and keeps her eyes on the road.

"I'll bring Stella over tomorrow to check on you too," Gemma says. She opens her window.

"Hey, Gem? Did you read any other headlines?" I might as well face whatever is coming my way. I lean my head near my window and let the breeze take me away.

"I didn't. Do you want me to?"

"No, I've read enough for one day."

Soon enough, I am back inside my apartment. When I first moved in, I stood in this empty room filled with possibility. As soon as I got the offer to go on tour with Jax, I quickly slammed the door on some of my goals. Opting instead, to chase a life-changing opportunity. I wasn't wrong. This trip did change my life. Just not for the better. Now, I'm still divorced, once again jobless, and suffering from a traumatic heartbreak that I didn't even feel during my divorce. Oh, and this time, the whole world knows it. Not just my social media followers. Go me.

JAX

I should have known something like this would happen. It's like I'm not meant to ever escape my past or my reputation. It always comes back to haunt me. When I first read the headline, all I could do was curse my life. Now I'm sitting alone on this plane and have to walk off without Cailin.

I thought hooking up with Kelly's friend would bring me out of my funk. Only, I didn't feel anything special while I was sleeping with her. I felt like garbage because I was once again using a woman to make myself feel better. Someone I knew I wasn't going to keep around. I know I used protection. Granted, condoms are not one hundred percent effective, but I really didn't think this would be something I'd need to worry about. I've never had a situation like this before, so why now?

I haven't even given this girl an afterthought since I ended things. She didn't try to contact me, and I didn't contact her. It was a clean break, or so I thought. But it turns out the break wasn't our relationship.

Now, I'm paying the price. I've lost the love of my life. Cailin won't even give me a chance to explain. I saw the tears in her eyes and my heart sank, knowing I caused that pain. I told her I would never break her heart. I told her I would never do anything to make her cry. I would rather die than to have to think of going through life without her now that I've found her. And look at the pain I caused Cailin.

She fled the plane so quickly she left her suitcase. I tried to run after her, but I couldn't catch up. Part of me wanted to get a car and go chase after her. Start a search party or something.

But I don't want to draw attention to what happened. I need to give her space while I get to the bottom of this. And then I need to get Cailin back.

By the time I get back to the buses, everyone has seen the headline. I have a pretty perceptive crew and they all know how to read my mood. No one is going to mess with me. No one, except Harry, that is.

He knocks on the door of my bus. "Jax, let me in to talk."

I don't answer.

"Okay, I'm coming in," Harry announces before he opens the door.

"I messed up, Harry. I don't even know if it's true. But it could be. And now everything is ruined. Hayley and Jayce's spur of the moment wedding inspired me to do something special for Cailin, so that's why I asked you to get the jet. This whole tour, we've been on buses because I've wanted to keep it real. But the reality is I'm not a backstreet boy next door. I can offer her more than she's had before. I wanted her to enjoy the perks of dating a pop star. It turns out that we got a night to remember, but now it's one I'd rather forget."

Harry, ever the voice of reason says, "Let's take things from the beginning and work with what we have. First of all, the media didn't name the source that came forward."

"No name, but there was a woman. It's only a matter of time before she contacts me."

"And if she comes forward, then we do a DNA test. We can court order one before the baby is born to prove whether or not you're the father."

That gives me a plan, but it doesn't solve the fact that I lost Cailin. "And what happens in the meantime? I can't expect Cailin to sit around waiting for me. She's done with me. You should have seen the way she ran off."

"If she loves you, which I am more than sure she does, she will give you a chance to explain." Harry pats my back. I know he wants to be here for me right now, but I made this mess on my own.

"As long as she loves me, she isn't going to stand by while I have a baby with another woman. I never thought I'd become a dad with a woman I don't love. I guess I deserve this after my reckless past." I'm so angry with myself, I couldn't cry even if I was alone with no witnesses.

"I'll give Marisol a call and see if she spoke to Cailin. Or we can ask Hayley."

"No, don't. The less people involved, the better. I want to request that everyone give Cailin space. No one reaches out to her. The last thing I need is anyone feeding her information from my past or adding to her negative thoughts."

"Ok, I'll send a memo out. We're going to fix this, Jax. We're going to get through it."

"Easy for you to say. Your life isn't falling apart. And you don't have to get up on stage and perform a show tonight. Do you know how I feel? How am I going to get up there and sing love songs after what just happened? Everyone is going to be looking at me and hate me for breaking Cailin's heart. I just went public about how much I love her. I look like such scum now. I'm lucky if people even show up tonight."

"We can't cancel the rest of the tour. We only have a few dates left."

"I'll pull myself together," I tell Harry. "But cancel all the fan events tonight. No interviews either. Oh, and who is going to manage press now? I've not only lost my girlfriend, but also my publicist. My life is officially a mess."

"I'll handle the press," Harry says. "You get yourself together. The show must go on."

Then I remember. I have Cailin's things here. I can write her a note. She's blocking my calls and social media, but she can't block deliveries to her door.

Trash the Dress Online Chat

Sara: I used to think divorce was a terrible word, but now I see it as a new beginning.

Cora: Let's start a national campaign for divorce.

39

CAILIN MCCALL CHECKS "SAVE A LIFE" OFF POST-DIVORCE GOALS

CAILIN

I MISS WAKING up as the little spoon, with Jax's body wrapped around me. I miss the feel of his scruff on my back as he rests against me under the sheets. I yearn to kiss him good morning or feel his touch just one more time. I feel like I lost my center of gravity. Now I'm just floating through the world, aimlessly. I'm torn like Natalie Imbruglia.

Then it hits me. I don't have to go through this alone. Sure, I have my mom and Gemma, who are always there for me. But what I need is someone who is literally always going to be by my side. Someone who will love me unconditionally, no matter what.

I need a dog and now is the perfect time to finally adopt one. The thought of finally getting my dog is enough to launch me out of bed and into the shower. If I hurry, I can make it to the local shelter as soon as they open. I will find the saddest, loneliest dog who has been at the shelter for years and take that dog home with me. Even if this is a senior dog on its final days, I will adopt it and shower it with love for as long as I can, because every creature deserves the comfort of love.

I am so pumped to do this that I get to the shelter in record speed, while obeying all driving laws, of course. Inside, the shelter smells like animals, but everything is oddly quiet. Why aren't all the dogs barking?

"Hello. Can I help you?" asks a shelter volunteer. She is wearing a T-shirt that says, "My Favorite Breed is a Rescue." I need that shirt.

"Yes, hi. I'd like to adopt a dog."

"That's wonderful! Unfortunately for you, but lucky for us, we don't have any dogs at the moment."

"What do you mean, you don't have any dogs?"

"We just had a big adoption event over the weekend and cleared the shelter. We do have some kittens that were just brought in this morning, if you're interested."

I feel so defeated. The universe is laughing at me again. "I don't want a cat," I cry. "I just want a dog. Is that so much to ask? For the heavens to part and give me one thing that will love me?" The stunned volunteer stares at me, unsure of what to say.

"I'm sorry, Miss. There's another shelter about ten miles away."

"What's the address?" Nothing is stopping me from adopting a dog today.

As I pull into a parking space at the next shelter, a variety of howls fill the air. A volunteer is walking a shepherd mix along the side of the building. The dog stops every few seconds to sniff grass. It's a sign from above that I need to slow down and focus on the simple things again. Just like this dog.

"Hi, I'm here to meet some adoptable dogs," I announce as I enter the shelter.

"Hi there," the male volunteer says. He is older, with a salt and pepper mustache and a beer belly. "Any type of dog in particular?"

"I'm open to options, but I live in an apartment, so that will be a factor. Dogs are allowed in the building though, and I own, so I don't need approval from a landlord."

"Okay, that's great. What about your lifestyle? Are you active? That will help me determine which dog here will be a good fit for your pet."

Does doing sit-ups in bed to reach the remote or scooping spoonfuls of ice cream count as active? Because that's how I plan on spending the immediate future.

"I like to go for walks." When I'm not hiding from the world, that is.

"I think you'll love Coco over here."

He leads me past a few cages and all the dogs perk up and run to the front of their crates to compete for my attention. I stop to give each of them some love and manifest that they all get homes soon.

Coco, a black hound mix about thirty-five pounds, is sitting politely behind the bars of her cage. Her tail slowly thumps behind her as her big, droopy ears perk forward.

"Hi, Coco," I say. "Can I pet her?"

The volunteer, whose name I learn is Stuart, opens the gate to her kennel. Coco is reserved and curious as she walks over to sniff me. I hold out my hand for her to get my scent. Once I earn her approval, Coco licks my hand and begins wagging her tail. She rubs her body against my thighs, as I kneel down next to her.

"I'll take her." She's perfect.

"Do you hear that, Coco?" Stuart shouts with joy. "You got a home!"

"What's her story?" I know black dogs are one of the least adoptable ones at shelters. It's referred to as Black Dog Syndrome. There are theories where people feel that black dogs are more aggressive than those with light fur. Total bull. Coco and I are going to break stereotypes together. I'll shatter the stereotypes against divorced women and ex-girlfriends of pop stars, and show I can be strong without a man. I'll post photos of Coco around town being a lovebug that I know she will be, and raise awareness for other black dogs in shelters.

"Coco has been here about four months. Picked her up off the street, no collar. Looked like she recently had a litter of puppies. The owners probably used her for breeding and let her loose once she was no longer useful to them anymore. No other way to explain why no one came looking for her."

My heart breaks for Coco and what she must have gone through. "That's horrible."

"Unfortunately, Coco is one of the happier stories of shelter dogs. We have had a lot worse in here. But thanks to people like you, who adopt and donate to shelters, we can help save more lives."

"Happy to do my part. Let's get this girl out of here." I don't need to look at any other dogs. There's no need to look at more options when I know my perfect fit is right here. Funny, that's what I thought about love. Once you know, you know. Now, I feel like I don't know anything.

I sign the paperwork, get a temporary leash, and exit the shelter with hope. Hope for my future, whatever that may look like. Actually, I love the idea of Hope.

"Hey, Coco. How do you feel about being called Hope from now on?" I ask. I pet the top of her head and confirm that I'm already one of those people who talks to her dog.

My first order of business as a new dog owner is to go to the pet store. We need a name tag, collar, leash, bowls, food, treats, poop bags, and of course a cute dog sweatshirt because in a few months it'll be fall. Hope has short hair so I want to keep her warm—and trendy. Who am I kidding?

A dog's first car ride after being adopted is often referred to as a freedom ride. We need to celebrate our new beginning. But unlike my divorce freedom ride from the City to Jersey, I'm not going to sing along to boy band anthems. I'm in the mood to blast some empowering female punk rock. I remember a song Hayley played for me by one female singer, type the name of the song into my phone, and press play. This is what I need for my new start.

When Hope and I return from the pet store, we go for a little walk around my neighborhood and then I take her inside to show her around her new digs. Hope wags her tail as she explores every room. Eventually, she settles on the couch. I sit down next to her and she rests her head on my lap.

"My sweet girl," I say to Hope. "You'll never be alone again." I wish I could say the same about myself. But right now, I feel like I am destined to be single forever.

Trash the Dress Online Chat

Alexandra: Cailin, are you OK?

40

CAILIN MCCALL FINDS OUT WHAT'S IN THE CARDS

CAILIN

HAVING a dog is great because it forces me to be active. Hope loves walking around the lake, and getting out and moving my body is just what I need too. It's our new routine. This morning, I try to find the beauty in the reflection of the trees on the lake, so that's progress. But then I cross paths on my walking trail with the mom of a childhood friend.

"Cailin, hunny, I'm so glad to see you're out and about and not at home crying over that man. He's such a dog."

I simply nod my head, return a weak smile, and tug Hope to keep moving forward. I disagree with her, for one thing. Jax isn't a dog. Dogs are loyal creatures and they never let down the ones they love. I can't say those things about Jax. Despite all of that, I can't help but think about how I wanted to bring Jax here after tour and hold his hand as we walk around the lake. Instead, my hand is stuffed into the pocket of my shorts and I can't stop thinking about what he's doing on tour. I deleted all my social media apps, so I haven't seen if he has posted or made a response. Marisol is thankfully giving me some space and told me to take the next week off to figure things out. And by figure things out, I mean watch soap operas with Hope.

There's a knock on my door. "I know you're in there, Cailin. Open up!" The bangs continue until I reach the door. Gemma is relentless.

"Hey." Hope is right by my side, eager to meet our guests.

"You got a dog already?" Stella is perched on Gemma's hip.

"This is Hope. I'm not sure if she likes kids, but she's very friendly."

Gemma pushes her way through the door and throws down her diaper bag, followed by her purse. She sighs and sits down on the couch, handing Stella a rattle toy. Even frazzled, Gemma is elegant. Impeccable hair and clothes are motherhood-proof on her. "I came to check on you. And it looks like you need it."

Granted, I have takeout bags scattered across my table. But that's only because I haven't walked down to the garbage yet. "I'm showering. Hope and I went for a walk. I'm fine."

"Thank goodness she is giving you a reason to leave your apartment. You can't hide in here forever, Cailin."

"It's not like I have anything else to do. My laptop didn't arrive yet. I can't look for a job."

"Have you checked the news or talked to your boss?"

"No, I don't want to see or hear anything about him. Marisol told me to take some time off to myself."

"Well, I know you don't want to talk about Jax, but I saw an article that says no one has contacted him personally claiming to be pregnant with his child. Sources say her name is Ana, but I haven't seen a photo. Why don't you check your direct messages online? Maybe he tried to reach out to you?"

"Nope, I don't care. I don't want to hear what he's going to say. He's probably releasing those statements to hold off the media." I'm hurt even more now that I know her name is Ana.

"I would probably feel the same way if I was in your position, but I hate seeing you like this. You need closure."

"Jax getting someone pregnant is all the closure I need.

Now, are you here to cheer me up or are we going to talk about Jax all day?"

"You're right. New topic. Do you want to come work at my shop until you figure things out?"

"Thanks, Gemma, I appreciate the offer. But that's too public for me right now. I don't feel like dealing with people."

"Understood. If you change your mind, my offer stands."

"Thanks for being a good friend, Gemma."

Gemma entertains me for a while, but eventually she has to go and put Stella down for her nap. Once I'm alone again, I take out a piece of paper and begin to write. Putting ink to paper helps me process my feelings about Jax and grieve for the career change that stopped before it barely began. I release the disappointment I have with myself for falling into a slump over this breakup. But at the same time, I find grace and try to be gentle on myself. This crushed me. And I don't know how I am going to bounce back just yet, but I know I eventually will. Experience has shown me that as tough as things may seem at the time, I'm strong and will prevail. I will never give up my faith to find love.

I wish I had a glimpse into the future or something to guide me. Maybe my horoscope predicted this. I can read the monthly post for my sign from my favorite astrologer. Or better yet, I can consult a psychic.

That's what I'm going to do—search online for spiritual healers. My soul needs serious care right now. I find someone simply named Ms. A, who has a lot of five-star reviews. Her website notes that she is available for video chats. I pick up the phone and call Ms. A.

"Hello, Ms. A," the voice on the other end greets me.

"Hi there. I was wondering if you can do a reading."

"I'm available right now. Would you like a tarot reading?"

"Yes, please. Do I need to go on video chat?"

"I can work over the phone if you prefer."

Perfect. The less she sees or knows about me, the better.

"This works for me." I give her my credit card info and pray this won't cost me a ton of money.

"I'm just going to shuffle the deck. While I do so, think about the question on your mind. If you were in person, I'd have you cut the cards. But since this is a virtual reading, I'll be channeling your energy."

My mind focuses on the way I felt when I was with Jax. I think about how foolish it was to fall for him. And of course, how much I miss and love him.

"I see a lot of change going on in your life. There's been upheaval and you're upset. The card I just pulled is showing me deceit from a man who was once close in your life."

"Yes, that is right on." Wow, she's good. She already picked up Jax. He was once close to me and was hiding something from me.

"I'm also seeing that you're heartbroken, but you left the relationship."

I don't want to reveal too much information. I think Jax caused his own heartbreak through irresponsible actions. "I did leave the relationship, but his actions were to blame."

"The cards are telling me a man has more to say to you. I also see a move."

I wonder if she sees me going to Antarctica. It's probably the only place where I can escape hearing the name Jax Slater for the immediate future. I'm over this reading. I'm not moving anywhere now that Jax and I are broken up. I'll be living in my hometown for the foreseeable future. She obviously read my cards wrong. Why do I amuse myself with these scam artists? I decide to end the session before I spend hundreds of dollars that would be better allotted on professional therapy. Jax might have more to say to me, but that doesn't mean I have to listen.

Trash the Dress Online Chat

Cailin: There's a new dog in my life and this one is the good kind.

    Alexandra: You're a mommy!

41

CAILIN MCCALL GETS A SPECIAL DELIVERY

CAILIN

Usually, when a package arrives at my door, I get a surge of excitement. The joy of holding the box, peeling back the tape, and opening it to see the long-awaited contents gets me every time. This, however, is not one of those times. I know what's in the boxes outside my door: the bags I left on the plane. Those boxes are my last connection to Jax. As soon as I open those packages, we'll be done. I will have to face life where I'm not his girlfriend or his publicist. We will no longer have pieces of each other.

Eventually, I open my door and drag in the boxes. I choose to open a small, flat package first because I know that one holds my laptop. I set the box on the table, pull out my computer, and lift open the lid, as if I'm going to actually check my email or start job hunting. Before I can hit the power button, an envelope with my name on it slides across the keyboard. I'd know this handwriting anywhere. Jax always writes in capital letters.

He wrote me a letter. I thought I blocked off all forms of communication with him, but Jax is indeed clever. He told me he doesn't stop until he gets what he wants and that clearly still stands. I hold the letter in my hands and contemplate. I want to read it, but at the same time I need to protect my heart. If I don't read it, it'll be easier to move forward (yeah, right). But if I do read it, it's only going to resurface everything I'm trying to push aside.

Since my legs are literally wobbling, I sit down and carefully slide my fingers under the fold of the envelope. I slowly split apart the envelope at the seam and then stop midway. Jax wants me to read this so he can feel better about breaking my heart. It's probably a proper apology to send me off so he can start fresh with his baby mama. Do I really need to go through that? I don't owe him anything. I should just put the letter down, or better yet, throw it out. But curiosity gets the best of me. I rip open the sealed half of the envelope and pull out a sheet of lined paper that's been torn out of Jax's songwriting book. My hands continue to shake while I open the folded letter.

Dear Cailin,

I'm resorting to writing you a letter and hope you find and read this. I'd like to think that you've come to know me completely in just a short amount of time, but the recent events have made you doubt me. I'm begging you to dig deep and draw on how you felt about me before this happened. How you feel when it's just me and you. When the outside world doesn't matter. How safe you felt in my arms after the bus accident.

I want to continue to be that source of security and happiness for you. But you have to give me a chance. Please give me the opportunity to explain. When I told you I love you, I meant it. No one has ever made me feel the way I do when I'm with you. And no one ever will. Love like this only comes around once in a lifetime and I am going to love you forever, whether we are together or apart. You have this picture of me in your mind right now, that I'm trouble. And maybe my life is a little chaotic, but I need you to see that loving me is worth it.

This letter is my last hope of trying to reach your heart. I need you to know that I want to do everything we talked about. I want to meet your family, see where you grew up, show you where I was raised. I told you that we are going to travel to a romantic island, do yoga on a mountaintop, and lay in bed all day and watch movies. I believe we can still do this.

I'm enclosing the final lyrics to the song I wrote about you one day when we were together on the bus. The music will be the guitar parts I played for you. I recorded it at a local studio on tour. I miss you on the road with me. I want you—us—back.

You make me a better person. I hope when you read these lyrics you'll see how much you mean to me. I am selfishly pleading with you to stand by my side as I work through this. You are the partner I want for whatever life throws our way. Please. Call me.

If you choose to ignore me, just know that you changed my life and a piece of my heart is always beating alongside yours. I love you more than words and am sending you three hand squeezes.

Love,

Jax

I'm a blubbering mess by the time I finish reading the letter. He really got me at the end when he mentioned our three hand squeezes. Jax knows how much our secret hand signal means to me. I can't deny that I love Jax and I want a life with him. I wish with all my heart that things would have turned out differently for us, but he has caused me deep grief. I can't let that happen ever again, so I can't respond to Jax. This needs to be a clean break.

I should clear my mind and get some fresh air. That will help. I fold the letter and grab my sneakers. "Hope! Let's go for a walk," I yell to my girl who is curled in a ball on the couch.

As Hope and I walk along the lake, I recycle Jax's letter in my mind. I can picture his voice speaking to me. I miss his voice. I miss his soft and tender touch. I miss my life with him. I want us back, too. It's all so much, I don't know what to do. But I can do one thing: I sit down at a picnic table and cry. Thankfully no one is around.

"Cailin?" a voice calls out to me. I know that voice. It's Ethan. The last person in the world I want to see me crying right now. I wipe my face.

"Ethan, I'm not really in the mood for company right now."

"I noticed you look upset. Anything I can do to help you? Is it that jerk Jax? I read the headlines. And I know you were involved with him. I saw it on your social posts." Ethan seems more satisfied in calling Jax names than worrying if I'm actually all right.

"I prefer not to talk about this, if you don't mind."

Ethan sits down next to me. "I care about you, Cailin. I always have and I don't like to see you upset."

"Then you should just get up and walk away like I'm asking you. Because right now my world has been turned upside down and I'm devastated that I had everything I ever wanted and then it got ripped out from under me."

Ethan goes against my wishes and wraps his arms around me. I want to push him away because he's not Jax and I'm still mad at him for what happened before I left for tour. But at the same time, I'm in need of comfort and he's been that for me before. So, in a stream of muddled thoughts, I lean in and accept his offer to hold me. We remain that way for a while, in silence, except for my sniffles between tears.

I don't have feelings for Ethan. On the outside of my heart hangs a No Vacancy sign because there's no room to love anyone other than Jax. My heart has lost more than the Rose family on the first episode of Schitt's Creek. If I can't have Jax, it doesn't matter who I'm with because none of them will be him. I'll never have a love like I had with Jax. Ever again.

Some people don't ever get to experience love, let alone the level of soul-blending Jax and I shared. I should be grateful for the gift. I had a moment of living in a fantasy and now I've crashed back down to the mundane. Maybe I should just accept it and move on with someone like Ethan, whose whole world would revolve around me.

Ethan always wanted me, that's why he was so protective. We were given a second chance and I dismissed it. Maybe the third time is the charm and I just need to spend more quality time with him so my feelings can grow. I know this goes against everything on my post-divorce bucket list and any new goals I have been chasing for myself. I know. I know. But against my better judgment and self-talk, I feel like I have nothing left to lose.

Ethan pats my hair and I lift my head, wondering if I should kiss him right now. One kiss and I would remove Jax as an option in my life. Not like he's an option anymore, anyway. As I inch closer to Ethan's mouth, I tell myself that all I have to do is...

"Cailin." Ethan's voice stops me in my tracks. "Did you really love him? Honestly? In that short amount of time?"

I sit up, pulling myself out of my moment of weakness. I feel like I just made a serious mistake letting Ethan console me. Even worse, through my hysteria, I almost kissed him.

"Yes, I loved him. Time doesn't mean anything. You can spend years with someone and not have the meaningful connection or conversations that Jax and I had. And now it's gone."

Yet, I still feel like I just cheated on him. The pit of my stomach turns.

Ethan is silent for a while. As we sit next to each other, I wonder why he doesn't get up and leave. Until finally he says, "I'm sorry you're going through this. I hate to see you in such pain. Know that I'm here if you need me. My door is open anytime."

I don't reply as Ethan walks away. Did he not see that I was going in for a kiss? This is what he wanted. And instead of taking advantage of me, he just left me. Did he finally get the hint from earlier in our conversation? I was rejected by someone I don't even want. My brain hurts and I can't think about what happened with Ethan while I am still in shambles over Jax. I go back to wallowing alone and lay my head on the table, careful not to hurt my face on the splintering wood.

There's only one problem with that plan. I can't wallow alone because one minute later, Ethan comes back. I have no strength to lift my head and instead opt to look at him with one eye open and the other shut closed against my arm, along with the rest of the right side of my face.

As he stands in front of me, Ethan says, "I just want you to know that you're crying over this guy, but you can do better. With me. Someone who has a stable life and doesn't have a job that puts your life at risk." Ethan begins to walk onto the dock.

I stand up and follow him. "Jax never put my life at risk, Ethan. He's a pop star. Sure, his fans might be a little overzealous at times, but they're hardly dangerous."

"You could have died in the bus crash, Cailin. Don't you see?"

I stop walking mid-step. "How do you know about the bus crash, Ethan?" No one knows about the bus crash. We never released that information to the media.

Ethan takes a moment to reply and his stare focuses intently on the sand beneath our feet.

"That truck almost ran your bus off the road. You could have been really hurt just because you're trying to prove you're the number one fan of some unworthy guy."

"Ethan. How do you know about the bus crash? Did you have something to do with it?"

Ethan pauses to gather his thoughts as guilt slathers across his face.

"I never intended for you to get hurt or anything. I just wanted to freak you out a little so you could realize that you will never be happy with life on the road. And the rain, obviously, I didn't know there was going to be a storm. The driver was just supposed to tail your bus, making you think that they were fans trying to get close to Jax. The rain caused the accident. I was terrified when I found out."

My body freezes, but I manage to inhale a deep gulp of air. "You are on another level. Are you telling me that you hired a truck to run my tour bus off the road?"

"I'm sorry, Cailin. Please forgive me. I don't know what I was thinking. I just... I just wanted you to leave the tour and come back and give us a chance. I didn't expect you to stay on the road and fall in love with him. And now I see how much you're hurting over this pregnancy scandal and I hate seeing you in this state, knowing I caused it."

"Are you crazy? I can't even believe what I'm hearing right now. You're insane. You are a lunatic. I don't even know what to think right now. You *just* wanted to scare me off tour with the bus accident? And what do you mean that you caused my pain over the pregnancy scandal?"

"It's not true. The headlines aren't true. Jax didn't impregnate that woman. She's not even pregnant. She never even met him." Ethan looks at me, waiting for some sort of response.

However, I can't respond. I wish I could call a Zack Morris time-out. I'm so stunned that I stop crying. Ethan uncomfortably stands in front of me, his left leg nervously twitching.

"I did it."

"You did what exactly?"

"I was jealous," Ethan says. "After you ended things with me and I saw you went on tour with your old crush, the pop star you talked about non-stop when we dated in high school, I got really mad. Like I lost you to him again. And then I saw all the posts and headlines. This guy who doesn't even know you just swoops in and wins you over, when I've been wanting you for years. After you got divorced, I thought I finally had my chance. And he took you away from me. I hired someone to make that claim against Jax to the tabloids."

This is unreal. I knew Ethan was the jealous type. That's why I broke up with him the first time and quickly stopped things from progressing between us again once I found out I was going on tour with Jax. I feared he may not have changed and I was right. But I never would have expected that he would sink to this level. I can't believe I almost kissed him. Ethan was the man the psychic warned me about, not Jax. Ethan was also once close to me and he definitely deceived me.

"You destroyed my life! *You* broke my heart, not Jax. Even worse, you might have destroyed the life and career of a completely innocent man in the process. I can't believe this."

I grip onto Hope's leash and inch towards Ethan as he backs up. He stands inches from the edge of the dock.

"Are you at least happy I told you the truth?"

"I'll be happy when you get your source to clear Jax's name. Or else I'll be contacting lawyers."

As I speak, I close the gap between us and fix my gaze into Ethan's eyes. I press my finger into his chest and open my palm. Then, I push Ethan off the dock. He's a good swimmer, which is lucky for him because he'll be treading deep water from this point forward.

Take that.

Trash the Dress Online Chat

Cora: I'm doing it! I'm road tripping and will figure out my life.

Harper: Which one of us are you going to visit first?!

42

JAX SLATER GETS MORE LIFE-CHANGING NEWS

JAX

THE TRACKING from the mail delivery service shows that Cailin's things were delivered to her apartment. I don't know if it's a good thing or bad thing that she hasn't made contact. On one hand, if she got my note, I would think she would break down, remember how she feels about me, and call me. That didn't happen yet, which tells me she's really through with me. Or, just maybe, she didn't read the letter. I'm assuming she's home, but she might be out, moving on with her life because she's done with me. On the other hand, if she loves me like I think she does, I don't think she can move on right away. Maybe she has the boxes, but she's holding out to open them. I'm gonna go with that because it gives me a sliver of optimism, but the suspense has me in overdrive.

I've been going through the motions these past few days of tour. It has not been easy. I keep to myself on the bus as much as possible. Since fans pre-paid to meet me, I don't want to let them down, but I also don't want to answer any, "Are you the baby daddy?" questions. So instead, we changed up how I meet the fans. Rather than everyone coming backstage for a little and hanging out, I sit behind a table. Everyone can come up, get an autograph, and pose for a photo. Then they're escorted out to the lobby.

One, dare I say, positive thing that came from this disaster is that I wrote my hit song. The A&R reps love it. I recorded it at a local studio one day before a show. It only took a few takes. The engineer and sound guy were easy to work with and everyone said I brought raw emotion. I want to play it for Cailin and let her know this is my ode to her. She'll know when she reads the lyrics I attached to the letter.

Tonight's the last night of the show and I'm really trying to get in a gratitude mindset. I should be proud of myself for all that I've accomplished: I embarked on my first solo tour and it sold out everywhere. I moved past my anxiety and started going out in public (thanks to Cailin). I wrote and recorded a song that can be released as a single, and I made my fans really happy.

Despite all that, I'm devastated. I discovered what true love feels like and realized I won't settle for anything less than Cailin. I need Cailin to know that even if there is a baby on the way, I want her to be part of his or her life.

I can't wait to be a dad and I thought Cailin and I would start our parenting journey together. It's not ideal to raise a kid with a woman I don't love, but I am going to make it work and be the best father possible for this child. I'll give them everything I never had. I don't have to be in a relationship with someone to raise a kid with them. I want to say all of this to Cailin. But why would she want to be with a guy who is having a kid with someone else? I can't say I blame her and I'm not sure what I would do if the situation were reversed. I do know that Cailin has changed my life.

I have a lot to think about, but right now I need to focus because the audience is seated, my opening act is finishing up her set, and I have to take the stage.

Harry enters my dressing room. "Jax, do you need anything?" Harry asks.

"Can you get my girlfriend back?"

"First order of business after this show." Harry surveys the state of my dressing room, which is as messy as my life. "I know it's not the best timing, but I think we should still do the end of tour wrap party tonight as we originally planned."

"I'm really not in the mood to party or deal with the public."

"What if we do something private with just the crew? Everyone has worked so hard. We're here in New York, and some east coast label reps want to meet you. It's good business."

"I don't know. Can't they just come backstage after the show?"

"Jax, I know your head is not in it right now, but my job is to look out for your best interests. We have a lot to be proud of on this tour. And we have to show the label that your personal life won't impact your work. Not if you want another solo album or more tour dates."

This is why Harry is my manager. I worked really hard for this and I can't let the fact that I might have fathered a child during a short-lived fling deter my career goals. The one thing I haven't done during this entire scandal is actually reach out to Kelly's friend. I asked Kelly to touch base and feel her out. I need an update. And I need to know why she's telling the media that her name is Ana, when her name is Chelsea. Probably to protect her own privacy, until she can start to collect child support from me. Once I get an update from Kelly, I can focus on moving forward.

"I'll do it," I tell Harry. Then I ask him to give me some time alone because I have something important to handle.

The phone rings five times before Kelly answers. In that time, I envision various outcomes to how this call will play out. I need to know why Chelsea isn't contacting me directly. Is she going to tell Kelly that she's involving lawyers to ensure I support the child, or will she want to file for sole custody because my career involves travel? Is that why she went to the media first, instead of me? To start building up public support in case I refuse to cooperate?

"Took you long enough," I say.

"I just got off the phone with Chelsea. She took a few days to call me back. I figured she was ashamed that she betrayed my friendship by going to the tabloids. But it turns out she was upset with me for setting her up with you because you were dating someone else around that time."

"That makes no sense. I was only seeing Chelsea." I've never dated two women at once. I'm not that much of a dirtbag. Just being accused of that irks me.

"Right, that's what I thought. I asked her to explain. Turns out, she read the headlines and was just as shocked as we were. She felt disgusted with herself for sleeping with you when you were allegedly sleeping with another woman."

"Let me get this straight. She didn't go to the press? She doesn't think she's pregnant?" A wave of relief lifts me up and I feel like I'm riding through the barrel of a maverick. If she's not pregnant, then this is all a tabloid scandal.

"She's not pregnant."

"This changes everything. That means I can be with Cailin," I say. "She needs to know the truth."

"Do you want me to reach out to her? She hasn't blocked me on social. Maybe she'll listen to me."

"I appreciate it, but she needs to hear it from me." I just need a strategy. What would my publicist suggest? I need to think like Cailin.

Trash the Dress Online Chat

Alexandra: Big news. I've forgiven myself for cheating. I'm going to start dating.
　Tori: Finally!!

43

CAILIN MCCALL AND JAX SLATER REUNITE

CAILIN

As I rush off the dock, I think back to the tour schedule. What day is it? Tonight is the last night of tour. New York City. If I hurry, I can drop Hope off with my mom and make it to the show on time.

Once there, Hope is happy to see my mom, but I feel like I'm leaving my child at daycare for the first time. I just rescued her and now I'm leaving her. Will she be confused and think I abandoned her like her previous owner? How much more pain can her heart take?

I remind myself that my mom loves dogs and Hope will probably be spoon-fed dog-safe peanut butter while getting a belly rub by the time I leave the house. My mom was a bit confused as to my hurry, but I told her I would fill her in on the details later. I'm sure she already texted Gemma and they're going back and forth with their own theories.

As always, I follow the speed limit as I drive home, but inside, my heart is racing. Hurry, hurry, hurry; it urges me with each beat. I need to shower and find the perfect outfit. Then I need to figure out the best route to the city without hitting traffic. I can take a train, or maybe I should take a car service. I won't drive in because then I'll spend an hour trying to find parking.

As I quickly shampoo and condition my hair, I decide to take the train. There's a direct line that will bring me close to the venue. I'll wear sneakers so I can run if I'm pressed for time. I don't know what exactly I'm going to do or say when I see Jax. First, I want to tell him I forgive him for something I know he didn't even do. Then I need to beg forgiveness because I jumped to conclusions and didn't give him a chance to explain his side of the story, like he pleaded. I'm no worse than the tabloid reporters who spread lies about him. And I'm the one person who should know better than anyone the kind of man Jax Slater is: humble, fiercely protective of those he loves, incredibly giving, and someone I can rely on to lift me up through anything life throws my way.

I quickly towel dry my hair, lather on the scented lotion that drives Jax wild, and pull my hair into a loose bun. It will dry on the way to the show and I don't have time for anything more. I'm not flawless and I've proved that loud and clear. I slip into my favorite pair of blue jeans that are ripped at the knees. I just need a shirt.

I packed all my favorite tops. I dump my entire suitcase onto the floor, get on my knees and dig through the pile. I throw everything I don't want across the room. It's not until I reach the bottom of the pile that I find the perfect tee. The "I Love Jax Slater" fan shirt that Hayley gave me when tour first started. That will let Jax know the moment he sees me that I'm sorry and I'm his.

Dressed and ready to go, I throw my essentials into a black mini quilted nylon backpack, and dash to the train station. If my estimates are correct, I'll get to the concert just as the show starts. I have my crew badge, so hopefully there will be no issues getting past security. Technically, I can text Harry or Hayley, but I don't want anyone to know I'm on my way.

JAX

Harry is right. The show must go on, even if I am still waiting to hear from Cailin. I tried to call her and text her again, but I still must be blocked. She's still not reading the messages I send on social media. There's another way I can contact her, but it's too risky. I have her work email, but I don't know who monitors that and I don't want anyone else to read about our private matters. I'll have to sort this out later because it's time to hit the stage.

Before each show, the band and I stand in a circle with our arms around each other and express our gratefulness for this opportunity. Then, we all throw in our hands and chant something. Each night, a different person chooses the word we end on that gets us all pumped to perform. Tonight it's my turn, but I can't think of anything other than, "Let's get this over with!"

I wait a few moments alone behind the curtain while the band takes their places behind their instruments on stage. The entire arena is black. I see dim lights from cell phones that fans have raised into the air, waiting for me. Not 5 Leo Hearts, just me. This entire tour, I've been worried about how people would respond and it turns out I have some of the most dedicated fans. Even through this chaos, my fans are defending me on social media. I don't know what I've done to deserve them.

This is it, the last show of the tour. It might not be one of worldwide tours that I did back in the day with 5 Leo Hearts, but it's just as significant in my life. Standing here, alone, as the headliner for a New York City show, I'm reminded of how far I have come.

From the young boy whose mom signed him up for dance, music, and acting classes, with the pure goal of doing activities that I enjoyed, to the teenager who was given the opportunity of a lifetime to turn the talents he honed into a career. I never went to high school like a normal kid, but I had a tutor and graduated from the school of life. I never even wanted to be famous. I just wanted to entertain people and make them happy as my contribution to the world.

But music also contributed to my own life. It gave me an escape from my broken childhood. Growing up without a father, I sometimes doubted I was worthy of love. Yes, I have my mom and my grandmother, who dedicated their lives to my needs. But if my own father didn't love me, how could I expect other people to care? The band became my family. Harry became my role model.

When 5 Leo Hearts became successful, it hit me like a tornado touching ground and flailing up everything in its path. I wasn't prepared for fame at that age. I hadn't developed into the person I wanted to become. Instead, I allowed the media to craft my identity. To them, I was the stereotypical bad boy. So, I lived up to it. I let others define me, and today that is the opposite of my definition of success.

I learned that you achieve what others deem as success, but it's nothing if you aren't being true to yourself. This album and this tour were also the reveal of the real Jax Slater. The man who never yearned for fame, but always dreamed of a normal life where he had the luxury of making a career from his passions.

After meeting Cailin, I can confirm that happiness doesn't come from material items. It's not the big house or the private jet. It's the little moments with people you care about. It's looking into someone's eyes and knowing they can read your mind. It's sitting next to each other in comfortable silence.

I found that in Cailin. Yes, she had my photos on her walls, which can be a bit uncomfortable to think about at first. But she saw past the posters and recognized that I am more than a centerfold and worthy of being loved for who I am outside of fame. That's what's so refreshing about her compared to all the other girls I've dated. I can see a real future with Cailin and I will not give up until I can talk to her about the situation.

Cailin has inspired me to get out of my comfort zone and do things like go out in public. Honestly, I don't even know if I would have written that hit song for the A&R department if I didn't feel the emotions I've experienced with her presence in my life. I can only manifest—as Cailin likes to say—and envision that she has read my letter, teared up over the lyrics, and will come back to me.

After I get off stage, my dream of a solo tour will have been accomplished. The crew will pack up and go home to their loved ones. And I will go home, alone, to the most materialistic city in the world. My heart, as empty as my house.

Trash the Dress Online Chat

Cailin: I made a big mistake! Will explain later. PRAY FOR ME!

Harper: OMG! Details!! Praying. Xo

44

JAX SLATER PERFORMS STUNT THAT
MAKES CROWD WEAP

CAILIN

BREATHLESS. Again. For someone who loathes running, I sure have been pounding the pavement a lot during my relationship with Jax. First, running out of the jet, and now, rushing to get to his final show. Luckily, I make it to the venue and get cleared by security without any problems.

As I dash through the lobby, I see Hayley. Her jaw drops and I yell that I'll explain later. I ask security guards to point me in the direction of the stage. Finally, I make it. Harry sees me and nods his head.

"Really happy to see you," he says. "Jax will be, too. He's been a mess without you."

"Harry, I have news. This has all been a setup. It's not true."

"I know. Jax told me. But how do you know already?"

"Wait, Jax knows? What do you mean, how do I know?" He looks at me quizzically.

Suddenly, I'm confused. I thought I had all the pieces of this story. But maybe I'm missing something. I don't even care at this point. All that matters is that Jax and I both know the truth. And I am here for him. My feelings are even declared on my shirt.

Someone comes and pulls Harry away. I don't want to waste any more time. I want Jax to know I'm here. Obviously, that's a bit of a challenge being that he's on stage. But, there is something I can do.

I push back the curtain and walk onto the side of the stage like I've done many other times on tour. Jax is at the part of the show where he's about to transition into the 5 Leo Hearts melody. That's when he turns to the side of the stage, and sees me. Jax pauses mid-sentence and takes a second to compose himself.

Then he does something unscripted. He walks over to the band and whispers something to Chris, who then walks off stage, followed by the others. A stage tech walks out with the acoustic guitar Jax plays on the bus.

"This is usually the part of the show where I bring up a fan and serenade her with a 5 Leo Hearts song," Jax tells the audience. "But tonight, we're going to change things up."

I wonder what he's going to do and if seeing me had anything to do with this change of set list.

Jax continues, "When I signed on to do a solo album, I wrote a ton of songs. But none of them were hits according to my label. Sure, I was writing songs about my life and journey, but I guess they lacked that big emotion. It took me falling in love, true love, for the first time on this tour, and then abruptly losing it all because of a lie. It took that pain, that hunger to get it back, to write the most honest song I've ever written. And that song, I recently recorded and will be released as a single."

The crowd cheers and breaks out in thunderous screams. Jax gives his fans a minute to calm down before he resumes. "That song was inspired by a woman who is here tonight. And I'm going to sing it to her for the first time, right now."

Jax looks at me. Oh my gosh. I'm already crying by the time he walks over and takes my hand, leading me out to the center of the stage. He places his microphone in its stand and picks up his acoustic guitar. A tech quickly brings out a chair for me to sit in for my serenade. I am secretly praying that fans record this and post it online because it's the most romantic moment of my life.

Jax looks me in the eye with every word he sings. There may be a few thousand people in the room, but it's like Jax and I are the only two people who exist right now. All the time we spent together, this is the first time he's singing a song to me. My heart might burst.

On paper, the song reads poetically. The verses basically highlight our relationship. The chorus echoes his feelings for me. This is our love, between the lyrics. I'm still a blubbering mess by the time the song ends and Jax kisses my cheek. With the microphone out of range, he whispers in my ear, "I love you, Cailin."

"I love you, too," I whisper back. Jax draws me into his arms and the crowd breaks out in applause and a bunch of "aws." Everyone backstage begins to cheer. I wish I could explain everything to Jax right now. But he's still in the middle of his show, so I glide through the air, and off stage.

***

JAX

The rest of the show can't go by fast enough. I considered cutting out a few songs to make the time go faster, but I can't deny my fans the experience they expect. The important thing is that Cailin is here. She knows how I feel, and she feels the same. On top of all that, the crowd loved my new song. I'm ending this tour on a high note.

After my encore, I take my final bow on the tour. In that moment, I'm filled with emotion. I'm proud of what I've accomplished and feel blessed to be able to live this life. While living my dream, I met the woman of my dreams and she helped give me confidence for my future. I know I can navigate life in the public eye and that she'll be three hand squeezes away.

I thank everyone and say good-night. Before I walk off stage, I turn and take one last look. The fans are gathering their belongings and walking out. Anyone else in this room would see crowds of people pushing their way out of the exit doors. This scene means more to me, though. I see joy, friendship, and a supportive community who has my back. This is confirmation that I am indeed, not an imposter. I am worthy of all of this. Now, to show Cailin that I am worthy of her love.

I find her waiting for me by the stage door. Everyone quickly scurries off to give us space. "You have no idea how happy I am to see you right now." I motion to say more, but Cailin silences me by placing her finger over my lips.

"Jax, I'm so sorry for rushing to conclusions. I should never have stopped believing in you or what we have. I let you down. All for a lie. I know it's a lie. I know who is behind this."

Cailin doesn't know that I thought there might actually be a pregnancy scare, so I'm eager to hear what she knows that I don't. "What do you mean?"

Cailin sighs. "It's a long story that I will fill you in completely on later. For now, I'll just say that someone in my life was jealous of my relationship with you and set this whole thing in motion. I was shocked, but they admitted it to my face when I went back home."

"Wow." I shouldn't be surprised as people make up lies about me all the time. But I never suspected the lies would come from someone in Cailin's circle. "The truth is out and that's all that matters," I say.

"I agree. But I do want to discuss this all in-depth later," Cailin says.

I plan on telling her everything as well. This new slate will begin with complete honesty. "Does that mean you're sticking around?" I ask after I lock our fingers together.

"I never plan on leaving you again. That is, if you'll have me."

"I'll never let you go," I tell her before I grab her neck, press our bodies together, and reunite our lips. I missed her vanilla-flavored lips and the tiny bits of sparkle they always leave behind on mine.

CAILIN

Jax is stripping out of his sweat-soaked clothes and changing into a fresh outfit for the wrap party. His body is shimmering under the low lights of the bus. Those abs are mine. Those illustrated arms are mine. Those toned legs? All mine. I didn't think I'd ever be back on this bus or that Jax and I would reunite. In just a few weeks of being on tour with Jax, I survived a bus crash, fell in love, proved myself in a new career, got my heart broken, quit that new career, adopted a dog, and found myself being serenaded on stage by the love of my life. I can't imagine what's coming my way next, but with Jax by my side—and I mean that because I'm not letting anything come between us anymore—I know I can conquer it all.

Jax catches my gaze as he zips his pants and asks, "What's on your mind?"

"Just thinking of everything we've been through and how lucky I am to be your girlfriend."

He comes over to me and places his hands on my waist. "I'm the lucky one. I have a gorgeous, hard-working woman who may be a little hard-headed at times, but fights for what she believes in. And I'm just happy that you fought for me and came back here tonight. Now, let's get out of here before I take both our clothes off."

At the party, Hayley runs over as soon as she sees me. "I am so happy to see you back. I missed you. I've needed our girl talks. You need to fill me in on everything." We head to a private booth so we can talk candidly. I fill her in on everything that happened with Jax.

"I really wanted to reach out to you, but Harry told us that Jax asked that no one contact you."

"Don't even sweat it. I was so upset, I probably would have blocked your calls too, just so I wouldn't have a reminder of Jax."

"I don't blame you. I've actually been having some romantic problems of my own."

"Uh oh. No newlywed bliss?" I feared this would happen, but I didn't expect it so soon.

"I think I made a mistake marrying Jayce spur of the moment. I got caught up in the excitement, but I think it would have been smarter to sit with the engagement for a little before making that final commitment."

"Is he feeling the same?"

"He's content with his life. But as tour began to wind down and we started to talk about our next steps, we're just not aligning again. I think I want to end things tonight, go back home alone, and spend some time working on myself and my own goals."

"I know that's not an easy thing to do, but I think that's a great idea. I know you've been struggling with this for a while and I can tell you're not as happy as when we first met. I'm here for you and I support you."

"I appreciate that. It just hurts ending a relationship that I invested years of my life in, ya know? But I know it's time."

"Believe me, I know. But if there's anything I've learned, it's that people come into our lives for a reason. It's not always meant to be forever. Sometimes it's just to teach us a lesson. Or to fill chapters of our story. But you should never settle."

Hayley hugs me. "Thanks for your support."

"Speaking of support," I have a great idea. "I'm going to add you to this online support group for young divorced women, called Trash the Dress. It's really helped me to find a community of women who understand in ways no one else can relate."

"That sounds amazing! Please do."

Just then, Jayce and Chris wander over and crash our booth. Hayley asks Jayce if they can go outside for some air. I give her a "see you later" hug because I know we'll stay friends. But I have a feeling that her night out is going to end after her conversation with Jayce.

I excuse myself from Chris and some other crew members who have now gathered around and look for Jax. When I find him, I sneak up and rest my head on his shoulder. I plan on standing behind him in everything that he does moving forward.

Trash the Dress Online Chat

Cailin: I never thought that my teenage dreams would ever come true, or that any of these experiences would come my way. It took mistakes, loss, falling down, and dancing in the dirt, for me to start living the life I was meant to lead. Without my divorce, none of this would have happened. I would not have found my soul-mates (Jax and Hope). And even more importantly, I would not have met all of you—the sisterhood of divorcees that I know will be with me every step of this journey happily, even after.

45

JAX SLATER DISCOVERS CAILIN MCCALL HAS A SECRET

JAX

ALTHOUGH WE WERE all on the same tour, everyone on my crew had a different experience. During my conversations with everyone at the wrap party, I learned that each person got out as much as they put into their time on the road. Chris took advantage of every pub in the area, eager to try the local homebrew beers. I didn't know he's thinking of starting his own business and used his travel with me to do research. Manny took a cue from my old playbook and hooked up with different girls in each city, wooing them with backstage passes. Jayce and Hayley got married, for crying out loud. Harry found a new band performing at a pub and wants to sign them to his management company. Others laid low and worked hard to ensure that things went off without a hitch for me, and I'm lucky to have them on my team.

By the time I say goodbye to everyone, it's after midnight and I'm beat. My plan was to go back to my hotel and catch an early morning flight back to LA. But I don't want to leave Cailin and I know she's not prepared to jet off in a few hours without notice.

"You did it." Cailin stands on her tiptoes and touches her lips to my forehead. I may have to physically look down on her, but I look up to her in a lot of ways too.

"It was all one big whirlwind. It's going to be weird tomorrow, not being on a bus or playing a show. I thought I was going to have to adjust to life on the road, but I slipped back into routine just like the old days."

"Speaking of tomorrow, I would love to wake up with you in my bed. Will you come home with me?" Cailin seems worried I might reject her because then she says, "I understand if you have to fly back to LA. I know this wasn't planned."

Before she can babble any further, I say what we both want to hear. "That sounds perfect. I'll grab my stuff off the bus and call us a car service."

On the ride back to Jersey, Cailin sleeps on my shoulder. This night took a lot out of both of us. I'm appreciating every minute of being close to her again. Soaking in her messy hair, the scent of lingering shampoo. The smoothness of her well-moisturized skin. The way her chest stretches out the text of her, "I Love Jax Slater" T-shirt.

As we drive through her town to get to her apartment, I take in its charm. We pass through residential areas and cruise past a quaint downtown with boutiques, bars, and specialty restaurants that look delicious. Signs point in all directions for lake communities. It's easy to understand why Cailin loved growing up here. Through moonlight and dim street lamps, I can already see the allure.

Cailin wakes up as we pull into the parking lot for her building. "Here we are," she says, gripping my hand.

We grab my bags and I follow Cailin inside. She lives in a small, two-floor complex that hosts about ten units. A flower garden outlines the building, blending with hearty bushes that offer privacy around the windows of the basement apartments. There are two-seater benches placed along the front lawn and I already feel welcome.

"Remember that I just moved in before we went on tour, so the space is not fully designed," she says.

Leave it to her to be worried about the presentation of her apartment. That's the last thing on my mind right now. Cailin digs through her backpack and pulls out her key. As she unlocks the door, I flash back to the night on the bus when we discovered my skeleton key tattoo and the vintage lock inked on her wrist. Things were fitting together then, and now we're unlocking a new start for not only our relationship, but also our lives. I can feel it.

Cailin swings open the door. "Here we are."

I throw down my bags and Cailin gives me a quick tour. Her apartment has everything I would expect to find in her personal space. There are vases filled with dried wheat and lavender, scented candles that have never been used, a plush fluffy area rug, and a collage of framed quotes on the wall, among other feminine touches. She said she hasn't been here long to finish decorating, but I can't imagine what else is on her to-do list. When we get to her bedroom, she gasps. "I forgot about this. I was rushing to get to the show and didn't have anything to wear, so I dumped out my suitcase."

"That explains the concert tee." I can't help but tease her, she's too adorable when she pouts. Our banter is one of my favorite things about our relationship.

"I actually picked that on purpose, Jax. You can't make fun of your own merch."

"Relax, I love it," I say. "But I'd love it better back on the floor."

CAILIN

I woke up in silk pajamas (thanks, Gemma) with Jax Slater in my bed. Being on tour and in hotels with him was one thing.

But having him in my apartment brings a whole other level of realness. I don't even know what to do with a pop star boyfriend in small town, USA. Before I can obsessively think about this any further, Jax wakes up.

"Mmmm, morning."

"How did you sleep?" I hope he thinks my mattress is cozy. It's not the luxury quality that he's used to, and truth be told, I got it on sale.

"Best night of sleep I've gotten in a while now that you're back pulling the covers off me."

I sit up and throw on the matching silk robe that's lying on the floor. "I promise that cleaning up this mess is on this morning's agenda. But first, I need coffee and I have to text my mom."

"She must be worried about you."

"Actually, I'm the one who's worried. She has my dog."

"Hold up, when did you get a dog?"

"I adopted her when I thought you broke my heart. Her name is Hope and you're going to love her."

Jax breaks out in a grin. "Of course you would go and do something wonderful like adopt a dog when you're heartbroken. I can't wait to meet her. And your mom."

Right. I didn't consider that. I'll need to tell my mom to make sure she doesn't embarrass me when she meets Jax. I can just picture her asking him to sign a copy of the magazine with his face on the cover. Then telling him she'll be the envy of her book club.

Jax takes a shower and I text my mom and Gemma to touch base. Over coffee, Jax and I have a no-holds-barred conversation about everything that happened during our brief breakup. I didn't expect him to tell me that he slept with someone before tour began. I was under the impression that he didn't date at all after he broke up with Maxine. The girl, Chelsea, obviously wasn't significant to his life, even if she is one of Kelly's friends. Jax said that he would have told me during our past discussions if he was seriously involved with someone. I also feel relieved to know that he always used protection.

Likewise, I spilled everything about Ethan, starting back to high school. And yes, I even admitted that Ethan was jealous of my crush on Jax back then. By this point, there's no trying to hold onto dignity. Jax knows I was a hardcore boy band fan. However, he also knows that's not why I love him. I see beyond his celebrity and how freakin' hot he is, for what's inside his heart and all that he wants to achieve. I would love him even if he chose to get off social media and give up a public career.

On the way to my mom's house, I warn Jax that my mom might go a little overboard asking questions. What I didn't expect was to open the door of the house and see Gemma sitting on the couch. Of course, they are in cahoots. Gemma could not let my mom meet Jax before she did. And rightfully so.

I just start laughing. Gemma strides over like she was born in stilettos.

"Jax, this is Gemma."

"Ah, the best friend," Jax says, taking Gemma's hand and then pulling her in for a hug.

Gemma fans her hand in front of her face and mouths, "Hot!" though Jax can't see.

"I'm sure Cailin told you everything about me and I can't wait to get to know you. That is, if you're sticking around a while."

Insert awkward moment. Made only more awkward by my mom coming in from the yard with Hope.

"Jax, it's a pleasure to meet you. I'm Patty. I've heard so much about you over the years between Cailin and the tabloids. I feel like I already know you."

"It's an honor to meet the woman who raised Cailin. She's amazing and you should be very proud." Jax takes my mom's hand and kisses it.

"He's a keeper," my mom says. Points for making Mom

swoon. By now, I've already given Hope 500 kisses and belly rubs to make up for leaving her. Jax bends down to pet her and Hope leaps into his lap and begins licking his face.

"Looks like you've got another fan," I observe.

"Safe to say I'm pretty fond of the ladies in this town," Jax says.

JAX

Cailin's best friend, Gemma, is a trip. I can only imagine the two of them being classic 5 Leo Hearts fans. And her mom, despite Cailin's warnings, is harmless and very welcoming. Pretty sure I won them both over as we ate some pastries from the local bakery. The bagel I had far surpasses LA bagels. I'm starting to really like Jersey.

Now, we're walking Hope at the lake where Cailin grew up. She's letting me hold the leash. I've missed having a dog and now that I'm with one, I decide I need at least one dog or more in my life from this point forward.

"So, this is where you spent your summers."

"Not just summer. There were activities here every season. In the winter, the lake freezes and we have a festival, burning firewood and making s'mores. Everyone is dressed in layers because it's frigid, but it's so much fun."

"Can you believe I've never really experienced winter?" I say.

"What do you mean? Not even on tour?"

"Not really. I grew up in Florida, joined the band and toured the world, and then moved to California. Sure, we toured places in the winter. But the most I did was walk from my bus to the venue in a puffer jacket. When it was cold, we never ventured out on the town. We were divas in that sense, I suppose."

"Wow. I can't imagine not having a white Christmas, or playing in the snow, or any of the fun winter activities. But you had other experiences just as a special."

Hope stops to sniff some bushes. "I want to make winter memories with you," I tell Cailin. "I want to get snowed in and drink hot chocolate and do all that basic stuff."

"Does that mean you want to stay a while?" she asks. We have yet to really talk about our next step.

"I was thinking that we can stay here for a few weeks and then go to Florida for my birthday. You can meet my mom. After that, I should go back to LA to check on my house. But I want you to come with me. I know that's asking a lot. We haven't talked about you going back to work." This has been an issue for us, so I am a bit apprehensive as to how she will respond.

"I've actually been thinking a lot about work and I'm pretty sure my days in music PR are over," Cailin says.

Part of me is relieved. One obstacle is out of our way, but I know Cailin won't be happy until she finds a job she loves—and I want that for her, because what's important to her is important to me.

"Was working with me that bad?"

"Tour was great because I was with you, but I don't see myself touring for work long-term. I have Hope now, and you."

"We do have Hope," I say as I pat the dog's head.

"We?" Cailin asks.

"Send me the paperwork, I'm adopting her with you. I love this dog. She's coming with us. We can't leave her behind."

"I think Hope would be honored to have you as her dad. I guess that would make us dog parents." Her cheeks turn pink.

"Look at that. I can still make you blush."

"I'm not blushing."

I give her a look.

"Okay, fine. You win. Again."

"So now that we have that settled, I was also thinking that

when we're in LA we can pack up my stuff. I want to put my house on the market. I never liked it and LA really isn't my speed. I still want to make music and explore other possibilities. But I can do that anywhere really, and travel when necessary. We can both take the time to figure out what's next for our careers, together. But there's one catch. I think you should sell your apartment, too." I hold my breath and wait to see how she will react.

"Sell my apartment?"

"I already told you that you have to want for nothing financially and I will support you. But I know you are also stubborn and want to be able to support yourself. Also, Hope needs a yard and I need space for my music equipment and home gym. Wherever we land, it's not going to be your apartment. You can sell it and use the money until you figure out what you really want to pursue."

"That's actually a really good idea."

Well, that surprised me.

Trash the Dress Online Chat

Tori: The dude I met up with last night just sent me a pick of his D.

Leanne: Is he getting it in?

46

BFF DREAMS COME TRUE! CAILIN AND GEMMA MEET THEIR FAVE BOY BAND!

JAX

As CAILIN and I board my jet, I have a brief flashback to her running off not too long ago. But I brush that image out of my mind and focus on coaxing Hope. She's a bit apprehensive about the plane. Since treats aren't doing the trick, I swoop down, wrap her in a protective hold, and carry her to our seating area.

"You're such a good dog dad," Cailin says.

Over the past few weeks staying with Cailin in her hometown, we've gotten a taste of reality. Overall, things went rather smoothly, considering this is our first time cohabiting and adjusting to our relationship in a normal environment. We spent a lot of time getting to know each other on a less accelerated level since we were no longer sneaking around or rushing to squeeze in moments together in-between tour responsibilities.

We savored everyday things, like cooking meals together. Cailin learned that she'll be taking on most of the duties in the kitchen after I burned pancakes. Luckily, the smoke alarms didn't blare. But we did end up leaving and going to a café for breakfast that morning.

Going out in a small town where Cailin knows everyone is a lot different than going out in LA or on tour. The locals are respectful of our privacy, but are also very friendly and always come over to greet Cailin and introduce themselves to me. I've come to form my own camaraderie with the baristas, who have our order ready within minutes of our arrival.

I haven't seen that guy Ethan, which is lucky for him. Apparently, he went out of town on business. He timed that perfectly to avoid the shame of what he did to me and Cailin, I'm sure. But he'll be served with papers from my lawyer as soon as he gets home. With Ethan gone and no paparazzi present, I haven't felt the need to look over my shoulder. Since I've had Cailin by my side on tour, I've gotten used to going out in public again and that original worry I agonized over subsided. I feel joy and freedom, a lot due to Cailin's support and encouragement.

All of this is true, but that's not to say there haven't been a few bumps along the way. We've discovered new quirks about each other that we've had to learn to navigate. Cailin gets annoyed when the cap is left off the toothpaste. Living solo for so long, I never had to worry about little things.

Despite Cailin insisting we keep the dog leash in a closet instead of close to the door, where we have quick access, it's easy for us to share a roof. We've lived in close quarters on the bus, and now have a little more space to spread out in the apartment. But we need more square footage to grow, not only in our relationship, but to attain our personal goals.

"My mom is so excited to meet you."

"I hope she breaks out the baby albums," Cailin says.

"I don't doubt that she will, actually. Good thing you've already seen my bare butt."

CAILIN

Fortunately, Hope was great during the three-hour flight to Florida. But she is more than ready to flee the jet. She nearly pulls my arm off onto land as Jax grabs our carry-on bags. The summer Florida heat packs a punch to my face. I've only been in the humidity for a few minutes and I'm ready to find air-conditioning.

"You get used to it," Jax tells me.

"I don't know about that," I say.

"We'll check Florida off our list of potential residences."

"I'm totally open to a vacation house, though." I say this as if Jax and I have made some formal commitment to each other. Though we plan for the future in all aspects and have started down this path, we're not yet engaged. I don't know when, or if, that time will come, so I want to maintain level headedness. I'm not going to push the issue of marriage. I just got divorced and Jax might have that lingering in the back of his mind. Plus, this would be his first marriage and he is going to want to take all precautions.

We check into the dog-friendly hotel we'll be staying at during our time in Florida. Jax wants us to have our personal space, but I look forward to meeting his family. After a quick nap and showers, we get ready to head over to the house Jax bought for his mom with his first big paycheck.

Jax opens the door for me to the luxury car we're renting. He insisted we ride in it because after weeks of roughing it on a bus, he wants me to enjoy the finer things his lifestyle can offer. I am not going to argue.

As he turns the key to the ignition, Jax tells me, "We're going to take a detour first. There's something I want to show you."

I love fun surprises. "Any hints?"

"You'll just have to wait and see," he says.

About 20 minutes of anticipation later, we pull up to a

small white ranch house. There are a lot of palm trees on the property. I think I know where we've arrived. Jax takes my hand and says, "This was my grandma's house where I grew up."

I warm like a plate of freshly baked chocolate chip cookies because Jax cares about me enough to show me this intimate part of his life. A place only those closest to him before fame had access. I ask Jax if he wants to get out and walk around, but he doesn't want to draw too much attention. Instead, we pause and take it all in before getting back on the road to his mom's house.

On the way, Jax tells me more stories about growing up there. When we arrive at his mom's, which is situated in a gated community, it hits me how her life was also upgraded by her son's success. The house Jax gave his mom is far from modest. It's far bigger than the needs of any woman living alone. But I know it's important to him to share his wealth.

Jax's mom opens the door and starts to cry as soon as she sees him. It's so sweet to see their bond. After she dries her eyes, she hugs me and welcomes me inside.

"It's so nice to finally meet the woman who captured my son's heart," she tells me while Jax brings Hope to the yard.

"Jax has told me so much about you. I'm really glad I have the opportunity to meet you, Ms. Slater." I immediately worry that they might not have the same last name. I would certainly consider changing my last name if my husband walked out on me. However, as a mother, I would also consider keeping the last name of my kid.

"You can call me Michelle, no formalities here. Did he tell you that you're the first girl he's brought here? That means he's serious."

"That makes two of us." I've been wanting to talk to his mom in private so I take advantage of the opportunity. Her eyes widen with excitement as I quickly fill her in on an idea I have to celebrate Jax's birthday. This covert mission will require secret texts so I have a feeling we're going to get to know each other pretty well.

The rest of the afternoon and evening is spent as Jax predicted. We share stories, flip through Jax's baby books, and enjoy a home cooked meal. I can see a lot of Michelle's qualities in Jax. I feel like I've unpeeled another layer of his identity.

JAX

The smell of French toast swirls through the air and stirs me awake. At first, I assess the situation to see if I'm dreaming. I reach out my hand next to me on the bed and pat around, but all I feel are covers. Cailin's warm body isn't next to mine. Rather than stop to think if I'm having a nightmare, I open my eyes. There she is, looking adorable in her leggings and T-shirt. Her hair is pulled into a high pony hail, with loose strands framing her face. She wipes them out of her view and greets me.

"Happy birthday," Cailin says. She pushes a room service tray towards the bed. "This is just your first surprise of the day."

"This is already the best birthday ever. I've got all I could ever want."

Hope jumps on the bed and tries to steal some bacon. "Looks like you got something your girl wants," Cailin says.

"Our girl." Saying that makes me think about the day we might have our own child. Cailin would make such a nurturing mom. I want to be the dad I never had and experience childhood through the eyes of my children. Find the magic in everything I missed.

We've talked about families and kids before, so I know we're both on the same page. I just don't know Cailin's exact timeline of when she would want to start a family, and I don't want to put any pressure on her, just getting out of her divorce. Instead of bringing that up, I simply ask, "Can I have a hint about my surprise?"

"Nope, and there's nothing you can do to bribe me either. You'll just have to let the day unfold."

CAILIN

Breakfast in bed was just the beginning to the day of fun I planned for Jax. We spent the morning riding bikes along the bay, soaking in the sun on the deck of a private boat, and enjoying an air-conditioned lunch at a local artisan restaurant. Hope had a blast at the doggy daycare in the hotel, but we made sure to also take her on a long walk. By late afternoon, we're both exhausted, so I suggest we rest at the hotel before we have to get ready for the big surprise at night.

The undercover birthday mission I've been planning with Michelle has been slightly tricky. Every time my phone dings, I tell Jax it's Gemma asking for details. By now, he must think she's super co-dependent on our friendship. But I can't tell him I'm texting his mom. Only a few hours left and then all will be revealed. Luckily, we both pass out and wake up just in time to start showering.

"We have to hustle," I tell Jax. "Can't be late." I instruct him to wear the nicest shirt he's packed, which basically means any shirt in his collection and he just has to decide on a color. He chooses navy.

Likewise, I put on a berry floor-length tiered boho dress with tropical flowers on it, because when in Florida, dress cute and comfortable. The A-line fit and V-neckline add a touch of sexiness. I pull my hair into a side braid to salvage it from the southern humidity. Since Jax and I are official, I brought back my lip color. But rather than ravage him in red, I choose a light cranberry gloss.

"You look gorgeous," Jax says. He comes up and places his arms around my waist. Holding me close, Jax says, "Thank you for today."

"Hold the applause until the grand finale."

———

JAX

Cailin refuses to let me drive to our destination, because it would ruin the surprise. At this point, I'm just grateful she hasn't blindfolded me yet. Maybe I shouldn't speak so soon. When our rideshare stops at a local club, I give her a look. I was hoping for something more intimate, but I'll appreciate whatever she has planned.

Cailin checks her phone and looks nervous as we exit the car. For a mother with a young baby, Gemma sure has a lot of time on her hands to constantly check-in on Cailin. But I'll approach that subject another time. I get a weird feeling as we enter the club. For one thing, the music isn't blaring. And it's oddly dark.

"Are you sure they're open?" I ask.

"For us, yes."

"What are you up to?" There's no way she would rent this whole place. It would cost a fortune and also not make sense for just the two of us.

Cailin takes my hand and leads us inside. I hear a scuttle and then a light switch being flicked. The entire room illuminates in string lights. A crowd of people yell, "Surprise!"

She got me. She genuinely got me. I never would have expected this. "I cannot believe you did this. No one has ever done something like this for me."

I scan the room and see my mom. She runs over and informs me, "This one is special, Jax. It was all her idea. I only helped her make contact." So that was all the secret texting.

One by one, people who have held important roles in my life circle around me. Ridge, Oliver, Mario, and Jack are here. It's the first time in years that 5 Leo Hearts are all in the same room. Harry takes that opportunity to snap a photo. Some of my cousins and childhood friends that I've stayed in touch with patiently wait their turn to say hello. Past them, I even see Cailin's mom and Gemma.

"This is incredible," I say out loud to anyone close enough to hear.

CAILIN

Phew! I pulled off the surprise. The tears I saw in Jax's eyes were worth the stress. At Michelle's urging, I even invited my mom and Gemma. Of course, neither of them would pass up this opportunity. I'm really glad I did though.

Gemma comes up and pinches me. "If you would have told me over a decade ago that today our dream of meeting 5 Leo Hearts would come true, and that Jax would be in love with you, no offense, but I wouldn't believe it." We break out in girlish giggles at the absurdity of this whole situation. It's just unbelievable really.

My mom is talking Michelle's ear off and I take that as a good sign that they are getting along. That's my cue to do something that's long overdue.

"Come on." I grab Gemma's hand. We walk over to Jax and I excuse myself for interrupting him with his bandmates. I whisper in his ear, and a minute later he pulls his fellow 5 Leo Hearts members into a huddle. Then they make their way towards me and Gemma.

"I don't believe you all have met," Jax says. He introduces us to everyone during an epic moment. Gemma swoons with each hug. As conversations begin, Jax interrupts, "One more thing, fellas. Let's get these ladies a photo."

No shame. This photo of Gemma and I with 5 Leo Hearts represents years of friendship, memories, and dreams. It represents how far we've all come to be standing where we are at this moment. It's about never letting go of your inner child, because within her lies a guide to happiness and finding your purpose in the future. We look into a lineup of cell phones in front of us and smile in front of the flashes.

The rest of the night flows better than I could have imagined. Gemma even convinced the guys to sing an a cappella version of her favorite song. They are happy to oblige and end up liking the sound so much, they begin discussing a reunion to record an acoustic album. They have a big anniversary coming and we all agree it would be a special way to celebrate and thank their fans.

After we sing Happy Birthday to Jax and cut the cake, we all wander outside. My mom and Gemma are jet lagged and have an early morning flight back home, so they wish me safe travels. Everyone disperses into little groups under the moonlight.

Jax takes my hand and we stroll along the sidewalk. Tomorrow concludes our time in Florida. Every stop of our post-tour travels has brought us closer together. In Jersey, we learned to live together and accept each other's flaws. In Florida, we dug deeper into our backgrounds and how our experiences made us who we are. Tonight, our families and friends came together as one. New dreams for 5 Leo Hearts were realized. One longtime dream for Gemma and I came true. I can't imagine what California will bring our way, but I'm here for all of it.

Trash the Dress Online Chat

Cora: He signed the divorce papers!
  Cailin: Now it's time for YOUR comeback story!

47

LOVE WILL SAVE THE DAY FOR JAX SLATER AND CAILIN MCCALL

CAILIN

"And that's everything," Jax tells me as he concludes the tour of his estate.

"Thank heavens. I need a break after all that walking." A laugh escapes my mouth, but I'm only half-kidding. "In all seriousness, it's gorgeous. I love it. But I can see how half of the rooms have never been used. I do have some ideas for the elevator."

"Which is exactly why I want to sell it," Jax tells me. "And, I'm taking you up on your elevator ideas later. I'm glad I gave Lily a few weeks off."

We move to sit out by the lounge chairs at the pool and sip on watermelon sugar lemonade. Hope has discovered a love for swimming, apparently. We each take turns tossing her a rubber ball to fetch in the water. Ever protective, Jax says it has to be a rubber ball and not a tennis ball, because the fuzz can be dangerous.

"Any word on the sale of your apartment yet?" Jax asks. My mom has been maintaining the apartment and preparing it for potential showings.

"Actually, no. What time is it in Jersey now? Around three in the afternoon. I'm going to give the realtor a call."

I step away from the splashing water for some quiet. When my realtor answers, she delivers frustrating news. Not one person has expressed interest in the apartment. Her theory is that because it was recently sold and back on the market so soon, buyers feel they should beware. I understand the train of thought, but it's not true. This is a lovely apartment and I need the sale of this to be able to afford to live. I can't count on Jax paying my way forever.

I'm feeling anxious as I hang up the phone and begin to panic. I have an apartment I can't sell, and I can't afford to pay the mortgage on it much longer since I officially quit working for Marisol. For a minute, I debate begging her to take me back. But I won't sink that low. I firmly decided that I don't want to work as a tour publicist or spend nights at countless shows now that I am in a relationship with Jax.

Maybe I can rent the apartment. Or I can move back home for a while and go work for Gemma like she offered. I don't know if Jax wants to go right back to Jersey. He has a lot to sort through here. There's so much to think about. I walk back to Jax and sulk on the lounge chair.

"Not good news, I take it?"

"Not good news. No interest in the apartment. Maybe I should market it as the place Jax Slater slept in and I'll get some offers." I know that was rude and I feel bad for saying it aloud. I'm just frustrated.

"That's one option. Or we can just not worry about it right now." Jax lets it slide, but he is also brushing away the real issue.

"I can't not worry about it, Jax. I have a mortgage to pay and I don't have a steady stream of income. I feel like, besides you, my life is a mess."

Jax leans over and takes my hand. "Hey, we're in this together now. Your problems are my problems. We're a team."

But are we really? I don't have any formal commitment

from Jax. We're not married. There's no engagement ring on my finger. I have no security other than his word. Yes, I trust him. But I'm also a self-sufficient woman who has never had to rely on a man before. And I don't want to be in this situation.

"It's different for me," I say. A mix of emotions bubble up inside as I try to explain. Before I get any more words out, tears begin to spill out of my eyes. I just need some time alone to clearly think. I get up and run out his front door.

JAX

Cailin already ran away from me once before and I'm not going to make the same mistake twice. I run after her, making sure Hope follows me inside. She's soaking wet and shakes her fur like a scene from a home cleaning commercial. Dirty water splatters everywhere. Serves me right for having white furniture, I suppose. It doesn't matter now. Nothing matters except for Cailin. I shut the door behind me, knowing the future is wide open.

"Cailin, wait!"

She doesn't look back, but she runs out of steam and stops at my front entry gate. Gasping for air, she puts her hands on her knees and looks up at me with a mascara-smeared face. I've seen this look way more than I would like to during our short time together.

"Where are you going, Cailin?"

"I don't know, Jax. I just need to think. I appreciate everything you are offering me, I really do. But I need to be able to support myself. It's very scary not having that security right now. There's so much uncertainty."

"Come here," I say, pulling her into a hug and leading her away from the gate. The last thing we need is any paparazzi passing by and shoving cameras in our faces.

As we walk to the front entrance of the house, I lay it on the line. "You're so used to being the breadwinner and holding the weight of your marriage on your shoulders, that you don't know what it's like to have someone to count on. I need you to trust me. I am not going to let you fall. I am here to support you. I want to support you. I want to use the gifts that have come my way to help you build the career you want. To build our life together."

Cailin wipes her runny nose and sniffles. This is not how I planned our first day in LA going, but then again, some of the best things in life are spur of the moment. I get down on one knee in front of Cailin and grab her hand.

"Marry me."

<hr>

CAILIN

Somehow my near nervous breakdown led to Jax asking me to be his wife. Obviously, I want to marry him. But I need to know he is seriously prepared to propose.

"Jax," I say.

"Shh... Just listen."

I oblige.

"The first day I met you in person, we were standing right here. As soon as I touched you, I felt electricity. In just those few minutes of hugging you, this big empty foyer felt like home for the first time. Because I had someone in it that I wanted to share my blessings with. I knew right then that you were someone special."

"I felt it too," I say.

"And now we're back to where things began between us. We made it through an accident, a tour, publicity scandals, even burned pancakes. We're still standing by each other's side. There's nowhere else I'd rather be and I bet you feel the same."

I simply nod my head.

"When you called me from the airport and asked about getting in the car with my driver, I told you to take a leap of faith. You did. And look at the journey it led us on. Now, I'm asking you to take another leap into the unknown, where the only thing that is certain is I will be by your side with whatever comes our way."

By now, I realize that Jax actually means this. Either he has prepared this speech or he is insanely good at professing his feelings on the fly. No matter which it is, he has my attention.

"Wait right here," Jax says.

A minute later, he's back on his knees in front of me.

"Will you marry me?"

This is really happening. There's a round solitaire diamond ring in the box. How did he have time to go shopping for a ring?

"This is the part where you say, 'yes,'" Jax nudges.

"Yes! Yes!" I say. "Yes, Jax, I will marry you." I loved him then, as the guy whose face on my wall taught me to dream for big love. I love him now, as the man who has shown me what real love is and has helped me grow as an individual. I will love him always, as my partner through the ups and downs of life. I seal my commitment with a kiss as Jax stands up and slides the ring on my finger. It's a little snug, but we get it past my knuckle.

"This was my grandmother's. My grandfather gave it to her. My mom showed me when we were visiting the house and I asked her if I could have it. I wasn't sure if I wanted to give it to you, because I want you to have a ring you love. We can still pick one out together, but at least consider this a place holder."

"I love it. I can't believe you thought to pass on your grandma's ring."

"I hope to keep it in our family, and pass it down to our kids one day. Let the legacy of love continue for generations."

"Stop it or you're going to make me cry again."

"No more tears caused by me from here on out, only happy ones." Jax wipes my eyes.

"This means we're engaged. Like Jax Slater is off the market."

"Jax Slater and Cailin McCall are both off the market. Don't underestimate yourself—everyone knows you're a catch."

"So, I guess eventually we'll have to make an announcement," I say.

"That we will. Do you happen to know a good publicist?"

EPILOGUE

5 YEARS LATER

CAILIN

THERE ARE SO MANY BOXES. I can't wait to dig in and unpack everything. I'm standing in the middle of the "yellow" bedroom of the house Jax and I designed and had built at a lake town nearby where I grew up in Jersey. I'm holding a coffee mug that says, "Trash the Dress" over my bulging belly. But the decaf brew is not enough to fuel me for preparing a nursery while our three year old daughter, Piper, runs rampant with Hope. This room is being prepped for one of our twin boys, who are arriving in a few weeks. Our other little bundle will be his neighbor in the room next door.

"Mommy! I have to go potty," Piper says.

Of course, she would declare this the second I bend down to open a box. This belly doesn't make chasing a toddler easy, but I am determined to get Piper fully potty-trained by the twins' arrival. Small wins will make life with two newborns a tad easier.

Luckily, Jax will be here to help me. Let me rephrase that. Jax is excited to take on more daddy-duty to our growing family. He's especially ecstatic about having two boys on the way. He texts me name suggestions all day, even though we're usually in the same room.

As I get up to waddle down the hall to Piper's bathroom, I glance at the gallery of family photos lining our upstairs hallway. Each snapshot transports me back to that moment in time. The selfie we took right after we got engaged is low-resolution quality because it was taken on a cell phone, but it's one of my favorites. My eyes are watery and Jax is beaming with pride.

There's one of us on the beach for our island elopement, which we planned for just the two of us at the spot Jax always wanted to honeymoon. This took place before our big California wedding where we exchanged vows on a mountaintop surrounded by close friends and family. Next to it hangs a photo of Jax serenading me at our reception.

Every time I look at the photos of Piper, I am in awe that we made this amazing little human. The day Jax and I got a positive pregnancy test, he started to cry.

We couldn't even wait the full three minutes to check our results. Some people might walk out of the bathroom and set a timer. Not us. We stood over the bathroom sink for what seemed like an eternity until two pink lines appeared after two minutes. Jax grabbed my hand and squeezed three times.

"You're going to be a daddy," I said, holding my hand over my mouth.

Jax already had salty tears streaming down his face. I knew at that moment, he was going to be the best dad ever. He even teaches Piper how to play some instruments. She can't follow directions quite yet, but she has a blast pounding the piano keys and strumming her tot-size guitar. I only ban the drums, for now.

I love the photo on our wall that documents the moment we became a family. My teary face after a C-section with Piper, where Jax is holding her near my cheek behind the operating sheet, always makes me emotional. We didn't plan on a C-section, but after 24-hours in labor with no dilation, we all decided it was for the best. It was scary, but at that point, I just wanted to meet our baby. It doesn't matter how she came into the world, as long as she's here.

The headlines over the past few years have cheered us on:

Off The Charts: Jax Slater And Cailin McCall Reunite And Prove Love Is More Powerful Than Gossip

Jax Slater Pops The Question To Cailin McCall

Exclusive Photos: Jax Slater And Cailin McCall Elope During Gorgeous Island Ceremony

5 Leo Hearts Reunite To Record Acoustic Album Inspired By Cailin And Her Best Friend

Jax and Cailin's Love Reaches New Heights: First Look At The Couple's Star-Studded Mountain-Top Wedding

The Boy Band Is Back: 5 Leo Hearts Acoustic Album Debuts At Number One

Oh, Baby! Jax Slater Announces Newest Adventure: Fatherhood (We're Positive Caitlin Is Pregnant!)

Exclusive: Cailin Slater Reveals Her #1 Pregnancy Craving And More

It's A Girl! Peek Inside Jax And Cailin's Gender Reveal Party

Oops, They Did It Again: Jax And Cailin Reveal Twins Are On The Way

I'm grateful the tabloids have stopped reporting fake news about our relationship and have let us live in harmony as a normal family. I cherish the everyday things, like potty training.

"Mommy, I want to go see Daddy and Rowdy," Piper says.

Rowdy is our one-year-old doodle puppy we rescued. Jax had been wanting a second dog for a while, one that he could personally rescue. One weekend, we were out running errands and saw a sign outside a pet store that a local shelter was there for an adoption event. We looked at each other, nodded, and Jax zoomed to a parking spot. Once inside, it was love at first sight for Jax and Rowdy. The puppy jumped right into his arms, followed by Piper.

Rowdy lives up to his name in every sense. He eats paper, so we have to be sure to hide all garbage cans. At night, when we're settling down to rest, Rowdy starts running laps around the house until Jax gets up and wrestles with him. He's also a food thief and jumps on the coffee table to steal whatever is accidentally left unattended. Rowdy keeps us on our toes for sure, but I wouldn't have it any other way.

A few minutes ago, Jax took Rowdy outside with him while he gathers wood for our fireplace. I can't wait to cozy up under a blanket in front of it this winter, drinking hot chocolate, and watching family movies. Jax and I will each have a baby boy in our arms and Piper will be nestled in a pile of blankets and dogs. And it will be one of the greatest moments of our lives, because the little things are the biggest.

As Piper washes her hands, I hear the front door open. "Cailin," Jax yells. "Put Piper's jacket on and send her outside. It's snowing."

Piper rushes down the stairs and grabs her jacket before I even make it down the first step. Walking when pregnant with twins is a challenge. Walking down stairs might as well be considered a sport. I break a sweat carefully taking each step. It's getting hard to lift my legs with the pressure of two babies in my abdomen, and my belly is so big, I can't see my feet. When I finally get outside, I watch Jax lift Piper up and demonstrate how to catch snowflakes on her tongue.

Jax loves winters on the east coast. After we got engaged, we decided to just sell my apartment (which thankfully, sold one month later) and stay in LA to plan the wedding. That ended up taking one year because at that time, 5 Leo Hearts also reunited to record their acoustic album, on which Jax even played the guitar. It released at Number One on the charts and the band made appearances on all the morning and late-night shows, which Carlos booked. They didn't tour, though.

While Jax was doing his thing, I was figuring out my next move. I decided that I really loved mentoring Hayley through her divorce and career change, and got certified as a coach. Many of the Trash the Dress girls have become my clients. My specialty is helping women pursue their passion. In addition to private sessions, I contribute articles to news outlets, putting my PR contacts to use. Last year, I also released a book. I'm fortunate that Jax championed me along the way and I had the time to figure out my true calling. Every day, I get to work on my own terms, create my schedule, and take part in fulfilling work that also helps change lives.

After we sold the LA house, we bounced around to different locations. Nashville was fun and where Piper was born, but we decided we wanted to set down roots back in Jersey before she begins school. We rented, until this house, our dream home, was complete. We're close enough to New York City so Jax can commute into studios as needed. He's found new pride and success in writing songs for other artists. He's still always recording on his own, but doesn't want to tour anymore until our kids—can't believe I am saying that—are older.

Needless to say, my mom is thrilled to have her grandbabies nearby and has been a huge help with Piper. As it turns out, Piper is the same age as Gemma's second daughter, Amanda. I love watching the girls grow up together. They're already the best of friends.

"Would you look at this?" Jax says. "It's sticking." A coating of white glistens across our lawn. Ice crystals capture the sun's rays and twinkle. Wonderland in progress.

"Mommy, catch a snowflake in your mouth." Piper sticks out her blue lollipop-stained tongue.

Who am I to deny such an adorable request? I open my mouth and try to catch a flake, but nothing lands. Figures. I've never been good at anything that involves coordination, whether it's walking in heels or catching snowflakes on my tongue. The three of us break out laughing, which is all fun and games unless you're pregnant and then realize you might pee your pants.

"Mommy needs to go sit down," I say. That's enough physical activity for the day. The couch is calling my name. Unpacking the nursery will have to wait until tomorrow.

Jax puts Piper down and she slips between us, holding both our hands as we walk inside. "Don't run," Jax tells her. "We don't want mommy to slip."

That's Jax. Always looking out for his girls. He's been so supportive of me through this pregnancy, waiting on me hand and foot. He doesn't even mind running to the 24-hour pharmacy at 11:00 p.m. when I get a craving for a caramel chocolate bar. However, he did learn his lesson after a straight week of requests, and now we're fully stocked at home with value-pack bags.

When we get to the foyer, Piper throws her coat on the floor as usual and scoots off to her playroom. The dogs follow. She has become their favorite person because they've come to realize she leaves a trail of crumbs from whatever she's snacking on, wherever she goes.

Jax helps me take off my coat and hangs up all three in the closet. Is there anything more attractive than a man who tidies up without being asked?

"Hey," Jax says, walking over to embrace me in a hug. I reflect back on the first time we hugged in his foyer and how he also proposed to me there. Now, we have a foyer we designed together. "Pretty soon we're going to be walking into this foyer as a family of five. Can you believe it?"

"5 Slater Hearts," I kid.

"Now there's a headline."

A NOTE FROM JOELLE

As I write this, it's been a few days since I took my daughter, Genevieve, to her first boy band concert. While watching Big Time Rush—a group we discovered after binge watching the TV show—I looked around the stadium at the 16,000 people in the crowd and thought to myself, "This is why I wrote my book." For so many of us, boy bands are our first loves. Posters of our favorite member line our bedroom walls, we dream of meeting them, and fantasize about being the girl in the song. Yet, I haven't seen a tribute to them in novel form. It was time for someone to capture this and it was gonna be me. Cue *NSYNC.

My love of boy bands begins with New Kids on the Block. I was in third grade when the group first came out, I saw them in concert, and named my pet goldfish after the members. By high school, I stood outside TRL with signs and gift baskets for Backstreet Boys, covered *NSYNC as a writer for Teen People magazine, and met 98 Degrees when the guys signed CDs at a mall. I saw Five, LFO, walked a mile barefoot with Hanson (I don't count Hanson as a boy band but they fall into the category of bands we crush on), and traveled to New York City's biggest record store in Times Square just to buy import CDs from UK acts Boyzone, Take That's Robbie Williams, and Another Level. These adventures filled my youth with cherished memories and provided me with a soundtrack that lifted me up no matter what trauma was going on in my life. Boy bands are happiness. Throughout this book, there are hidden references to these groups and more. I hope you've caught some of them and smiled.

During my college years into my 20s, my musical taste transitioned into indie and punk music. Whereas boy band music provided me with an escape, the punk scene lent a platform for me to channel creativity and chase my dreams as a music journalist and publicist. These bands inspired me and made me feel alive. By the time I had my first major heartbreak, I was quoting Unwritten Law songs in emails to my ex-boyfriend. The character of Cailin is named after my favorite Unwritten Law song. I named Cailin's love Jax because it pays tribute to my favorite soap opera, General Hospital. The plot twist revolving around Ethan's character is one of the other soap-opera inspired elements of this story.

I wrote my original draft of this book in three months, but it took much longer for me to go back and really figure out how to weave in the Trash the Dress divorce support group and pay tribute to the awe-inspiring community of women we have. All the chats in the story are made up, as our real convos in the group are top secret. It was important for me to have my main character be a young divorced woman because this area is underrepresented in romance novels and there are really amazing stories of happily *even* after. *The Comeback Tour* is the first book in my Trash the Dress fiction series and I am excited to tell the next character's story of finding love and living her dream post-divorce.

If you're going through a breakup, considering getting married, or simply want to read about empowering women, please read my memoir, *Trash the Dress: Stories of Celebrating Divorce in your 20s*.

Self-publishing this book brought creative passion back to my life. I am so grateful for everyone who cheered me on to write this story (esp. Katie Schnack during our Skype convos at work). Fatema Ahmadi and Jackie Obeid—I appreciate you reading multiple versions of the book and replying to all my texts! Thank you to Melissa Gould, Alana Ortega, Nicole Baker, and Jennifer Tucker, for reading early drafts, offering feedback, and helping brainstorm titles. Fun fact: I had three working titles and versions of this book! My fiction go-to expert Olivia McCoy (@oliviathebookpro)! It was our Zoom that helped me connect the dots and bring in the Trash the Dress chat, which completely transformed the book.

I also appreciate every rejection letter I'm still getting from agents because they led me to continue self-publishing and I love having a project that is completely my own. I am beyond lucky to have inspirational Best-Selling authors offer me advice and encouragement along the way. I'm talking about you, Jessica Buchanan at Soul Speak Press and Octavia Goredema. I'm so lucky to know you both and be a small part of your author journeys.

Thank YOU so much for buying this book. The real work has just begun for me and I'd really appreciate it if you can leave me an online review on Amazon or Goodreads and write a social media post and tag me in an effort to raise awareness of my book and announce me as a new independent fiction author.

Cindy Ras—your illustrations of Cailin and Jax are amazing! I am obsessed with the cover design. Thank you for bringing my vision to life and working through all my ideas. I am grateful to have found Michelle Files at The Author Files to proofread for me. Jackie Dorey—you always back me up! Thank you for your notes! Anthony Middleton DiIonno, Esq. at Sharma Law—thank you for your guidance.

I'll be here, cherishing moments as I listen to my son, Luca, sing along to my favorite songs with me, and searching music videos with my daughter to teach her boy band history. (Fun fact: I taught her the names of every Backstreet Boy when she was one-year old). Sometimes we'll be driving in the car and my husband, Frank, will sing along to a BSB song and I'll yell at him for ruining my vibe, but it goes to show the impact of boy bands. Everyone secretly likes at least one song. When you close this book, I hope you play a song from your favorite boy band, raise the volume, sing along, and forget about everything else for a few minutes.

For all those that have a dream, take this as your sign to go for it. Start now. You don't need anyone's approval to live your best life. It's not going to be easy, but it will be worth it. If you can make a positive impact on just one person's life, you are successful. I took a risk starting Trash the Dress and each time someone writes me to tell me how my book helped them through one of the darkest times of their life, it brings tears to my eyes. By sharing my story and writing a book (one of my dreams), I have met so many special women. I hope this Trash the Dress fiction series continues to build on that legacy and by reading along, you're inspired to create your own.

ABOUT THE AUTHOR

Photo: Leanne Dolan

Joelle Speranza is a storyteller, whether she is in author, book publicist, or journalist mode. Her goal is to write and share stories that empower and inspire girls of all ages and life stages.

By day, she is a book publicist representing Wall Street Journal and New York Times bestselling authors. As a freelance lifestyle journalist, she has been published on outlets including Oprah Daily, Insider, HuffPost, and Today.com. Her acclaimed memoir, *Trash the Dress: Stories of Celebrating Divorce in your 20s*, was featured internationally in outlets including HuffPost, Cosmo Middle East, Glamour UK, Globe and Mail, Sunday Times, Yahoo! Health, Dr. Oz's You Beauty, and International Business Times. Her first children's book, *Princess Genevieve: The Hero with Girl Power*, features her family. Speranza lives in a NJ lake community with her husband, two kids, and three dogs. Learn more at www.joellesperanza.com and follow her on Instagram @thejoellesperanza.